A shadow fell across Hawk and he looked up.

Willow stood beside him, offering him baked cakes on a flat piece of stone. Hawk glared at her.

"Where is the meat?"

"There is no more. You have not been hunting."

Without answering Hawk reached out to grasp the dun-colored puppy by the scruff of its neck. He lifted it with one hand, and reached for his club. This was why he had brought the puppies; now let them serve as food. He raised his club.

Willow moved so swiftly that she was in and out before the heavy club could descend. She snatched the puppy from his hands, and stepped backward. Hawk stared, too startled to move. A woman had defied him! As he got to his feet with a growl of rage, she swung away from him, shielding the puppy.

"Do not kill it! We have food!"

Hawk took a threatening forward step. Willow stood her ground for a moment, then turned and ran. The gray puppy raced at her heels. Furious, Hawk ran after them, club in hand.

Willow ran across the clearing to the border of the woods. At the base of a huge, lichen-encrusted boulder, she stumbled and went to one knee. Quickly she rose, turning to face the enraged Hawk. Her eyes widened in fear, not of the man. She was staring over his shoulder.

Turning, Hawk saw the hunting saber-tooth between them and the safety of their fire.

232486

THE HUNTER RETURNS

DAVID DRAKE
JIM KJELGAARD

BAEN
BOOKS

THE HUNTER RETURNS

A Baen Books Original. Portions of this book have appeared under the title *Firehunter*, copyright © 1951.

Baen Publishing Enterprises
P.O. Box 1403
Riverdale, N.Y. 10471

ISBN: 0-671-72042-2

Cover art by Charles R. Knight

First printing, March 1991

Distributed by
SIMON & SCHUSTER
1230 Avenue of the Americas
New York, N.Y. 10020

Printed in the United States of America

FOR
LOUISE RASHIG

TABLE OF CONTENTS

Author's Note

Modern ideas of what life was like in prehistoric times are based on two sources of information. One consists of actual remains, such as stone implements and fossilized bones, and their location and relationship to each other. The other is scientific guessing—reasoning, for example, that if primitive tribes today do so-and-so, then under similar conditions prehistoric men would do thus-and-thus. So, by knowing a little and deducing a lot, a general picture is built up, which is incomplete only in details.

Still, a story must have details, and to get them I had no choice but to make them up. I have, however, always tried to keep them plausible, as what might have happened, in the light of scientific facts and theories. An exception is the telescoping of time. The developments that occur in the time-span of this book undoubtedly took many generations. And yet who is to say?

JIM KJELGAARD

FIRE-HUNTER

The top of the hillock which the tribe was climbing was studded with boulders, some so big that they overhung both sides of the hill. The rank scent of feeding bison was borne over the hill and down the side by a shifting wind.

Hawk, the Chief Spear-Maker, licked his lips. Though the tribe had seen much game in the past few days, most of it had been either too agile or too fierce for the hunters to attack. Even the mammoths had learned that only in numbers lay safety from human hunters, and aside from occasional small game the tribe had seen nothing except herds of big, dangerous beasts. It was suicide to attack a herd of mammoths, even with fire, for one such animal was capable of engaging every hunter in the tribe. But the giant bison were a different matter.

1

Hawk licked his lips again. In eight days they had eaten only seeds and wild fruit which the women had gathered, and one doddering old camel that had been about to fall from old age when the hunters overtook it. Seeds and fruit were all right when nothing else was to be had, but a wandering tribe needed red meat to maintain its strength.

As they drew nearer the top, the smell of the giant bison became stronger. It was a herd of more than two hundred animals, and had not yet taken alarm. That was good, for not in four seasons had the tribe run across a herd of bison as big as this one. If they were successful in the hunt, there would be all the meat they could eat, and much left for the scavenging wild dogs, dire wolves, and saber-tooth tigers that always gathered wherever game was killed.

Wolf, the Chief Hunter, remembered and spoke of the time when such herds had been fairly common. Tribal legend recalled when the earth had trembled to the pounding hooves of countless giant bison, but that was no more. Hawk had never wondered why.

Like all the rest, he was ruled by simple tribal laws and taboos, which were the accumulated wisdom of generations. It was tribal law that Hawk should be Chief Spear-Maker, because he was the most skilled in the methods and rites of spear-making. Similarly, the tribe must have a Chief Fire-Maker who thoroughly understood the magical properties of fire, their greatest protection. Aside from the Chief Fire-Maker and the Chief Spear-Maker, the rest of the men were, most of the time, hunters, for the demand for food was never-ending. And all food, whether meat brought in by the hunters or seeds or berries gathered by the women, must be shared, no matter who had found it. When the tribe was in danger, everyone, women and children included, helped defend it. Most important of all, the tribe must always live and travel as a group; one human alone was at the mercy of wild beasts.

Other than that there were few laws, but these few were inflexible. The tribe was a unit, and every member must contribute his share. If anyone failed, all might die.

Hawk paused a moment, and glanced backward to take mental tally of the women and girl children. The boy sons of hunters, armed with spears and clubs to fit their size, were at their fathers' heels, up ahead. But, as Chief Spear-Maker, Hawk's place was not with the hunters. It was with the women and children, and he did not like it.

For a second his eyes dwelt on Willow, daughter of Wolf, and his face lightened. Willow was lithe and swift, and already skilled in basket-making and a knowledge of seeds, roots, and fruits. The only reason she had not yet been taken by a hunter of another tribe lay in the fact that not in two moons had they met another tribe. All were scattered, desperately seeking the fast-disappearing giant bison.

Hawk grunted his annoyance. He was a man in his own right, for he had seen sixteen summers. Eight years had he sat at the feet of his father, to learn the mechanical details, the rites and incantations, that went into spear-making. Now he was Chief Spear-Maker himself, for less than a moon ago his father had fallen to a saber-tooth tiger. But though Hawk had a man's responsibilities and privileges, he could not have Willow, because it went without saying that she must be taken by a man of some other band.

Suddenly Hawk stiffened, and sniffed another breeze that blew in from the north. The tribe was being shadowed by a pack of wild dogs, which hoped to scavenge after the hunters killed. But the dogs seemed to be merely following; there was no indication that they would attack. Hawk returned his attention to the bison.

They were grazing in a meadow, and remained unsuspicious. Turning around, raising his right hand as a signal that the rest must halt, Wolf, the Chief Hunter, went on alone. He seemed to melt right into the earth as he approached one of the big boulders and peered around it. Hawk watched keenly.

It had never occurred to him to question why there had once been numberless giant bison and why there were now so few. He knew only that his tribe were bison hunters, and that they lived largely on bison flesh. Because the tribe's sole idea was to get enough food any way it could, Hawk had never considered the hunters wasteful in spite of the fact that they often wiped out an entire herd of bison with one fire drive. They might kill hundreds when they could use no more than ten, but that was their way of life.

For an hour, while the sun approached its noontime high, Wolf remained silently in position. He was watching the bison, and because he had not yet signaled the hunters, Hawk knew that the herd was not in position for a fire drive. He turned around to place the positions of the women and seven girl children.

As Chief Spear-Maker, he could not hunt, but he could wield a club or spear in common defense, and when the hunters went out for game, it was his duty to help protect the tribe's more helpless members. Hawk sniffed the breezes from all directions, but could detect no alien scents save those of the giant bison, the pack of wild dogs, and, faintly, the odor of a wooly rhinoceros. There was no immediate peril.

Hawk toyed idly with a spear shaft he had been fashioning. It was a well-balanced, carefully scraped piece of wood, with a curiously flattened knob on one end. But the shaft was just a little too slender and flexible for a hunting spear. Something in that very quality had kept him from casting the shaft aside.

Four days ago, entirely by accident, he had thrust the knobby end of this shaft into a litter of loose pebbles and leaned on it. The shaft had bent under his weight, then the end had snapped suddenly out of the pebbles. Hawk remembered vividly what had happened, and was still puzzled by it.

When it had snapped away, the end of the shaft had shot a small pebble straight into the middle of a pond. Afterward Hawk had picked up a similar pebble, and tried to hurl it into the pond. He could not throw such a light object half as far as the shaft had snapped it. There was something in the flexible shaft, some mysterious power which he lacked, and he had spent much time wondering about it.

After an hour and a half, so slowly that he seemed scarcely to move, Wolf raised his hand. At once Kar, the Chief Fire-Maker, went to his side. Hawk quivered eagerly.

The time was here; the bison had evidently moved into a suitable position and the fire drive was about to take place. One by one the hunters moved up beside Wolf and Kar, the boy hunters imitating exactly everything they did. The sight made Hawk writhe with impatience. He, too, wanted to be with the hunters, but he dared not join them. Whoever violated tribal law was banished from the tribe, and banishment meant sure death, for no lone human being could survive in this savage wilderness.

Kar and Wolf disappeared over the top of the hill. One by one, in order of experience, the hunters and their sons crawled past the boulders and down the other side. Presently, their spears and clubs with them, all were out of sight.

Hawk glanced once more at the women and girl children, who were sitting and lying in the tall grass. They were safe, for the wild dogs were still far away in the deep forest, waiting patiently. The dogs knew that they had almost no chance of making a kill should they attack the giant bison. But they were an experienced pack, familiar with humans. Always, after a fire drive, there were numerous dead animals that the hunters did not use. The dogs could afford to wait.

Since there appeared to be no danger threatening the women, Hawk was unable to restrain himself any longer. He could not join in the hunt, but he could watch it. If danger came, he could reach the women and children in time. Crawling toward the top of the hill, he lay prone behind a boulder. Cautiously he peered around it.

He looked down on a wide river meadow where rank grass grew shoulder high to a man. But no men were in sight. Hawk knew that they were crawling through the grass, dispersing themselves at strategic intervals to intercept any bison that tried to break through their encircling ring. As they advanced, they gave no sign of their presence. Nothing but a stray breeze that carried their scent to the bison could betray them now.

Hawk turned his eyes toward the bison. The entire herd, bulls, cows, and calves, was feeding toward the river. Hawk looked toward the river, and uttered a puzzled grunt.

Getting enough food was an always-present problem, and an opportunity such as this could not be missed. But was Wolf not risking too much in his present preparations? The herd could be ringed with fire, but there was only a six-foot embankment at the edge of the river. Driven down that by the flames, more bison would escape than would be killed or injured. Maybe the entire herd would get away. Hawk wondered if it would not have been wiser to follow the herd and wait until it could be driven into a deep canyon or over a high cliff.

Reluctantly Hawk put his doubts aside. Wolf was a mighty hunter; it was unlikely that he would fail.

The unsuspicious bison fed on, moving slowly

nearer the river as they did so. To all outward
appearances the meadow was a peaceful one, con-
taining nothing save the herd of bison and a few
bright-colored birds that flitted about the tall grass.
Even the wary birds had not yet detected the
hunters.

Then, after another hour, a wisp of smoke arose.
Hawk's excitement mounted, and he burned with
an inward tension. The fire drive was under way.

Several hunters were on their feet now and
running as fast as they could, flaming torches of
twisted grasses in their hands. They paused at
twenty-foot intervals to touch their torches to the
dried grass, and ran on.

Leaping fire crawled up the grass where the
hunters had first lighted it, and long tongues of
flame licked hungrily out toward more grass. In a
matter of seconds, behind the racing men, a curving line of fire sprang up and began to spread both
ways. In a frenzy of excitement, Hawk leaped to
his feet and shouted hoarsely. Then he was aware
of the women and girl children beside him.

Now that there was no further need for concealment or quiet, they had come up to watch. Their
faces were alight with anxious hope, for they and
their men would eat well only if the savage scene
below worked to their advantage.

A great, rumbling bellow came from the be-
sieged herd. Cows with calves at their heels trotted nervously toward the river. Massive bulls stayed
in the rear, shaggy heads lowered toward the approaching flames, alert to meet any danger. Watching, Hawk scarcely breathed.

It was an alarmed herd, but not the panic-stricken

one it should be. Obviously the bison had been in other fire drives, and refused to be stampeded toward the dangerous river bank. Some of the bulls wheeled in ahead of the cows, turning the whole herd. For a few moments they stood still, the calves in the center and the bulls and cows in a protecting outer ring. Then, at a swift run, the entire herd started away from the river, toward one side of the encircling fire ring.

Hawk turned his attention toward the hunters. They had leaped into the burned part between the blaze that was burning toward the bison and the fire that was running back into the forest behind them. They were advancing behind the fire, but something was wrong; the far side of the meadow was too wet to burn. Yellow smoke rose from it, but scarcely any flame. The bison, too much hunted and too wise to fall into the trap designed for them, were going to try to break through the weakest part of the fire ring.

The wind freshened, keeping the smoke low and blowing it toward the river. The meadow was covered by a thick blanket of smoke that rose halfway up the running bison, so that only their shaggy backs and heads were clearly visible to the watchers on the hill.

Hawk stood still, watching with growing despair as the running hunters raced toward the herd's line of escape. Only one man blocked it. He was Short-Leg, one of the poorer hunters, and as the shifting smoke revealed him clearly, Hawk's keen eyes could see that he was holding his spear wrong. He gripped it too high, so that he could not get the weight of his body behind any thrust he made, and he was sure to miss. Hawk looked anxiously toward the other hunters.

They were running as hard as they could to put themselves in position for a strike, but the herd's sudden shift of direction had left them at a disadvantage. The bison had too much start and were running too fast. Hawk groaned in dismay as he saw Short-Leg stab at a huge bull. Neither well nor strongly thrust, the spear was pushed lightly aside by the bull's ponderous leg.

Then the smoke closed in and quarry and hunters were lost to sight.

Hawk turned away, not having to see any more to know the outcome of the hunt. But the tense women continued to stare at the swirling smoke blanket, as though the very fierceness of their gaze would help the men who were trying to get the desperately needed food.

Moodily Hawk toyed with his spear shaft. He thrust the knobby end against a pebble, bent the shaft, and watched the pebble snap away. With respect that was close to awe, he picked up the shaft and twirled it between his fingers. He bent the slender stick, feeling the tensile strength within it. The shaft had life and power of its own, but he knew of no way to control it and make it serve him.

There was something about that mysterious power of which he was just a little afraid. His father had told him, over and over, that the spear-maker's secrets lay in the strength of certain resilient hardwoods and the cutting edges of certain stones. These properties were strong magic, his father had said, and never, under any conditions, were they to be treated lightly or trifled with. Human skill could combine the wood and the stone to make a properly balanced spear, but if the spirit of each part was not treated with respect, the spear would not fly true.

His father had also said that there was a way, by combining a short piece of wood with a spear, to throw that spear a very great distance. He had been given such a magic throwing-stick by an old spear-maker of another tribe. Although Hawk had carefully preserved it since his father's death, he did not understand the secret of its power, for his father had never felt that the time had been right to reveal it. The ways the tribe knew, and had always known, were good ways, his father had believed.

Now, handling the slender shaft, Hawk wondered if there was some connection between its power and the magic of the throwing-stick. Going over to his pile of extra spears, he picked up the mysterious implement.

It was the length of his arm, a carefully polished stick with a short piece of branch protruding at right angles from one end. The branch had been cut off so that only two inches remained. Where the branch joined the stick, a smooth hollow had been scraped or worn. Hawk looked at the throwing-stick in bewilderment. He grasped it at both ends, and bent it in his hands. It was stiffer than the slender spear shaft that had snapped the pebble, but he could feel the same living strength. But he did not know what to do with it; the magic would not reveal itself to him.

A bedraggled, discouraged little group, the weary

hunters straggled back. After the bison had broken
through their fire, they had chased the herd a long
way without overtaking so much as a calf. There
was no meat.

As the hunters joined their hungry women and
children, the wind ruffled the grass, and a bouncing little antelope-like creature appeared suddenly.
It stopped forty feet away, head alert and ears
erect as it studied the group. One of the hunter's
sons threw a spear that fell short by ten feet. The
little animal skipped away, and the boy listlessly
went out to retrieve his spear. Except for Hawk,
the hungry men paid no attention. From time
immemorial they had lived chiefly on the giant
bison, and other game was only incidental. The
boy should have known he couldn't hit anything so
small and fleet.

Hawk stared intently at the place where the
little antelope had disappeared. The problem of
finding meat was becoming more and more serious. Except for large beasts such as bison, which
could be trapped in fire drives, and were conse-
quently becoming scarer, the land was alive with
game. But the tribe had never had much success
in hunting the smaller animals because they were
so agile; they could avoid the ordinary hurled spear.
So, in the midst of plenty, the tribe was hard-
pressed for food of any kind.

Kar, the Chief Fire-Maker, went into the forest
and returned dragging a small tree for his night
fire. He went again, bringing back an armful of
dead branches and dry tinder. Kar stamped about
the place where his fire was to be, one step sideways with his left foot and one with his right.

Hawk looked disinterestedly on. All this was fire ritual, and no business of his.

Short-Leg, the hunter who had missed his strike at the bison, had been standing moodily by himself. Finally he spoke.

"My spear failed me, Spear-Maker."

"My spears do not fail," Hawk replied shortly.

"I struck at a bull. My spear missed," Short-Leg insisted.

"I saw you. You did not hold your spear as a hunter should, and it is your fault because you missed."

Short-Leg's eyes gleamed redly, and he snatched at the club dangling from his girdle. Hawk sprang to his feet, ready to defend himself.

"Peace," Wolf commanded. "We have trouble enough, without you two fighting. You will make Short-Leg another spear?"

"I will."

Kar and two young apprentice fire-makers had by now brought a great load of wood and piled it by the night fire. It leaped high, spreading welcome warmth over the hungry people who huddled around it. Kar passed his hand over the fire and it glowed blood-red. Hawk watched, and wondered.

The customs and beliefs of the tribe were deeply ingrained, a part of him, and it was not for him to question them. Yet, sometimes, he was puzzled by them. The incantations and rituals he himself used in the making of spears—just what connection did they have with the true worth of a spear? He knew that it had been Short-Leg, and not his spear, who had been at fault in the bison hunt. Yet he must make a new spear—and it must be made in a certain fashion, and in no other way. Puzzling over this idea, Hawk idly began drilling his slender spear shaft deep into the ground.

Wolf stiffened suddenly, his nostrils distended as he sniffed the breeze. A moment later Hawk had the scent, and almost at once the rest of the hunters were alert.

For three days, always maintaining a respectful distance, the wild dogs had been trailing them. But until now, as their scent had proven, they had been interested only in scavenging any excess game killed by the hunters. Now the harmless scent had changed to a threatening, dangerous odor. Hungry, and having failed to get any bison, the wild dogs were aroused.

Spears in their hands, clubs swinging at their fur girdles, the men arranged themselves in a protecting circle around the fire, facing outward toward the gathering darkness. The women and children snatched whatever stones they could lay their hands on and took up positions behind the men.

A fierce pleasure surged through Hawk. Forbidden to hunt lest his spear-making skill be endangered, he had to content himself most of the time with chipping flint heads, fashioning spear shafts, and binding the heads to them. He found action of the sort he craved only when the camp was attacked, and everyone called on for defense. He leaped erect, snatching up a spear, but still hanging tightly to the shaft he had drilled into the ground. Its supple length bent under the pressure of his hands and the weight of his body.

He looked beyond the ring of light cast by the
fire, the only haven in the savage wilderness, into
the brooding shadows. Most of the time the tribe
was safe near the fire, but not tonight. Now the
hunger-maddened wild dogs were stalking the
camp. They knew that the tribe was not in a good
position for defense; thick grass provided concealment right up to the light of the fire. The only
visible evidence of the impending attack was an
occasional ripple in the grass.

A sudden strange idea seized Hawk and he
gripped the imbedded spear shaft so tightly that
his knuckles whitened. The stick, the live green
stick with so much supple strength! He had been
looking for a way to make it hurl a spear, and now
he had found it! Hawk bent the shaft back, and
placed the butt of his spear against the flattened
knob at the end. Supporting the spear with both
hands, holding the shaft back, he searched the tall
grass.

The next time he saw the grass move, he bent
the shaft a little farther and released the spear. It
shot from his hands into the tall grass, and disappeared without striking its intended target. Hawk
groped for another spear.

The next moment the dogs closed in.

With no time to use the shaft again, Hawk
grasped the second spear in his hands and braced
his feet. Leaping gray shadows in the tall grass,
the dogs appeared. Seeing one, Hawk hurled his
spear. It flew as straight as the wood from which
its shaft was fashioned. There was a shriek of pain,
then a few bubbling growls.

Almost before the spear left his hands, Hawk

snatched his club and sprang forward. A big black dog, a beast fully as tall as Hawk, leaped from the grass with jaws gaping wide. Its polished ivory fangs glinted in the firelight as it sought a throat-hold. Agile as a cat, Hawk side-stepped and smashed the dog's skull with his club.

All the men, having thrown their spears, were busy with clubs. Hawk saw a hunter drop his club when a great dog sprang at him, and throw up his hands to shield his face. Wolf dashed to the man's rescue.

The next instant Hawk pivoted on the balls of his feet and, club raised, raced toward the fire. He hadn't seen any dog break through the line of men, but one had, for the women were smashing at it with their stones. Hawk whirled among them, and brought his club down on the dog's head. The beast took two staggering steps and collapsed.

But he had not been quick enough. One of the girls was on her knees beside the fire, red blood bubbling from her mangled thigh.

It was Willow.

SPEAR SHAFT

For a moment Hawk stood still, the club dangling idly from his hand. The scene was commonplace; someone was always being hurt or killed by wild beasts. But, though ordinarily Hawk would not have given a second glance, he felt troubled because it was Willow who lay there on the ground.

Slowly Hawk turned his back on her and walked away from the fire. He could do nothing here anyway; he had no knowledge of the secrets of the medicinal herbs and grasses, and was a little afraid of the incantations with which the old medicine woman of the tribe applied them.

The wild dogs had retreated, leaving five dead behind them. Back in the forest there was a confused chorus of growls and snarls, then a few high-pitched screams. The pack had set upon and torn apart one of their wounded members, and now they would eat. The humans around the leaping fire relaxed. The pack had suffered a crushing defeat, and it was unlikely that the dogs would attack again, at least until they had marshaled their ripped forces.

Wolf came in, dragging two of the dead dogs by their rear paws. He took them to the fire and dropped them near the one Hawk had killed. Other hunters came with the other two dogs.

The tribe arranged themselves near the fire, the women and girl children nearest and the men making an outer ring. Save for the fire, and the people around it, the wilderness was a dark and menacing void. This was the way it always had been and, as far as anyone knew, the way it always would be. Merely staying alive was a desperate business.

Kar threw more wood on the fire, and its leaping flames brightened. The little knot of humans sat close beside it. Life during the day was never without its danger, but at night, when prowlers were rampant, anyone who went beyond the fire's outer circle of light took his life in his hands.

Thus would it be all through the hours of darkness. Not one minute would lack a hungry beast that hoped to catch and eat a human being. There was no way to strike back. Fire and unity, the ability to throw many spearsmen against any and all attackers, were the tribe's only protection.

But the dangers of the night were only normal. Death threatened, but life must go on. The women were working with flint knives, preparing the dogs for cooking, and presently the mingled smell of cooking meat and scorched hair filled the air. At-

tracted by that odor, a pair of saber-tooth tigers
came near and beat a restless patrol around the
night camp. They coughed and snarled, but nobody moved. The tigers feared the fire, and as
long as they were there no lesser brute would dare
come near. In one way the tigers' very presence
was a guarantee of safety.

While the women cooked, the men rested. Hawk
again fell to studying his slender spear shaft.

. He realized that there would be a great advantage in hurling a spear farther than the strongest
man could throw it. If the hunters were able to do
that, they could remain a proportionately safe distance away from a maddened bison or cave bear.
They could strike their enemies that much farther
away, and kill game which now stayed out of spear
range. Again Hawk drilled the spear shaft into the
ground, and pondered.

Using the mysterious power of the shaft, he had
hurled a spear much farther than even Wolf, the
mighty, could throw one. But he had hit nothing.
Hawk braced another spear against the flattened
end of the imbedded shaft and bent it back. Yes,
the power was still there.

Slowly, snarling in anger because they dared
come no nearer, the pair of tigers were still beating a measured patrol around the camp. Now and
again one or the other would make a short, savage
rush, rippling the tops of the tall grass at the
farthest reach of the firelight, but coming no nearer.
Hawk studied their routine.

They were making a rhythmic, methodical beat.
They always traveled at about the same speed, so
that they were in the same places at the same time

as their patrol led them around the fire. They always charged toward the camp at one place where the grass was thickest. Seized with a sudden, bold idea, Hawk bent the shaft a bit more, and took a new grip on the spear.

His senses were nearly as keen as those of the wild beasts against which the tribe constantly fought, and after he had studied the tigers' motions a few minutes he knew exactly where they were. He waited, his eyes on the patch of dense grass, measuring the fierce pair's progress. At exactly the right moment he shot his spear.

As he released it, the tall grass rippled from the tiger's half-rush toward the fire. There was the solid impact of a spear striking flesh, and the tiger's growl changed to a high-pitched scream. The wounded tiger's mate roared threateningly. The grass bent as before a powerful wind while both great cats charged angrily about. Continuing to scream, the spear-stricken tiger leaped so high that his blocky form showed for an instant over the tops of the grass. Then there was only a string of coughing snarls that grew fainter as both beasts sought a refuge in the forest.

Hawk stood still, trembling at the thing he had done and not at once able to comprehend it. The fierce tigers had always been part of the night, a routine portion of the dangers of darkness. They never came near the fire, but neither did even the mightiest hunter ever think of molesting the creatures. Now, at night, a man had deliberately attacked a tiger. Furthermore, it had been a spear-maker who had done so, not a hunter.

It was too much to understand all at once. The

hunters, awe-stricken, sat in silence. Women and children stared wide-eyed toward the faint snarls that marked the retreating tigers. Even the smell of cooking meat seemed for the moment to be suspended. Then Wolf spoke heavily.

"What demon possessed you, Spear-Maker, that you dared do such a thing?"

Short-Leg was on his feet, chattering angrily. "He broke the law! He hurled a spear without cause! I saw him!"

"Tell us!" Wolf repeated sternly. "Tell us why you did it!"

Hawk found his voice. "I did not throw the spear! The power of the wood threw it." He faltered, and pointed to the supple shaft, lacking words to explain because he himself was not entirely sure what he had done. He had acquired a new power, so new that there were no words for it. To show them all its magic, Hawk snatched up another spear, braced it against the shaft, and shot. The spear made a long, clean arc, flying above the grass tops and falling in the darkness. Nobody, not even Wolf, could throw a spear half that distance, and in spite of his uncertainty, Hawk was proud.

"It is forbidden!" Short-Leg shrieked. "Trouble will come because the Spear-Maker meddles with that of which he knows nothing!"

The hunters made a little half circle, awed and fearful. This was magic of the blackest sort. There was a prescribed way to throw a spear, and since time began men had thrown them in just that way. Sacred custom had been violated, and anything could happen now. The only flicker of real interest was in Wolf's eyes, but he, too, shrank back from the mysterious thing he had witnessed. He stared hard at Hawk.

"You know the law," he said. "All your spears will fly false unless you use them only in defense of the tribe. The tiger was not attacking us."

"It is true, Wolf," Hawk admitted. "But it is also true that I was not hunting, which is what the law forbids. I am Chief Spear-Maker and I accept my place as such. But this is good magic and great power which has come to me. Will you not use it yourself?"

The hunters were now staring at Wolf, their chosen leader. He was a brave and skillful hunter, but the Chief Spear-Maker's argument about the law was too much for his simple mind. He did realize, however, that the other hunters were afraid of this new power.

"It is not our way of hunting," Wolf said, turning away.

Hawk pulled the slender shaft out of the ground and laid it with his extra spears and shafts. To relieve his own awed excitement he counted them. There were a dozen shafts and a dozen spears, an extra one for each man. And when the sun rose, he must make another spear for Short-Leg, who was dissatisfied with the one he carried. Hawk looked sideways at the leader, the only man who had shown real interest in the spear-throwing shaft. But, in the face of opposition from all the rest, even Wolf dared not press that interest too far.

Hawk sat alone, shunned by the awe-struck hunters. He accepted a piece of half-cooked dog brought to him by one of the women, and gnawed hungrily on it. As he ate, he stole a glance at the little cluster of women and children. They, too, were now eating, the men having been given the best parts. Even Willow, lying on a bed of grass that the women had prepared for her, was listlessly nibbling a strip of meat. Her thigh was no longer bleeding.

Hawk gave all his attention to the food in his hands, tearing the stringy meat from the big bone with his powerful jaws. Dog was not the best of food. It lacked the strength-giving qualities of bison, or any of the other grass-eaters, but it would serve when nothing else was to be had. After he gnawed the bone clean, Haw lay down to sleep.

Black night still reigned when he awakened. Hawk sat up, locating by his odor the leopard that had taken over the tigers' patrol. The wind brought him the scent of wolves and, far off, the faint odor of the wild dogs. They had gone only far enough to lick their wounds, and had not departed. But it was unlikely that they would attack again.

Kar, sitting with his chin on his knees, rose to throw more wood on the fire. The flames flared brightly, revealing some of the men sleeping and a few wakeful. One of the women rose to bring them more meat. Hawk ate his slowly; he was not as hungry as he had been. When he had eaten enough, he lay down to sleep again.

This was their life. When they had enough to eat, they gorged. Uneaten meat would spoil anyhow, and tomorrow was far away. Keeping alive and fed today were the important parts of living.

The next time Hawk awakened morning had come and a warm sun was pouring through the tall trees. He stretched luxuriously, then looked to his sheaf of spears. When he rose and walked near one of the hunters, the man moved quickly away from him. The rest looked suspiciously at Hawk. Not forgotten was last night, and the witchcraft by which he had stricken a hunting tiger at a distance greater than any man should be able to hurl a spear.

Relieved of his night duties by another day, Kar was lying in the grass with his head pillowed on his arm. Kar must never sleep at night, for only to the Chief Fire-Maker fell the responsibility of the night fire. But he could sleep during the day whenever the tribe was not on the move.

Hawk glanced toward the women. Some were busy near the fire, cooking the remainder of the slain dogs, but two were grinding dried berries in a hollow stone, using a smaller stone to crush the berries into powder. Willow had risen from her bed of grass and was sitting with her back to a stone, staring wanly at the fire. A compress of green herbs bound her injured leg. Hawk looked at her pale face; obviously Willow was badly hurt.

Hawk licked his lips, and bolted his portion when a woman brought him another piece of meat. It was one of the last pieces, and when it was all gone the tribe would have to move on. Again Hawk glanced at Willow. If she could not go with the rest, she would be left behind to certain death; a hungry tribe could not risk starvation for the sake of an injured girl.

Hawk picked up the slender spear shaft and twirled it between his fingers. Respectfully he gazed at the shaft, a thing more powerful than any man.

Even now he had not acquired all of the secrets it contained. He knew only that there were better ways of spearing than any yet put into use by his fellow tribesmen. Perhaps more of the strange new power would be revealed to him. When Hawk caught Wolf staring at him, he put the shaft down.

Covertly he studied it, then glanced sideways at Wolf. Except for the leader, the hunters feared the spear-thrower. And Wolf did not dare risk their fear. Hawk cast about for something he might do to win over the leader. The power of the shaft was good, as had been proven by his striking the tiger last night, but how could he persuade the rest to accept it?

The sun climbed higher, and the women served the last of the meat. Carrying skin containers, two of the women rose and went to a spring that bubbled from beneath one of the boulders. They filled their containers, returned to the fire, and kneaded the coarsely ground berry powder into flat cakes. These they put on hot stones to bake.

The men looked disinterestedly at them. Having had meat, they wanted more. Baked cakes were acceptable to satisfy great hunger, but they were not good food. However, since their bellies were filled for the present, nobody was inclined to move. It was good to take full advantage of rest periods whenever they occurred because, soon enough, there would be none.

Hawk busied himself making another spear. He knew the capabilities of every man in the tribe and fashioned his spears to fit the user. Wolf could throw a large shaft with a heavy head and do deadly work with it. The rest took proportionately lighter spears and Short-Leg needed the lightest of all.

The Chief Spear-Maker selected a smooth shaft of the proper weight and balanced it in his hand. It had already been scraped smooth by one of his helpers, but there was one place that needed further scraping. Hawk worked with a rough piece of flint, the top of which had been chipped to fit his hand. Again he tested the shaft by balancing it, and this time he found it better.

From his pouch, he chose a head, a carefully chipped piece of flint to fit the spear, and lashed it on with bison-skin thongs.

Hawk balanced the completed spear in his hand, feeling it as a part of him. It was good, and would fly straight, but there was more yet to be done. Though Hawk knew it was good, the hunter who would use the spear must have confidence in his weapon.

He glanced at the willow-bordered streamlet that wandered away from the spring, and carefully studied the various small birds flitting about the branches. This was one part of spear-making which only he knew thoroughly. There were different birds with different flights, and much depended on selecting the right one.

The newly made spear in his hand, Hawk rose and walked down the hillock. At the bottom was a tar pit, and the hot sun had made it a sticky mess. He thrust a stick into the tar, and turned it until the stick was coated.

Carrying the dripping stick, he returned to the willows and lightly coated some of their thin branches with tar. The little birds took alarm when he approached, but returned as soon as the Chief Spear-Maker went back to the fire. Three birds alighted on the tar-coated branches, and fluttered wildly as they tried to escape. Hawk waited until another bird was caught, then trotted over to his captives.

He was conscious of the hunters' keen interest as he approached, but nobody offered to help. This was a part of spear-making that he alone could do.

Hawk slowed his steps as he came near the fluttering birds, and cast an expert eye over them. Two were little insect-eaters whose life depended on their ability to twist and turn; they had to be able to do so in order to catch the insects that dwelt among the willows. As a consequence, they seldom flew straight for more than a few feet.

But the other two birds were fruit- and bud-eaters, suited to his purpose. Hawk disengaged the two birds he did not want and let them go. They bobbed erratically into the willows. He closed his hand about one of the other prisoners. Gently, not hurting it, he worked its feet out of the sticky tar. As he did so, he noticed that in thrashing about, trying to free itself, the bird had broken its tail. It couldn't be mended, but that made no difference; it was the right kind of bird.

Ceremoniously Hawk thrust the spear's point at the sky, then at the earth, then at the four winds. He poised the spear in throwing position and let the bird go.

Bending and twisting, unable to keep itself straight with its broken tail, the bird wobbled into more willows a hundred feet away. Hawk stared, dumb-founded. This was the acid test of a spear. If the bird flew straight the spear would be certain to fly straight. Always before such birds had flown in a perfectly straight line, but now no hunter would accept this spear or dare use it. Hawk walked slowly back to the fire.

Two of the women were supporting Willow between them and guiding her about. Willow hobbled stiffly, painfully, unable to use her injured leg to good advantage. But she must move; the tribe would not stay here and the women knew it. If Willow could not accompany them, she would certainly be left behind.

Short-Leg looked up at Hawk. "Do not ask me to use that spear, Spear-Maker. I saw the bird fly."

Without replying, Hawk broke the spear shaft across his knee and threw the head away. Whether or not the flight of the bird had anything to do with the flight of the spear, it was tribal tradition that spears must be tested in this way. Hawk fashioned another spear.

This time, when he approached the willows, he was more careful. He had learned something—even a bird that normally flew straight could not do so when it had a broken tail. Hawk added this to his store of knowledge. When he selected another bird he chose the same kind but looked it over carefully to make sure there were no broken feathers.

Again he went through the exact ritual. When he released the bird, it flew straight as a dart to another bush. Hawk carried the spear back to the fire and gave it to Short-Leg.

Kar rose and stretched, and looked questioningly about for more meat. There was none. Kar grunted his disappointment and, stooping to pick up his spear and club, went into the forest for wood. From now until the sun rose again, Kar would maintain his vigil.

The women had put Willow back on her bed of leaves, and the girl lay there with one arm across her eyes, while the old medicine woman changed the compress of herbs that covered her wound.

Hawk stretched out by the fire and slept a few minutes. When he awoke, it was dark and the tribe had settled down for the night. Save for Kar and one sentry, the rest of the men and boys slept lightly. Hawk tested the night winds.

There were no scents save some far off, and the inevitable nearer one of the tiger that patrolled the camp, hoping somebody would stray from it. Then, from the distance, Hawk caught the scent of the wooly rhinoceros. It was still alone, and in almost the same place it had been when he first scented it. Hawk lay down to sleep again.

The camp awoke hungry, for during the night even the berry cakes had been eated and now there was nothing left. This, too, was a normal part of things. The tribe was a wandering unit with no settled home and not often at the same sleeping place twice. It must constantly follow the game upon which it depended for most of its food, and the time had come again.

Without ceremony, Wolf started out. The hunters and Kar fell in behind him, but Hawk lingered, as was his duty. Willow rose painfully, and would have fallen had not one of the women caught her. The two women who had helped her yesterday looked questioningly at each other, then at the backs of the men. Fear and doubt were in their faces; they wanted to help the girl but not if helping her would cause them to be left behind. They urged Willow along the line of march, while other women took up Hawk's extra spears and shafts. Up ahead, one of the men turned impatiently, gestured with his arm, then went on with the other hunters.

The distance between them and the women who were trying to bring the crippled girl along increased. Hawk stayed behind, spear and club ready. But the women were becoming restless now. Their strength lay in all the men, not in just one, and they knew it. They talked softly among themselves.

Then, below the crest of another hill, the men stopped.

Hawk knew why, for scent of the wooly rhinoceros came plainly to his nostrils now. The hunters had not stopped out of consideration for the women, but because they were near game. When Hawk and the women came up, Wolf was on the crest of the hill, looking over. Walking openly, for this was no herd of nervous bison but a savage beast that almost always stood to fight, the rest went up the hill when Wolf beckoned. Hawk looked down on the scene below.

It was another river meadow, but a barren one. The grass was short, scarcely high enough to cover a man's ankles, and the rhinoceros stood nearly in the center of the meadow. An armored behemoth with two long spears in his ugly snout, he was dozing in the midday sun. Nothing else was near.

The hunters talked softly among themselves, debating the possibilities. Here there was no opportunity for an effective fire drive, for the grass was too short to burn. Any assault on the wooly rhinoceros would have to be a direct attack, and that was always dangerous. Nevertheless, it could be done.

The hunters decided to attack.

Hawk walked down the slope with them, trying to conceal his great excitement. Here was the chance to use the power of the green shaft, the opportunity for which he had been hoping. At the very best, with every advantage on the hunters' side, a wooly rhinoceros was a dangerous beast, a snorting ton of fury that, once aroused, would turn aside for nothing. His hide could be pierced, but not by any thrown spear. Brute strength was needed to penetrate the beast's heavy armor. But if a hunter could stand at a distance, and shoot a spear that would sink into the creature's vitals . . . Hawk glanced at Wolf, who had apparently forgotten all about the shaft. It was no use; the hunters would have nothing to do with Hawk's new power.

The Chief Spear-Maker remained in his proper place, a little behind the hunters. The wooly rhinoceros came awake, and tossed his long snout viciously. Two of the more agile hunters feinted in front of him, while Wolf went in from the rear to thrust at the monster's tendons.

On a sudden, irresistible impulse, Hawk drilled his spear shaft into the ground. He braced a spear against the knobby end, bent the shaft way back, and shot. There was a sudden snap as the shaft splintered. The spear wobbled in flight, brushed the wooly beast's side, and bounded off.

Grunting in anger, the rhinoceros wheeled suddenly. Unbelievably agile for anything so huge, he twisted back, dipping his long head. When the sharp horns on his snout came up, the foremost one slithered squarely into Short-Leg's belly. The skin on the man's back bulged, then the horn broke through and Short-Leg was lifted from the ground.

He screamed once, while his dangling arms and legs writhed and twisted. The rhinoceros pivoted, and, still grunting, trotted across the meadow, bearing Short-Leg's drooping body with him.

Wolf turned on Hawk, his face dark with anger and fear. "This time, Spear-Maker, you have truly broken the tribal law. You are no longer of us!"

The hunters dived on Hawk's pile of spears, each man snatching the one made for him. They wheeled, and at a fast trot started across the river meadow. For a second the women hesitated. Then, as one, they followed their men.

Willow sat where she had been abandoned. Scarcely noticing her, Hawk stood in dumb despair. His new-found power had failed!

LEFT TO DIE

In the distance, the wooly rhinoceros was scraping its snout on the ground, trying to rid itself of its gruesome burden. The retreating tribesmen, sure that they were fleeing black misfortune in the person of their Chief Spear-Maker, did not look back. Even the women did not waste many backward glances at the pair who had been abandoned in the wilderness. They were as good as dead already. With no hunters to help them, and Willow crippled, very shortly they would furnish a meal for a pack of dire wolves, or a saber-tooth.

Hawk walked slowly forward and retrieved the spear he had shot. Then he stood still, leaning on the spear and watching the backs of the departing tribesmen.

A vulture flew overhead, and began to wheel in slow circles over the place where the rhinoceros had scraped Short-Leg's body from its horns. A moment later there were a dozen more in the sky. Vultures always seemed to know before anything else when there was food to be had. One by one, they planed to earth. The rhinoceros stamped his ponderous feet and snorted at them. He shook his massive head. Hawk watched dully.

The bent shaft, he knew now, was not a good thing. Its magic worked when conditions were exactly right, but one who lived by his spear must be ready to hurl it in a split second. He could not always depend on finding the right sort of ground into which he might drill the hurling stick, and drill it fast. Nor could he know when the power might choose to leave the shaft, and the wood break. And all of it together had led to banishment.

Willow moved painfully. Steadying herself against a stone, she stood up. Hawk glanced at her, as though for the first time aware of her presence. She was only a girl, and crippled, scarcely able to move without help. Therefore she was useless, and the tribe had been right in abandoning her. But as long as she was still alive, she seemed in some way to be his responsibility. Hawk looked again to his weapons, checking his spear shaft carefully for strength and making sure that the head was properly bound.

Fire was the first essential to keeping alive, and though Hawk had never built or tended a fire he had watched Kar and his assistants do it. He knew the stones from which Kar produced the spark to ignite his fires, but he was not sure he could find any along the river meadows. Nor did he know whether he could control the power of fire. However, the fire at last night's camp was sure to have live sparks buried in its dead ashes. It would be wise to return there.

Hawk swung on his heel and started away. Then he stopped and looked back at Willow. She was leaning against the boulder, her eyes fixed despairingly on the meadow grass. She had made no protest when Hawk walked away from her. It was the creed of the wild land in which they lived that cripples had no right to expect help. But they were both forsaken, and though Hawk knew that Willow could not help him in her present condition, her mere presence was reassuring. She was human, one of his own kind.

"Come with me," said Hawk with unaccustomed gentleness. "We will go back to last night's camp."

The dull despair left Willow's eyes, and hope flashed within them. She had been resigned to her fate, knowing that the wounded never lived long. Now, even though she knew that both of them together had small chance for survival, the will to live was strong. She let go of the boulder and took a stiff forward step. She stumbled, almost fell, and caught herself. Hawk picked up one of the extra spear shafts the departing tribe had left behind, and offered it to her. Then he started out, spear and club ready.

Twenty yards away, a small mottled wild cat crouched in the grass. Its tail twitched, tufted ears were erect, and yellow eyes gleamed. So silently had the wild cat come that even Hawk had not detected its presence.

Knowing that the smaller of these two humans

was wounded, and having marked her as its prey, the cat glared at the man in rage. But it made no move to attack because it had no wish to face an armed man. It crept back into the tall grass and disappeared.

Hawk's keen eyes followed the little cat's circling course through the grass, and he took a new grip on his club.

They walked slowly, Hawk suiting his pace to Willow's hobbling shuffle. He was aware of the cat that slunk around them, of furtive life represented by hares and other small creatures, but there was nothing large, nothing that meant danger. They stopped on top of a hillock and looked down at a grove of trees.

A monstrous ground sloth, a beast fully eighteen feet long, moved slowly among them. The dull-witted, harmless creature reared to curl its long tongue around a small branch and strip off the leaves. Bruising them between its hard, toothless gums, it swallowed the leaves and reached out for more.

Hawk looked questioningly back to where the tribe had disappeared. It wanted food, and here was easy game to last all of them for many days to come. The giant sloths were neither agile nor quick-witted. When attacked, they tried only to get away unless they were in some corner from which there was no escape. Then they fought fiercely, and were so big and strong that they could kill or seriously injure anything they could reach with their long, hooked claws. But they were unable to strike fast, and a group of skilled hunters could always kill one.

However, the tribe was gone beyond recall and just one man could not hope to kill a beast so huge. Much as he and Willow needed meat, the giant sloth would have to go on his slow, harmless way.

When they reached the site of last night's camp, Hawk poked in the white ashes with a stick, and uncovered a bed of glowing coals. Then he hesitated.

Secretly he had questioned some tribal practices and taboos, but now that it was necessary for him to take over another man's task he was filled with uncertainty. Kar had always been the Chief Fire-Maker and only Kar knew all the secrets of fire. Anyone else who tried to control its power would be interfering with something about which he knew little. Anything could happen.

Deliberately Hawk kept his eyes from Willow, who had seated herself on her former bed of leaves and was applying a fresh herb compress to her wound. Hawk looked all about, and discovered nothing dangerous. Spear in hand, club dangling from his girdle, he went into the forest.

He knew the various kinds of wood because, in experimenting with spear shafts, he had used limbs from most of the trees. But he had also watched Kar and his helpers bring wood in, and had noticed that wood suitable for spears was evidently not acceptable for fires. Almost always in starting a fire, Kar had used dead wood, whereas a spear-maker needed the straightest, hardest, and greenest shoots.

As he strode among the great trees he remained alert to everything about him. He automatically noted where to find a future supply of spear shafts, where small animals had their secret lairs, where there were nesting birds, and where beasts had been. The faint, stale odor of wild dogs still clung to the mat of fallen leaves, but the dogs had left.

Hawk soon found what he was seeking. A mighty tree had fallen, dragging others with it, and the place was now an almost impenetrable mass of dead and dying branches. Hawk broke a branch from the dead tree and dragged it back behind him.

When he cast his branch on the glowing ashes, a shower of sparks rose. Powder-thin ashes sifted into the air and for a moment hovered in a tiny gray cloud. Hawk watched, perplexed.

This was the way it should be done, for this was the way he had seen Kar do it. But no flame and scarcely any smoke rose from the tree limb. Hawk squatted beside it, his eyes intent as he sought to fathom the mystery of fire. He had never built one, and obviously there were secrets connected with the proper making of a good fire that he did not know.

"Use small pieces."

Hawk turned in astonishment to find Willow kneeling beside him.

"Break off small pieces and put them against the hot ashes," she repeated.

She seemed so sure of herself that Hawk broke some slender twigs from the end of the bough, and laid them on the ashes. Almost at once a little tendril of smoke leaped up and a second later there was a tiny tongue of flame. The flame grew, licking eagerly around the bough. Hawk glanced at Willow with a look of respect. Plainly there was more to this fire business than he knew. Even women, ordinarily the lesser part of the tribe, seemed to know more about it than he did.

The fire rose, and began to burn fiercely at the big bough. Again Hawk went into the forest for wood. He was worried because night was certain to bring wild beasts and they would need a fire all night. But the flames seemed to be eating the wood faster than he could carry it. Returning with the wood he could carry, he threw an armful of dry branches on the fire. Rising sparks made a bright shower, and the flames raged high.

As darkness began to fall, Willow wearily fell asleep on her bed, and Hawk began a frantic search for enough wood to last them through the night. Now he was no longer as careful in what he selected; anything would do. Green branches went with dead ones onto the fire. As he piled them there, Hawk noticed that the fire burned more slowly. He squatted beside his blaze, looking intently into it, seeking an answer to the puzzling question of why his fire did not now consume the wood so rapidly.

When he rose he had learned something new. Dead wood created a fierce blaze, but wood with sap still in it burned slower. Therefore, dead wood was the firemaker, but green was its keeper. Having found this out, Hawk brought in a large pile of both. As night shadows became deeper, he sat silently beside his fire. When a tiger coughed out in the darkness he scarcely even glanced up.

Never in the history of his tribe had a tiger attacked human beings who were sitting around a fire. Of course a pack of starving wolves or wild dogs might come, and if so they would have to be dealt with, but there was small use in worrying about anything before it happened. Let the next hour bring what it would. They were safe for this one.

Hawk picked up an extra spear shaft and began to toy with it. He drilled the shaft into the ground, bent it with his hand, and tried to brace his spear against it. He pulled the shaft out of the ground and examined it again. It was not good to drill it into the earth; there were too many things that could go wrong. But the slender shaft still retained its supple strength, and would, no matter where it was.

Hawk tightened his fingers around it, then squeezed so hard that his clenched knuckles whitened. He could not depend upon finding a place to brace his shaft whenever he needed it, but a man's hand was always ready! This, then, was the answer! Hawk laid the shaft back in his hand and tried to brace a spear against it. He could not. The spear was lying parallel with the shaft and there was nothing against which it might be held. The shaft needed a cross-piece or projection of some kind, something against which the butt end of the spear could be braced.

Feverishly Hawk took up the throwing-stick, which his father had never showed him how to use. At last he knew! The magic had finally been revealed to him. Hawk grasped the smooth end of the throwing-stick and swished it experimentally through the air. The smooth end fitted his clenched hand perfectly and, almost of its own volition, the other end rose easily into the air. All the power and strength, all the magic of wood, were there. Hawk was no longer in doubt as to how it should be used.

Holding the smooth end in his right hand, Hawk laid back the throwing-stick until it was level, and shoulder high. Then he fitted the butt of a spear against the hollow at the base of the branch. It worked smoothly, naturally, as it was supposed to work. The butt of the spear was braced against the short branch; the center of the spear shaft fitted easily into his palm, and the spear had an almost perfect balance. Hawk did not throw at once, but he felt that he could hurl the spear a great distance. The throwing-stick seemed to double the length and strength of his arm.

Hawk removed the spear, then put it back into position. Again and again, never releasing the spear, he swung his arm back, then forward. Then he looked around. Some distance away, faintly revealed in the fire's dancing light, was a tuft of withered grass. Hawk swung his arm forward and cast his spear at the grass.

The weapon landed almost two feet to one side of the tuft, but some hunters could never come within two feet of their targets anyway. Retrieving the spear, Hawk threw again, allowing for his previous margin of error. This time the spear landed within a few inches of its target. Again he cast the weapon. Out of a dozen throws, he hit the tuft of grass squarely four times. Had it been an animal of any size, he would have struck it every time. The magic of the throwing-stick was his!

Suddenly aware of danger, he raced lightly forward, snatched up his spear, and held it ready. Willow rose from her bed, struggled to her feet, and looked around. Painfully she bent to catch up a large stone lying at her feet.

The wild dogs were coming back. The wind told Hawk that there were only two of them, but that they were determined to attack. Theirs was a fighting scent, the odor of intent beasts of prey. As he followed their progress by the breeze, Hawk balanced a spear in the throwing-stick.

Had there been a pack of dogs he would not have done such a thing. The spear-thrower was new and experimental, and he had practiced too little to know much about it. If he kept the spear in his hands he could certainly kill one of the dogs, but there were only two and he thought he could handle both with his club, if the spear-thrower failed. He waited tensely.

He saw motion in the grass, but restrained himself. The instinct to hurl a spear was born in him; spears had always been the most important part of his whole life. However, all his life he had thrown spears with arm power alone. Now he waited because he was not sure; for a second he was tempted to remove the spear from the throwing-stick. Then the feel of it gave him confidence. It was strong and good. He must trust it.

He shifted the spear a bit, remembering the lessons taught by practice. To control the eager spirit of the green wood, the spear must be held exactly right and the throwing-stick must be given just the right motion. Hawk remained still until the wind and the gently rustling grass told him that the approaching dogs were about as far away as the tuft of withered grass had been. He squinted his eyes, trying hard to see. The head and fore parts of a dog were framed in the grass.

They were there for only a split second, but that was enough. Anyone who lived by hunting had to learn, first of all, to take advantage of opportunities. Hawk cast his spear.

He heard it strike, and saw a thrashing in the tall grass. Instantly he was running forward, his club upraised. Meeting the other dog, he side-stepped as it struck at his throat. Hawk smashed his club solidly down on the dog's head. It staggered, threw itself about, and went limp.

Scarcely pausing, for he was in the fire's outer glow and therefore in a very dangerous place, Hawk went forward to get the spear-stricken dog. It was a female, and the one he had killed with his club was a big male. Doubtless they were a mated pair with puppies somewhere in the forest.

Hawk dragged both dogs to the fire and left them beside Willow. Then he squatted down near the fire.

He still shivered with excitement at the power of the wonderful new weapon that was now his. It was a long-sought answer to two pressing problems: how to stay far enough from dangerous game and at the same time attack it; and how to reach out and kill small, agile beasts which hitherto had eluded the hunters. At last he had a weapon with which he could strike at an unheard-of-distance.

Hawk sat still, so entranced by the new and wonderful spear-thrower that he paid small attention to the familiar smell of burned hair and roasting meat. But when Willow brought him the roasted haunch of one of the dogs he tore happily at it. Finished, he looked to his fire and lay down to sleep.

His slumber was light. Ceaseless vigilance, an ability to be awake and on one's feet fighting, all in the same instant, was the price of life. Hawk awakened at intervals to tend his fire and to test the various winds. No danger threatened.

He slept sporadically, satisfied that all was well and still refusing to worry about what tomorrow might bring. Banishment should have meant death in a matter of hours, but he and Willow were still alive and had food in plenty. They also had fire, their surest protection. Hawk rested contentedly, knowing that at any moment he might have to fight for his life but accepting that fact as a normal part of existence.

With dawn he rose and ate more meat which Willow cooked. The day would bring its own special problems and the question of coping with them occupied his thoughts.

Until now his life had been a nomadic one. The tribe to which he had belonged had always found it necessary to wander, to follow the game herds upon which they depended for food. Often they passed one season hundreds of miles from where they had spent the previous one. There was no such thing as a settled or permanent home.

And the tribe, with a dozen strong hunters, had been able to wander. That many spearsmen, presenting a united front, could beat back almost anything that attacked. Even the ferocious sabertooth was not a match for twelve spears.

But Hawk knew that he could not possibly wander now. Even if he were not accompanied by the wounded Willow, one man alone was no match for all the dangers of traveling. He must have a haven, some place of safety, and the fire was the safest place he knew. He hauled more wood and built his fire up. Then he looked restlessly about.

The second absolute necessity for just staying alive was plenty of food. For the present he had plenty, but it would not last. He must get more, and the fact that he had to hunt meant that he must leave the safety of the fire.

Hawk carefully fashioned two more spears for himself, then lashed points to them from the flints and thongs in his pouch. He tried them both for balance, and fitted them to his spear-thrower. Satisfied, he glided softly into the forest.

Seeking game, Hawk walked as cunningly and as carefully as any four-footed hunter. He used his eyes, ears, and nose, as completely as any beast of the forest. Always he hunted into the wind, so that he might be sure of everything about him.

Suddenly he halted, his nostrils dilating as they detected a faint scent. The odor strengthened, bringing to him positive news of a great cave bear. Hawk stood still, smelling, looking, listening. Cave-dwelling bears were monstrous things, even more savage than the saber-tooth tigers. From time to time, when they were desperate for food, the tribe's hunters had attacked and killed a bear, but such a creature was far more than a match for one man. Still, for safety's sake, he had better locate the bear's cave.

Cautiously he stole forward, only to halt again as a new scent began to mingle with that of the bear.

It was the odor of dire wolves, giant beasts larger than the deer they usually hunted. A pack of them must be after the bear.

Just ahead of him was a small hillock crowned with a group of trees. Hawk ran swiftly up the slope and stopped beneath a tree whose low-hanging branches offered a quick climb to safety if need be. He peered around the trunk.

Across a small meadow, and against the side of another hill, the cave's black entrance made a gaping hole. Taller than a man, it was little more than a yard wide. Nothing was visible, but Hawk was sure that the bear was within his den. Wolf scent grew stronger.

They swept into sight, a score of them. Lean gray beasts, each almost as tall as a man, the pack was strong and knew it. Even a heard of giant bison might fear such a pack. Should they attack a marching tribe, one unprotected by fire, the best the hunters could do would be to climb the nearest trees. Unfortunate humans caught on the ground would be torn apart in seconds.

The pack was intent on the bear's den, and without hesitation swept in to attack. To Hawk, watching from the opposite hill, the cave's dark entrance seemed to become a shade darker, and then the massive head and shoulders of the bear were framed in it. The wolves were leaping now, crowding each other in their eagerness to close. They swept in from every angle.

Like swift clubs the bear's paws flashed. His great jaws snapped, and three wolves lay where they had fallen. More pressed in, so many that for a moment, the cave's mouth and the bear were almost hidden beneath a wave of wolves.

Then, almost as suddenly as it had started, the fight was over. Leaving its dead behind, the battered pack withdrew. For a few minutes the wolves milled uncertainly, as though they would attack again. Then they trotted away.

Hawk waited until he was sure they were gone before he left the sheltering trees. It had been a surprising fight. The bear should have been killed, and would have had he been caught in the open. But he had chosen his position well and defended it easily. His tender flanks and belly, his most vulnerable parts, had been protected on three sides, and he had won his battle.

It was something to think about. Hawk added the incident to his wealth of forest lore.

He continued his hunt, searching out those places where he thought game would be. Presently he stopped again. Just ahead, a herd of antelope was feeding. Hawk stalked the small beasts carefully. He fixed a spear in his throwing-stick, stepped around a tree, and found himself within a few yards of the antelope.

They reacted in their usual fashion. Leaping and jumping erratically, they seemed for a moment unable to decide just where they were to go. Hawk cast his spear and saw it transfix a buck. Entering one side, the spear head and six inches of shaft protruded through the other. Happily Hawk went forth to retrieve his game. Again he had done it. Again he had killed game at a greater distance than a man could throw a hand spear by strength alone.

As Hawk shouldered the little buck, he straightened and stood still, alerted by the scent of dog. It was a puzzling odor, last night's stale smell mingled with a faint but fresh one. Hawk followed his nose.

He looked beneath the roots of a great tree at two snarling puppies.

WOLVES

The mammoth had begun bellowing in the middle of the night. The men of Wolf's tribe awakened immediately. They squatted, shoulder to shoulder, just inside the glow of firelight.

The hunters murmured among themselves as they strained their ears to catch every detail of sound and scent which the wind bore.

The commotion might mean food, and the tribe needed food very badly. Wolf's belly pinched though he, as Chief Hunter, had eaten as well as any of the men in the tribe. The women looked gaunt, and several of the children cried listlessly with hunger.

When dawn was a hint so slight that stars still sparkled on the eastern horizon, Wolf muttered, "Come!" He got up, carrying his two spears in his

49

left hand. Several of the hunters watched their chief in concern.

"Men do not hunt in the darkness, Wolf," said Elm, the medicine woman. She was very old, perhaps a full generation older than anyone else in the tribe. Although Elm was a woman, age and the spiritual powers which she invoked in healing gave her freedom to speak where others would remain silent.

Wolf nodded toward the east. "It is not night, it is morning," he said gruffly. "Besides, we need meat.

"Come," he repeated. The hunters were looking at him. They got to their feet without objection. The ten adult men and their sons stayed close together as they slipped through the near-light.

Old Kar looked back once, toward the campfire which the women would now have to stoke. The Chief Fire-Maker had a duty to the camp, but his greatest duty was to the hunt; especially now, when the tribe's luck had been bad for so long.

The mammoth was alone. It was a young bull, perhaps one driven from its herd when it challenged another bull for leadership—and failed.

The beast's current problems began when it tried to cross a slow-moving stream during the night. The low creekbank shaded imperceptibly into a marsh of reeds rather than ordinary grasses. The mammoth was now bogged to its belly in sucking mud.

Wolf frowned at the sight. He and his hunters were not the only predators summoned by the beast's despairing bellows.

A pack of a dozen dire wolves snapped and

snarled among themselves at the edge of the marsh, waiting for dawn to provide them a better notion of how to proceed. The dire wolves were twice the bulk of ordinary wolves, and their powerful jaws enabled them to break up bones which their lesser cousins could not.

The increase in size and strength had not been accompanied by a comparable boost in brain capacity. The dire wolves were unusually stupid for carnivores. Their usual tactic was to charge straight in and overpower their prey. That would not work here.

The mammoth, though trapped beyond hope of rescue, weighed five tons. It was simply too big for the wolves alone to kill. Besides, it still swept a great arc with its trunk and curved tusks.

The morning sun was not yet high enough to lift vultures from the trees on which they perched overnight. They would come soon enough, drawn by the movements of other meat eaters even before the scent of death reached the birds' keen nostrils.

The killers on which all the would-be scavengers depended were the pair of great tigers pacing toward the mammoth from upstream while Wolf and his hunters approached in the opposite direction. The cats advanced with a degree of caution, heads up and sniffing the wind. A grown mammoth was a dangerous opponent, even for tigers whose fangs were six-inch knives.

"The tigers are already here, Wolf," said Boartooth, as though the Chief Hunter had not seen the big cats almost a minute before. Boartooth, an Assistant Fire-Maker, was a young man who wore a broad necklace of boar tusks to flaunt his name. He had vast confidence in his own abilities. "We must go back."

Wolf looked at Boartooth sourly. "No," he said. "We need meat, so we will drive the animals away and take the mammoth."

"Waugh!" said several of the hunters in surprise. Old Kar looked at Wolf with concern. The Chief Fire-Maker guessed what his own part in the plan would be, and he was worried that he would not be able to perform it.

"Wolf," Kar said, "the grass here will not burn well. There will be more smoke than fire, and the flames will spread slowly."

He nodded toward the pack of wolves, angrily sidling away from the oncoming tigers. "Besides," he added, "these are not bison to flee in panic from a fire. While there is so much meat around, they will not go far."

Wolf grunted. "We are men," he said. "It is right that the meat should be ours."

The Chief Hunter turned to Boartooth. "You, Boartooth," he said. "Go back and bring the women and girls. We will camp on the creekbank, and our campfire will keep the wolves and tigers away."

Kar grimaced. "Be sure they fetch all the dry wood," he said. "The alder saplings along the creek here will not burn well, and we will need a very big fire tonight."

As the Chief Fire-Maker spoke, one of the saber-tooths sprang with a terrifying scream. Its forelegs locked on either side of the mammoth's hump. They anchored the cat while the long fangs stabbed and slashed backward under the pull of the tiger's powerful neck muscles.

Arterial blood spurted from the deep cuts. The red streams pulsed, paused, and pulsed again. Blood soaked the black wool covering the mammoth's hide.

The stricken mammoth bellowed again and clubbed its trunk back over its head. The tiger was already leaping away. The mammoth's blow staggered the cat and caused it to splash sideways into the marsh. The saber-tooth twisted, then clawed its way to firm ground in a spray of water and shredded reeds.

The killer's mate began to groom it on the banks. The long saber fangs were bright with blood. The tiger licked them clean with obvious relish while the mammoth bled to death in the bog nearby.

Kar fussed with his preparations, plaiting the coarse, bottomland grass into torches. The outer leaves were golden and would burn well enough, but the core of each grass stem was still pale and juicy because the soil was so wet.

The hunters could see that they would have trouble even keeping their torches burning. The tigers began to eat. The smell of fresh meat outweighed the tribe's concerns.

Each hunter carried a hollow gourd filled with punk. Kar went from one man to the next, lighting the punk from the smoldering in his own gourd. By the time Boartooth returned, a little embarrassed at having been sent on a task that would usually have been given to a boy, all was ready for this unusual hunt.

Wolf gave a curt order. The men and boys lighted

their torches and moved forward slowly. This time instead of running ahead of the fire, they let the mild breeze advance the flames.

As Kar had warned, there was smoke but very little in the way of fire. The gray-white cloud clung to the grassheads as it blew toward the mammoth. The dire wolves had taken no notice of the tribe. Now the pack began to snarl and pace, uncertain of what was happening.

The male saber-tooth rose to its full height on the mammoth's back and roared a challenge while its mate hunched low. After a moment, the cats resumed eating, but their attention was now concentrated on the humans.

The hunters continued to walk forward, relighting their wall of protection wherever it had smoldered out. Their legs were smeared black from the ashes. Occasionally a man would yelp as he brushed the tip of a stem which was still glowing.

The women and girls, carrying all the possessions of the tribe, stayed close behind the males. Elm muttered, but even she was willing to accept that there was no traditional way to hunt a bogged mammoth—so Wolf was not going against tradition. If the tribe hadn't been so hungry, there might have been louder protests . . . but they were *very* hungry.

Bitter smoke wrapped the carnivores in memories of of instinctive fear. The cats stopped eating, but they held their position on top of the mammoth's carcase. The female growled. The male rose frequently onto its hind legs and slashed out with its widespread claws. The smoke swirled and reformed.

The line of hunters was within fifty yards of the mammoth. Vultures wheeled in the sky, but the birds would not come down while the smoke from the grassfire drifted over the ground.

"Hau!" the Chief Hunter shouted. His torch had gone out, but the fire had begun to leap ahead of him over the pithy reed tops closer to the creek.

He clashed the shafts of his two spears together. "Hau!" he called again. "Run, beasts, run! We are men and we come with fire!"

"Hau!" cried Kar, who did not have a spear. He waved his club to fan the flames. Other hunters took up the chant, clacking their spears together—tentatively at first, then faster and louder as they found the noise gave them courage and disturbed the animals. The wolves began to back away, then paused.

Wolf was afraid, but he knew that if the humans turned and ran now, the pack would chase them down and kill all but the swiftest. Without really thinking about what he was doing, he shouted, "Come!" to his men and rushed forward.

The fire singed his thighs as he ran through it. For a moment, the dire wolves were shadows twisting in the thickest part of the smoke. Then the pack broke and fled in the opposite direction. The ground trembled as a dozen 200-pound wolves galloped across it.

Boartooth threw a spear. It was a good cast, but the range was long. The spear struck a wolf in the haunch and penetrated to half the length of the flint blade—deep enough to cling, but not to disable its victim. The dire wolf, yelping in bass terror, ran even faster.

For the first time since he exiled Hawk, the Chief Hunter realized that the tribe no longer had a spear-maker to make up for such accidents. They would have to appoint a Chief Spear-Maker soon—

But first there was the problem of gaining the tons of good meat which were almost in their grasp.

When the wolves ran, the male saber-tooth leaped to firm ground with effortless grace. He roared a challenge while his mate crouched on the mammoth.

Kar had paused to plait together several reeds and ignite their dry heads. Though the reeds did not make a bright flame, they burned better than the wet grass, and the new torch had sufficient weight to carry it if thrown. Kar hurled the burning reeds straight at the tiger.

The bundle caught the cat on the side of the jaw. Its whiskers and the fine tufts of hair on its ears flared up. The tiger roared and sprang off in the direction the wolves had taken.

For a moment, the female saber-tooth held her place on top of the huge corpse. Then, with a blood-curdling roar, she jumped to the bank also. For a moment her body was a tawny shadow arching like a fish's back every time it leaped and disappeared again in the high grass. Then Wolf's tribe was alone with the corpse of the mammoth and a skyful of vultures which were afraid to land.

"We've driven them off!" Boartooth cried exultantly. "Our luck has changed, now that we've rid ourselves of Hawk!"

"Begin laying a proper fire," said Kar coldly. "We'll need more than smoke to keep those teeth away from us as soon as the wolves and tigers have time to get over their surprise."

But the whole tribe, including the women and children, was splashing through the marsh with hand-axes and flint knives to get pieces of the meat. They were famished. None of them would wait for the mammoth to cook before they ate their bellies full.

Kar sighed and began to gather dry wood from where the women had dropped it. He was as hungry as the rest of them; but his duty came first, and Kar's duty was to make the fire that would protect the tribe through the rest of the day—and the night which would follow.

The sun was two fingers beneath the horizon, but it still cast its red glow over the western sky. The moon would not rise until after midnight, and even then it would be a waning sliver. Through the twilight sounded the hollow *tok! tok! tok!* of a hand-axe on bone.

"Boartooth!" Kar shouted. The Chief Fire-Maker and Chinless, his other assistant, were dragging a bundle of alder saplings toward the fire. "Leave the mammoth alone and help us cut wood!"

Most of the tribe sprawled around the fire on their backs or sides, trying to find a comfortable posture. Their bellies were swollen with the huge amount of raw meat they had stuffed down their throats.

Many of the humans had eaten so much that they threw up. That didn't matter; there was plenty more to refill the suddenly-emptied stomachs. No matter what, tons of the rich, fat-marbled meat would spoil before the tribe could possibly devour it.

Even Wolf looked nearly comatose with his eyes half-open. His powerful fingers were laced over his belly as if to keep his guts from bursting out. With the exception of Kar—and Chinless, whom the Chief Fire-Maker had bullied into getting on with his duties—the tribe were not so much humans for the moment as they were like serpents which lay torpid as they digested the swollen lump that marked their most recent meal.

The campfire was near the mammoth. Kar had set his fire as close to the creekbank as he could in the jubilant confusion after the tribe gained the mountain of warm meat.

The fire *had* to be close if it was to keep the other predators away from the mammoth as well as protecting the humans during the night, but the constant procession of people jumping and splashing to and from the corpse made it impossible for the Chief Fire-Maker to build as near the bank as he wanted.

"I'm cutting out a tusk, Kar," Boartooth replied. In the near-darkness, it was almost impossible to tell where the young man ended and where the dead mammoth began. "I'll carve it with this scene, so that the mammoth spirit will be thankful and send us more of his children to eat."

"We need wood!" Kar shouted angrily. "We don't have enough fuel to keep the fire burning all night!"

Tok! went Boartooth's hand-axe as he resumed his self-appointed task. "The wood here is green, old man," he said. "It won't burn anyway. Tomorrow we can get dry wood from the forest and bring it here."

The sky was dark enough now that the eyes of animals glinted red in the light of the fire. The wolf pack lay in a loose semicircle facing the humans' camp and the partly-butchered mammoth in the marsh beyond. Soot from the grassfire stained everything and charged the air with a green, sickly smell quite different from that of the dry wood now burning in the center of the camp.

Kar threw down his load of alders. They made a swishing sound, not the bang that he could have achieved with dry wood on firm ground. Boartooth was right. These saplings would burn badly, with a crackling, smoky fire and very little flame—but they were the only wood available here in the bottomlands.

"Nobody listens to me!" he cried in frustration. "You'll be sorry!"

Wolf rolled into a sitting posture, looking uncomfortable from the amount he had eaten. The orange firelight darkened the hairs in the Chief Hunter's beard which were still brown, but it turned the grizzling of age into golden accents.

"Settle down, Kar," he called. "It's too dark to go out now anyway. In the morning, everyone will fetch more wood—even hunters."

Tok! went Boartooth's axe. *Tok! Tok!*

The opposite side of the creek was more than thirty feet from the mammoth. The tiger crouching there in darkness gave a terrifying roar and leaped to the back of the huge corpse.

Boartooth shrieked as though he had been disemboweled. He hurled his hand-axe away in panic as he jumped to safety on the bank. He was actually unharmed.

The tigers—the second saber-tooth followed the first in a flat, graceful arc, flexing its backbone like a willow bending in a fierce wind—ignored the man. Their whole attention was concentrated on the mammoth from which they had been briefly driven.

"Up!" shouted Wolf, active and alert despite his heavy meal. He held a spear in his right hand. With his left, the Chief Hunter snaked a burning branch from the campfire. The brand was alight along most of its length. The bright flames licked within inches of Wolf's hand and made the hairs shrivel on the back of his forearm. He ignored the pain. Other hunters sprang to their feet and joined him.

The two tigers balanced on top of what had been their prey in the first place. They glared at the men across the short distance separating them. The male coughed a bloodthirsty challenge.

Wolf whirled his torch around his head. Sparks flew off in a dazzling circle, falling to the ground and on the men beside him. The male saber-tooth roared and raised his right paw in a gesture like a human waving. The four toes were splayed, and the needle-sharp claws were extended from the pads to their full length.

For a moment, the scene was frozen. Then the tiger deliberately lowered its head and began to tear at the meat. Its eyes remained fixed on the humans.

Boartooth had snatched up a spear—in the confusion, not the one of his own which remained. He poised the weapon to throw.

Wolf clouted the younger man across the temple with the shaft of his own spear. "No!" shouted the Chief Hunter. "You'll only wound it, and then—"

He didn't have to complete the sentence. The whole tribe could imagine the infuriated tiger springing into the middle of them and slashing in all directions with claws and the fangs that had slaughtered a mammoth.

Both cats were now eating noisily, though they continued to watch the humans.

"We'll stay close to the fire," Wolf continued. "The tigers aren't interested in us, they have food to eat. In the morning, we'll build up the fire and drive them away again."

He backed slowly away from the creekbank. The other men followed willingly, glad to be offered an option which did not require them to fight a pair of saber-tooths. After all, the tribe was full of meat now. Not even the tigers could devour enough of the mammoth to make a difference.

Beyond the circle of firelight, the dire wolves crept closer on their bellies. They were drawn by the slurping sounds as the saber-tooths gorged on their prey.

The fire was beginning to burn low. Kar threw another branch on it. He was worried. Not very much dry wood remained, and Boartooth had been right when he said that the alders would not burn well.

Kar woke up abruptly at the sound of Wolf's voice shouting, ". . . the fire! It's too low!"

The campfire was a bank of red coals, shimmering angrily while the tribe sprawled around it.

Everyone had been asleep. The huge meal following days of hunger had acted like a drug on the humans, despite the predators encircling them.

Kar couldn't believe that *he* had fallen asleep in the midst of this danger, but even the sound of the tigers eating had become a neutral background instead of a threat. The cats weren't interested in human beings while the mammoth was available for food, after all. . . .

Kar scrabbled for wood in the darkness. There had been a bundle of alders beside him. His hand found nothing. One of his assistants—Chinless should have been on watch—had thrown the whole mass on the fire and gone to sleep. The alders would not keep burning without a careful hand to stir the green stems.

Awakening hunters shouted nervously when they saw the state of the fire. An infant screamed, terrified by the atmosphere of fright.

"Chinless!" Kar ordered. "Boartooth! Get more wood!"

The Chief Fire-Maker himself snatched at partly-burned saplings that stuck out from the heart of the fire. He stuffed them into the glowing center. The wood flared in a brief revival, singeing Kar's forearm and hand. The eyes of the dire wolves gleamed around the tribe, as close as a garnet necklace to the throat of a chief.

Hunters shouted. Some of them threw spears.

"Don't throw!" Wolf bellowed. "Stab if the wolves come close, but don't waste your spears!"

Chinless reached for the club he had left on the ground where he had been sleeping. "There isn't any more wood!" he said. A dire wolf rose from its crouch and clamped its huge jaws over Chinless's elbow. The man's voice rose into a scream.

Kar thrust his handful of alder stems into the wolf's face. His swift motion quenched the flames on the green wood. The smoldering ends left a smear along the carnivore's gray fur, but the wolf only growled deeper in its throat. It backed away from the camp, dragging Kar's whimpering assistant with it.

Another dire wolf grabbed Chinless by the leg in its bonecrushing jaws. More of the pack converged on the sudden prey—but a single man was no meal for a dozen animals as big as these. Several sprang into the camp circle, no longer afraid of the fire's sullen glow. Kar threw down his useless attempt at a torch and ran in the opposite direction.

The Chief Hunter tried to shout an order, but the whole tribe was running. The only light was that of the crescent moon. Screams of panic located humans in the night. Snarls and the horrible sound of bones snapping showed that the wolf pack pursured.

Kar was old, but terror drove him. He overtook a woman who was burdened by her infant child. None of the humans were fleeing some*where*; they were just trying to get away from where they had been.

As the Chief Fire-Maker wheezed past the woman, a huge shadow arched out of the darkness. It was one of the saber-tooths. The cat had been gorging on mammoth for several hours, so it cannot have been hungry. Perhaps the scents of blood and fear had triggered a killer instinct deeper than the mere need for food.

The tiger weighed four or five times as much as the woman. It crushed her flat, silencing the scream in her throat before she had time to utter it. The tiger bent its lower jaw back more than ninety degrees to unsheathe its long fangs. The moonlight was just bright enough to gleam on the teeth as they stabbed down in a duplicate of the blow which had killed a mammoth.

Kar closed his eyes and continued to run until he collapsed, sobbing with exhaustion.

In the morning the Chief Fire-Maker lit a fire on the edge of the forest. The smoke column called the remainder of the tribe to him. Most of them limped from thorn cuts or the shock of falls they had taken while running through the darkness.

Wolf's left forearm was bloody and swollen. He had wrapped it roughly with grass during the night. Elm tut-tutted about the coarse bandage. When she removed it to wash the area and replace the bandage with one of her own, the puckered holes and slashes left by a dire wolf's teeth stood out against the Chief Hunter's swarthy skin.

Wolf's spearhead was black to the bindings with predator's blood. Only four other hunters still had their spears.

The battered humans looked around at one another. Four women and three of the children were missing. Nobody suggested going back onto the plain to look for them.

Chinless was the only adult male who had not survived. The men had their weapons, and they had sprinted away from the camp more quickly than most of the women and children could follow.

"We need more spears," Wolf said heavily. "We have no spear-maker now."

"I can make spears," said Boartooth. "My spears will be better than those of Hawk. His spears brought us bad luck."

Kar had built his fire against an outcrop of gray-brown chert. It was not as hard or as uniform in quality as flint, but the rock was glassy enough to chip into serviceable points if the maker was careful.

Boartooth began worrying a block of chert out of the soft shale in which it was held. The Chief Fire-Maker wondered if the young man had gotten the tusk loose before the tigers drove him away from the mammoth. Ivory was the least of the tribe's worries now. . . .

"We have fed well," Wolf said in a forceful voice which compelled his listeners to believe him. "We will make more spears, and we will hunt much more food. Our luck will be very good from now on."

"We must appease the spirit of the bison," Elm muttered. "We will have no luck until the spirit of the bison forgives us."

But she spoke under her breath, and nobody wanted to listen to the old woman anyway.

SABER-TOOTH

Hawk knelt, examining the new sight. A large tree had blown down, and when its imbedded roots had been torn out of their resting place they had carried a great quantity of dirt with them. It still clung to the upraised roots, forming a roof of mingled earth and small stones. Beneath it, crouched as close to the back wall as they could get, the furry puppies slunk close together for comfort and safety.

They were too old to be sucklings, and beaten trails proved that they had already made short hunting expeditions of their own into nearby thickets and bramble patches. One was dun-colored, the other silvery gray. They snarled their defiance of the intruder.

As Hawk peered into the den, he realized that these were probably pups of the two dogs slain in attacking his camp. Deprived of their parents' protection, only miraculous luck had kept them from falling prey to some predator. If left alone, they would certainly be killed before long because they were too small to defend themselves. Hawk considered.

He should not leave them here, and thus let something else rob him of what, by right of discovery, was his proper food. But there was meat in plenty at the camp and now he had the little antelope buck as well. In hot weather meat spoiled quickly, and if he killed these puppies now the chances were good they would rot before he and Willow could eat them.

A happy thought occurred to him.

He needn't kill the puppies at all. They were small, and could be captured easily. If he caught them alive, and carried them back to the fire, they could be tied and held prisoners. They needn't be killed until he and Willow needed meat.

Hawk stood for a full minute interpreting the various sights, sounds, and scents. To capture the puppies he must get down on his hands and knees and crawl part way into the den. Before he did so he wanted to be sure that no danger threatened. But he could see nothing unusual.

He returned his attention to the puppies, who were pushing as hard as they could against the back end of the cave and watching him with bright, hostile eyes. Hawk crawled into the cave and reached out his hand.

Instantly the silver-gray puppy was upon it. Launching himself with all the fury at his command, he slashed with his white, needle-sharp puppy teeth. Hawk grimaced as he withdrew his scratched hand. The puppy took a stance in front of his companion, as though to protect him. He snarled and bristled fiercely.

This time Hawk struck hard, sweeping his hand forward and clenching his fist around the puppy's fore paws and body. The puppy squirmed, and tried to get his teeth into play. He could not because Hawk gripped him too strongly. Instantly transferring the silver-gray puppy to his left hand, Hawk snatched the other with his right.

As quickly as possible, dragging the pair with him, he withdrew from the cave. He stood erect and retested the winds, then looked and listened. All was peaceful.

The puppies were squirming to free themselves. The silver-gray had got hold of Hawk's horny left fist and was enthusiastically chewing on it. Unable to get any purchase, or to brace his body, he could not break the skin with his small puppy jaws. But he could make himself felt. Hawk took the puppy by the scruff of his neck, tucked him under his right arm, and kept his right hand tightly closed around the dun-colored one. The pups squirmed and wriggled, trying to get away, and Hawk cuffed them.

He stooped, shouldered the little antelope, clasped his spear and throwing-stick in his left hand, and started back toward the fire. As he neared it, he stopped and slunk into a thicket. A saber-tooth, a big one, was lying on a ledge of rock, studying the fire. Cautiously Hawk retraced his steps. He took a new direction, around the tiger, and trotted lightly into camp.

Having reached the safety of the fire, Hawk glanced back at the ledge upon which lay the saber-tooth, and sniffed the breeze to get the tiger's scent. It was a big male, and the very fact that it was so stealthily intent on the fire was proof that it was hunting. They would have to be very wary. Hungry meat-eaters had almost endless patience. If this one had decided to watch the camp, it might wait for days on end. But there was no danger as long as they stayed close by the fire.

Willow, who had been out gathering seeds, was grinding them in a hollow stone she had found. She left her work and rose, for the first time able to walk with some freedom. Now she had only a painful limp. Young and strong, she would now recover quickly from the wound.

She looked at the puppies in Hawk's arms, and took them from him. Then she sat down, cradling the pups and playing with them. They wriggled from her arms to the ground, and Hawk raised his club, scowling his annoyance.

This was not the way to handle the puppies; they would run away at the first opportunity and should be confined or crippled so they could not run far. But he stayed his descending club. The puppies seemed perfectly contented to stay near the girl. When one ventured a little way from her, it returned as soon as she snapped her fingers. Hawk forgot about them.

He stretched out beside the fire and went instantly to sleep. This he must do when he could, for only rarely was there an opportunity to rest. He dared not relax when he went hunting, and night required constant vigilance.

An hour later he sprang erect, his hand shooting out to the club at his side. Then, looking for what had awakened him, he saw the silver-gray puppy making a ferocious attack on his fur girdle. The other one was tumbling over and over in the grass, waging a fierce mock battle with a stick. Smiling at their antics, Willow became sober-faced as soon as Hawk sprang to his feet.

For a moment he was angry. He raised his club, tempted to smash the gray puppy's brains out with it, but the look of pleading on Willow's face made him desist. He lowered the club, pushed the puppy out of the way with his foot, caught up his spear, and stalked haughtily off to gather more wood. Unabashed, the gray puppy trailed at his heels.

A flock of big, turkey-like birds scattered ahead of him. One by one they rose to wing away. Hawk drew back his club to hurl it at one of the birds, but he was forestalled by the gray puppy. Yapping hysterically, he flung himself forward and leaped upon a running bird.

He fastened his small teeth on the wing feathers, and strained backward with all his strength. The running bird dragged him, but the puppy would not let go nor could the bird rise while thus encumbered. Hawk stepped forward, grabbed the running bird, snatched it away from the puppy, and wrung its neck.

He stood still, dangling the big bird by its twisted neck and smacking his lips. Such game was a delicacy which the tribe almost never enjoyed because the hunters could seldom get close enough to kill it. The Spear-Maker looked down at the panting puppy, who now reared against his knee, stretching an eager nose toward the bird. Hawk stared quizzically at him.

A few hours ago the puppy had been a wild, savage thing, ready and willing to fight him as best it could. Now it was almost tame. Too young to know any better, it had accepted the humans in place of its own parents, and had even aided in the hunt.

This was something entirely new to Hawk, and therefore something he could not understand. Certainly he would not have the bird had not the puppy caught it for him. This much he realized. But there was, in his mind, no possible connection between one single incident and the idea of using the puppy as a hunting companion. Men had always hunted for themselves and he would continue to do so. But at least he felt more kindly disposed toward his small prisoner.

He gathered an armful of wood and returned to the fire. The dun puppy gamboled happily out to meet him. Kicking him aside, Hawk threw the dead bird down beside Willow. The gray puppy sat expectantly on his haunches, turning bright little eyes from Willow to Hawk and back at the bird. He barked sharply, and wagged his furry tail.

Hawk ate a piece of antelope, saying nothing about the remainder. Certainly there was more missing than he and Willow had eaten, therefore she must have fed the puppies while he had been sleeping. That was all right as long as there was plenty.

His meat finished, Hawk tossed the bone to the gray puppy and moved restlessly about the camp.

The lurking tiger posed a very real threat, and one that must be dealt with. It was not the ordinary night prowler or occasional daytime visitor. This tiger had marked its quarry down and evidently had a plan. It seemed to know humans and their habits, and sooner or later would catch Willow or Hawk, or both, away from their fire and in a place where they might safely be attacked.

Armed with the two spears, his throwing-stick, and his club, Hawk left the fire. He circled through the forest to the rocky ledge upon which he had seen the tiger. It had left, and Hawk moved cautiously up to the place where it had been. He found the tiger's resting place in a ledge of rocks from which the camp could be studied to perfect advantage. Keeping a spear poised, and constantly on the alert, Hawk followed the tiger's tracks.

For a moment he was puzzled because they led downhill and away from the camp. He stooped in order to study the tiger's trail more clearly. The beast was a long way ahead of him, but there was always the possibility that it might circle and lay an ambush. Hawk hunted into the wind, always trying to know what lay ahead, and whenever the tiger's trail veered with the wind, he circled until he picked it up again. A half hour later he knew why the tiger had abandoned its watch of their camp.

A large herd of camels had moved into the area. Their scent came faintly at first, but as Hawk moved nearer, the odor strengthened. They had passed among the little hillocks and winding valleys toward the same river meadows upon which the tribe had unsuccessfully attempted to trap the giant bison. Hawk swerved from the tiger's trail and climbed a hill.

From the summit he looked into a partly wooded valley. The camel herd had passed here, so many of them that they had left a beaten road behind them. Below, in the valley, Hawk saw the tiger.

It was eating from a large camel it had pulled down. Vultures were wheeling through the sky, and others had already alighted in the nearby trees. Endlessly patient, they were waiting until the tiger was through before they descended to feast on what remained. Skulking in the grass were two other hopeful scavengers: a pair of wild cats that were also lingering until the tiger was finished before they fought over whatever was left.

Hawk had previously noticed that the saber-tooth was an old beast. Yet it was not too old to kill a full-grown camel. Even though some of its vigor was gone, it was a beast to watch carefully. Hawk went back down the hillock and started toward the river meadows.

From another vantage he looked down upon the camel herd. Hundreds strong, they were feeding avidly on the rich river grass. Judging by their condition, they had journeyed a long way from some arid, drought-stricken pastures. But at last they were here and now would give themselves over to satisfying their hunger. They would stay here until the river meadows were grazed bare or until they were driven elsewhere by raiding beasts.

Already the raiders were gathering. As Hawk watched, a small pack of dogs swooped upon a camel calf feeding at its mother's side. The mother whirled to defend her young, striking high with her big hooves. Three of the dogs feinted before her, luring her away and distracting her attention while three more went in and killed the calf.

Hawk turned away, satisfied. The camel herd was a blessing in more ways than one. He himself could hunt them, for one man could kill a camel. Also, it was very unlikely that any predator would bother to stalk a man when there was easier and safer game to be had. He was sure that the tiger would stay near the camel herd as long as the camels stayed.

But, though Hawk needn't fear the tiger in the near future, there were other things he must do. Never far from his thoughts was the fact that he was a lone man. Banished from his tribe, he lacked the safety which numbers alone could furnish. When faced with danger, he could not present the many spear points that the tribe could.

He needed more striking power, more weapons. But if he carried two spears and a club he was already burdened down with everything he could conveniently carry and handle. The throwing-stick was a thing of great power, but suppose he was confronted by a pack of dogs or wolves? After he had thrown his two spears he must still rely on his club, and that meant dangerous, close-quarter work. Hawk turned back toward the fire, giving all his thoughts to this new problem.

All about were the scents of small beasts: rodents, deer, antelope, and different tree-climbing creatures. According to their natures, they either bounded out of his way or froze tightly where they were, hoping to escape detection by staying quiet. Hawk paid no particular attention to any of them, for these were creatures he needn't fear and at the present didn't want. But suddenly he stopped, his nostrils dilated. The wind bore him the scent of another wild cat, and he knew from the odor that the cat was in a dangerous mood. Furthermore, it was coming his way. He fitted a spear into his throwing-stick.

The little cat came upon him suddenly, bursting out of the grass and hurling itself recklessly toward him. Hawk waited, not wanting to cast his spear until the right moment and not afraid of the little cat anyway. He could kill it with his club if need be, but the throwing-stick was a new power, and he wished to use it as much as possible. When the bouncing wild cat was about twenty feet away, Hawk smoothly cast his spear.

The flint-edged point snicked into the beast's neck and came out its back. The cat reared straight up, clawing at the spear shaft, then fell on its side. For a moment its paw twitched feebly, then it was still.

As Hawk walked slowly up to his fallen quarry, he understood why it had rushed at him in such an insane fashion. In the recent past, the cat had foolishly tackled a porcupine, and had become half-crazed from the pain of the quills. There were so many of the needle-sharp barbs in its cheeks and face that the tawny gray fur was almost hidden beneath them. The cat had evidently tried to bite the porcupine, and had succeeded only in filling its mouth and tongue with quills. Hawk looked at the little spears with respect.

He knew the porcupines, some of which were almost as big as dire wolves. They were stupid things that knew only how to gnaw bark, and to eat grass and roots. But of all the creatures in this savage land, porcupines were the only ones equipped to survive without fighting. Any beast that attacked those bristling arrays of small spears did so to its own sorrow and frequently its own death.

Hawk pulled his spear out of the wild cat and shouldered the carcass. It was meat, and therefore to be saved. But it had also given him an idea. A human could not carry and handle more than two or three full-sized spears, but what if, like the porcupine, he were armed with many small ones?

When Hawk returned, Willow was turning the bird over the fire on a long spit. The puppies crowded over to frolic about him, and he pushed them aside, his nostrils twitching from the savory smell of the cooking fowl.

Hawk tore hungrily at his portion, and looked appreciatively at the girl. Meat prepared this way was delicious, much better than that which was just hung over the fire on a green stick. Usually the outside of that was burned and the inside raw. The bird was cooked to a flaky turn all through. Hawk wiped his hands on his fur girdle, threw the bones to the puppies, and let them scramble for them. His stomach filled with hot food, Hawk sighed happily.

"I never had such food before," he said. "It is good."

Her own portion finished, Willow sat cross-legged beside the fire, weaving a basket from limber willow shoots she had gathered. Hawk watched her idly. The art of basket-making had long been known to the women of his tribe. When they gathered a

store of food, they used woven baskets in which to
keep it. But the baskets were never kept for very
long. On a long march nobody wanted to carry
extra or unnecessary weight. Only on those rare
occasions when the tribe stayed somewhere for an
extended period did baskets appear.

Hawk looked up quickly, distracted by a rustling sound. But it was only the skin of the bird
they had eaten. Pending some possible future use,
Willow had hung it on a limb and he had heard
the feathers rustling. Returning to his problem of
more weapons, Hawk went to the dead cat, pulled
a quill from its cheek, and looked at it.

Although he had tried many times, he had never
been able to make any practical use of the little
barbs. The quills served their original owners well
enough, but they were too thin and flexible even
to think of tipping a hand spear with them. But he
might make a small spear and see how it worked.

Hawk emptied his pouch of flint spear heads
and studied them intently. All had been fashioned
for heavy spears. Attached to a shaft smaller than
that for which they had been designed, they would
make it unwieldly and top-heavy. Nor could they
be reshaped without spoiling them. He put all the
spear heads back into his pouch.

Unmindful of the gray puppy that tagged at his
heels, he rose and walked to an outcropping of
stone on the side of the hill. He pried among the
tumbled pieces of flint that had broken off, examining every piece with painstaking thoroughness,
rejecting most of them. He was not concerned
with size, but rather with flaws, conformation, and
the way any given piece might be expected to

flake. Finally, after an hour's search, he returned to the fire with half a dozen rough pieces of flint.

Now it was necessary to haul more wood for the night's fire. Grudgingly, reluctant to leave his task, he rose and went into the forest. While he made trip after trip, Willow sat quietly, shaping her basket. When it was finished, she lined the bottom with grass, then put in a large quantity of seeds she had gathered. As Hawk brought in his last load of wood, she began cooking more meat.

Holding a long piece of flint in his right hand, Hawk pried a flake from one of the pieces he had selected. Carefully, making no sudden moves that might injure the small head, he pried another flake off. Ordinarily it took only a few minutes to make a good spear head, but these, being smaller, must be made with great care. The Spear-Maker continued to shape the head he had planned, using pressure to remove one tiny flake at a time.

When he was finished he looked critically at the point in his hand. It was very good, better than most of the spear heads in his pouch, but he thought he could make a still better one. By the fire's light he crouched down again and went to work. Willow had been sleeping for hours when he finally thrust the last half-finished head into his pouch.

With morning he resumed his task, so absorbed in it that he forgot all else, except to eat what Willow gave him. Finally he balanced half a dozen flint heads in his hand. Again and again he inspected them minutely, looking at each for flaws. He could find none. He went into the forest and returned with an armful of hardwood shoots.

He knew what he had in mind, but he was somewhat at a loss as to how to accomplish it. The darts must be lighter and shorter than spears, but they must be long enough so that he could rest them in the throwing-stick and still balance them. With a sharp piece of flint he scraped a stick until it was perfectly smooth. Working with painstaking precision he smoothed off all the uneven edges, so that the stick balanced perfectly. He made another, and another.

It was noon of the following day before he had finished his task. He had half a dozen darts, better fashioned and balanced than any hand spears he had ever made. All six of them did not weigh as much as two spears, nor would they be any harder to carry. With mounting excitement he fitted one into his throwing-stick, getting the feel of it in countless practice casts before he finally threw.

A grunt of disappointment escaped him. Lacking the weight of a spear, the dart wobbled in flight and fell three feet to one side of the tuft of grass at which he had aimed. Nor could he get as much distance with the lighter weapon. He tried again and again, and failed each time to strike the tuft of grass. Hawk sat before the fire, chin in his hands. There must be some way to make the darts fly straight, but what was it? A shadow fell across him and he looked up.

Willow stood beside him, offering him baked cakes on a flat piece of stone. Hawk glared at her.

"Where is the meat?"

"There is no more. You have not been hunting."

Without answering Hawk reached out to grasp the dun-colored puppy by the scruff of its neck.

He lifted it with one hand, and reached for his club. This was why he had brought the puppies; now let them serve as food. He raised his club.

Willow moved so swiftly that she was in and out before the heavy club could descend. She snatched the puppy from his hands, and stepped backward. Hawk stared, too startled to move. A woman had defied him! As he got to his feet with a growl of rage, she swung away from him, shielding the puppy.

"Do not kill it! We have food!"

Hawk took a threatening forward step. Willow stood her ground for a moment, then turned and ran. The gray puppy raced at her heels. Furious, Hawk ran after them, club in hand.

Willow ran across the clearing to the border of the woods. At the base of a huge, lichen-encrusted boulder, she stumbled and went to one knee. Quickly she rose, turning to face the enraged Hawk. Her eyes widened in fear, but not of the man. She was staring over his shoulder.

Turning, Hawk saw the hunting saber-tooth between them and the safety of their fire.

HORSES AND CAMELS

Wolf chewed determinedly at the root and berry mush which was all the tribe had to eat this morning. He tried to pretend that he didn't notice the bitter taste. Except for the bitterness, the coarse porridge had no flavor at all.

Elm swore that she had appeased the spirits of the plant by scraping the roots, putting them in a wicker basket, and soaking them for two days in a running stream. Finally she boiled the mass to a gelatinous solid by pouring it into a pit in the ground and dropping in stones heated by the fire.

Wolf was confident that Elm knew what she was doing and that she had performed the rites correctly. The plant spirits would not grip the Chief Hunter's belly with cramps and nausea, perhaps even with death, as could happen if the medicine woman made a mistake.

But the porridge tasted terrible, simply terrible. Wolf thought that for flavor and texture—each mouthful felt as if it were made of the skin that formed on tar after it oozed from the ground—he would rather chew the willow splits from which Elm had woven the soaking baskets.

Elm walked over and stood in front of Wolf. "Well, Chief Hunter," the old woman said. "How do you like your breakfast?"

Wolf dipped the index and middle fingers of his right hand into the porridge pit again and lifted another load of the glop to his mouth. "Thank you for making the food, Elm," he said formally. There were a few dried blueberries in the porridge, but they did nothing to flavor the horrible stuff.

"We have nothing else to eat," Elm continued, as if it were news to the Chief Hunter. She spoke in a loud voice so that the whole tribe could hear her. "In the old days we ate bison, but it is many days since we have had any kind of meat to cook."

"We will have meat again soon," Wolf said, trying to keep his temper. Under other circumstances, he would have knocked the old woman down to silence her. The Chief Hunter knew that now Elm was only saying what all the members of the tribe were thinking. If he struck her . . . well, Wolf was Chief Hunter, but there were many in the tribe. They might all turn against him at once.

He wondered if the medicine woman had deliberately made the porridge taste worse than it needed to. Probably not. Elm was eating the horrible stuff herself, after all.

"*When* will we have meat again, Chief Hunter?" the old woman demanded with her hands on her hips.

"A moon-phase ago we had mammoth," muttered one of the hunters. "I don't want to go through that again."

Wolf licked the porridge off his fingers. He grimaced at the taste despite his attempt to keep his face calm. He knew he had to change the subject quickly or he was going to lose his position as Chief Hunter. The tribe might even cast him out, as they had done to Hawk.

Deep in his heart, Wolf wondered if perhaps he really was the cause of the tribe's misfortune. He performed the hunting rites with particular care each night, drawing in the ground the shape of the animal they would hunt and setting an actual part of the beast—a horn, a swatch of hide, a hoof—in the outline.

When he had created the outline, Wolf led all the hunters in bowing to the spirit of the animal and promising honor to the spirit if it would lend the strength of its children to the tribe. Then the men danced and thrust their spears into the dusty drawing, chanting praise of the spirit of the beast while the women watched in respectful silence.

Wolf performed the hunting rites just as his father and other hunters of the former generation had taught him. He followed tradition perfectly— but the spirits did not bring game to the tribe. Was there some rite that he had forgotten? Had Wolf somehow, during an earlier hunt, offended the spirits so that they would not permit the tribe to have success in hunting so long as Wolf was the Chief Hunter?

Wolf thought of exile, of being thrust out of the circle of the tribe to starve alone or be devoured with no one to chant his name on the nights of remembrance when the moon was dark. He shuddered and said loudly, "Boartooth! Do all the hunters have spears now?"

Boartooth got to his feet quickly. He knew as well as Wolf did that the Chief Hunter was trying to focus the tribe's anger on somebody else. The young man held the shaft to which he had just bound one of his own chert spearblades.

"Heron, this is yours," he said loudly, holding out the spear. The shaft had an obvious crook in it. "Now all the hunters in the tribe have spears."

Heron reached out from the reflex of a man to take something that is handed to him. When he had time to look at the spear, he jumped back quickly.

"What is this?" Heron demanded angrily. "You have not tested the spear by bird flight! I will not accept it."

"I performed the rites in the forest yesterday when I was alone," Boartooth said in a haughty voice. "The birds flew straight."

"I will not accept this spear!" Heron repeated. "Look at it! The shaft hasn't been smoothed down like it should be. It isn't even straight! I want a proper spear, not this."

"Hawk's shafts were smooth, but his spears would not strike hard," Boartooth said. "I do not make my spears the way Hawk made his." His tone had changed. He was wheedling with Heron now, instead of trying to shout down the other hunter.

"I won't take it!" Heron shouted angrily.

"Heron is a woman," sneered Boartooth. "He doesn't think he needs a spear."

Heron grabbed for the spear-maker's throat with both hands. Boartooth tried to fend him off with the crossed spearshaft. All the hunters jumped to their feet, shouting.

Wolf saw that he'd let matters go as far as they safely could. He stepped between the angry men, placed one hand on the chest of each, and pushed them apart. "Enough!" he shouted.

Boartooth gestured as though he were threatening Heron with the chertbladed spear. The Chief Hunter slapped the weapon from Boartooth's hands. Wolf was really angry now. "Enough!" he repeated, glaring at the younger man.

All the men in the tribe had a club or a spear in their hands now. They relaxed when they saw that Wolf was fully in control of the situation.

"I will not take that spear," Heron said in a sullen voice.

Wolf grunted noncommittally. He looked at the spear-maker. "Boartooth," he said. "Do you still say this—" he pointed to the chert-bladed weapon which lay on the ground beside them "—is a good spear?"

"It is a good spear, Chief Hunter," Boartooth muttered. He would not meet Wolf's eyes. "I performed the rites in the forest yesterday, just as I said."

"Very well," said Wolf. "You will give Heron your own spear, Boartooth—the spear that Hawk made when he was with the tribe. You will keep the spear you just made yourself."

Boartooth looked up. "Yes," he sneered. "I will have the better spear. Heron will beg me to make him a spear soon, and I will not."

"Enough," the Chief Hunter repeated grimly. "It is time we were hunting. Now that we all have spears, we will bring in meat again."

He breathed a prayer to the spirits of the hunt that he was correct.

Wolf crawled to the knoll where Flash, a hunter with a patch of white hair growing from a birthmark in his scalp, waited for him. The Chief Hunter moved so silently that even the little gray birds hopping and chirping from one tall grass stem to another were unaware of his presence until he was directly beneath them.

The knoll was rocky and grew a crop of stunted beech trees. Flash lay on his belly. He braced his left hand on a tree trunk to raise his head enough to look out over the valley beyond. Even he was startled when Wolf appeared beside him.

"What do you think, Wolf?" he whispered. "Camel hump's the best eating there is, some say. And even horse isn't too bad for a hungry man."

The Chief Hunter looked at what his scout had found. He said nothing for a long minute.

In the rolling valley beyond was a mixed herd of camels and horses, about a hundred animals all together. The horses had keen directional hearing, but the long-necked camels could see farther across the plain when they raised their heads. The combined herd was therefore safer than either horses or camels would have been separately.

The grass was about waist high. Although the beasts traveled together, they did not eat grass at the same stage of growth. The horses cropped the fresh shoots growing close to the ground, while the camels took mouthfuls of the coarser dry blades which their huge stomachs and cud-chewing broke down over a long period.

"We could drive them," Flash muttered. "The grass is plenty dry enough."

Wolf squinted to the south. He couldn't see the other end of the valley. "It won't do us any good to drive them," he said, "because there's nothing to drive them *against*. The herd can run for the next moon-phase without coming to a drop-off or even a marsh."

"Camel hump sure is good meat," Flash said wistfully. His stomach rumbled unhappily on its latest meal of bitter porridge.

Wolf tested the wind with the tufts of fine hair on the peaks of his ears. There was a slight, fitful breeze here on the knoll. It was scarcely noticeable. Further down in the valley, the air would be almost perfectly still. It was just possible . . .

"We will not drive the herd," the Chief Hunter said decisively. "We will stalk them. Only the adult hunters will be join the hunt. The boys are not experienced enough yet, and they might startle the animals before it is time."

"Can we do this, Wolf?" Flash said, frowning. He was used to driving herds by the use of fire. He had expected that somehow the Chief Hunter would show him a way to kill meat under the present circumstances by using traditional methods.

"We will be very close to the herd before they notice us," Wolf said. He knew that in grass of this height, *he* could get within twenty feet of even a skittish horse. He had to hope that the other men of his tribe could do almost as well. "We will approach from all sides—there is no wind to carry our scent."

There was *almost* no wind to carry the hunters' scent.

"When the herd finally runs in panic, we will be all around them," the Chief Hunter concluded. "We will spear at least one of the animals. Perhaps we will spear many and eat meat until it spoils."

"Waugh!" said Flash. "It is good."

Wolf crawled back to gather the other hunters and explain his plan. The little birds hopped cheerfully above him.

Wolf moved as if he were a spike of winter ice which extended farther and farther along a rock face even though the seepage which fed it was imperceptible. The grass rasped softly. The edges cut the skin of the Chief Hunter's shoulders and forearms, but that was the least of the discomfort of his glacially slow stalk.

The heat was the worst. The valley floor was hotter than the knoll, and the dry grassblades seemed to weave through the sullen air and clamp it down, the way roots kept soil from washing away in a cloudburst.

Pollen and ordinary dust sifted onto Wolf's shoulders, then found their way up his nose. Several times he had to pause to keep from sneezing.

He wondered if one of other hunters would sneeze and waste all the effort thus far invested in the stalk. He hoped not. He had deliberately chosen the most difficult approach for himself, the long circle to get on the far side of the herd.

If all went as planned, Wolf would jump up and charge the herd when he got as close as possible. He might even be within the distance at which he could hurl his spear. Fleet-footed horses acted as sentinels on the fringes of the mixed herd. They would probably dodge a spear thrown to its maximum range, but Wolf's appearance should throw the beasts into a sudden panic. When they fled from the Chief Hunter, they should crash directly into the spears of the remainder of the tribe's hunters, who were creeping closer in a loose arc from the other direction.

The tribe would eat meat tonight!

Wolf slid his spear forward among the roots of the grass, as silently as a flint-headed serpent. Only when the weapon was advanced by the length of his forearm did the Chief Hunter begin moving his body again.

The grass blades were so thick that Wolf could not see anything more than an arm's length in front of him. He could only hope that his men were carrying out their part of the plan. Occasionally he heard one of the horses whicker or a camel give a peevish grunt. Wolf froze at each sound, but the animals were only chatting among themselves or complaining about an unusually persistent horsefly.

Insect-eating birds hopped merrily among the herd, snapping up prey which the animals' trampling feet had uncovered. A tick-bird gave a long, raucous call from very close by. From the apparent height of the call, the bird must have been standing on the shoulders of horse. Wolf was unable to pierce the screen of grass with his vision.

The Chief Hunter feared that the birds would notice him even though the horses and camels had not, but by now he was so close that it almost didn't matter. The smell of herd animals lay across the grass like fog rising from a pond in the morning. The camels had a ranker odor than that of the horses, but as Flash had said, camel hump was a dish as tasty as any a man could desire.

Wolf's stomach rumbled in sympathy with the thought. As if that were a signal, a stallion on the far side of the herd gave a shrill scream of warning.

The Chief Hunter jumped to his feet. In front of him was a chaos of dust and animals crying in terror as they wheeled to run. He had been so close—

But a hunt that fails by a hair's breadth puts no more meat on the table than a day when no game at all is spotted.

One of the other hunters had spooked the herd toward the valley's southern end, away from the main arc of spearmen.

If Wolf had been a little closer, the animals' flight would have been directly past him. Then the Chief Hunter at least would have had a chance to spear a single animal—only one meal for the tribe, but better than bitter porridge and black looks from his fellow tribesmen.

Instead, the nearest animals were thirty yards away, too far for an effective spear cast. Wolf raced toward the herd.

The horses and camels separated as they ran. The horses formed dense globes of a dozen or so, with a stallion in the lead and his mares formed behind him with their colts on the protected inner side of the group. The long-necked camels fled individually. Their knobby legs moved in a jerky, seemingly uncoordinated, motion which none the less covered ground even faster than the graceful scissoring of the horses.

Wolf heard human shouts, but the other hunters were hidden behind the cloud of dust. A camel bolted toward him. As the Chief Hunter poised his spear, the beast saw him and changed direction with the delicacy of a bird flaring its wings against the air. Wolf almost threw his spear anyway, but he had only a tiny chance of bringing down his prey with a hasty cast at this distance.

He might have tried despite the slight chance of success, but a slightly-wounded camel would run for miles with the Chief Hunter's spear stuck in its side. The spear—one of those Hawk had made before his exile—was a good one. Wolf did not throw because he knew that if the spear was lost, a weapon made by Boartooth would replace it.

The last family of horses thundered off to the south, too far for Wolf to reach with a spear cast, much less for him to hope to deliver a killing blow. The stallion leading the group was a powerful roan animal. Sweat darkened the dust on the beast's chest and forelegs. He ran easily, but a spear hung from his shoulders. The point had slid under the hide at an angle, so that it pricked the horse but did him no serious injury.

Any successful hunter had sharp eyes. Wolf's eyes were the best in his tribe. Even at this distance, he recognized the spear bobbing from the stallion's withers as the one Boartooth had made for Heron—and had been forced to keep for himself.

Now the Chief Hunter knew why the herd had been spooked too early. It was as clear to him as if he had been standing beside Boartooth when the boastful younger man stood and hurled his spear from too long a range, so that he could claim to have brought down the first meat of the hunt.

The remaining hunters puffed toward Wolf along the track the herd had torn through the meadow. Most of the men had thrown their spears. Wolf hoped they would be able to find the weapons again. The rumps of the trailing animals were barely visible through the dust of their flight. Occasionally a mare would flick her tail high, as if gesturing defiance toward the humans.

It was too much to hope that one of the hunters would have made a lucky throw that brought down an animal, but Wolf *did* hope that until he saw that all nine of his men were straggling toward him with sad looks on their faces. The tribe would have no meat tonight.

There was a sudden commotion toward the southern end of the valley. The herd had vanished into the distance and the cloud of its own dust. Now individual animals reappeared, scattering in many directions. Horses and camels alike screamed in pain.

"They've fallen over a cliff!" Flash said. His

face, gloomy and dispirited only moments before, was suddenly alive with laughter. "We'll have something good to eat after all!"

"My spear drove them!" shouted Boartooth as he joined the group gathering around the Chief Hunter. "I told you that my weapons would bring luck, while Hawk's spears left us hungry!"

"There is no cliff," said Wolf in a voice that sounded as if he were chipping the words out of stone. "We chased the animals into a hunting party from another tribe. If someone had not thrown his spear too early—"

The Chief Hunter glared at Boartooth.

"—we would have much meat to eat tonight."

Boartooth looked away. His necklace of tusks had become disarranged during the chase. His fingers straightened the decoration now, since they no longer had a spear to occupy them.

"Chief Hunter?" said Flash timidly. "They have meat over there." He pointed with one finger toward the south, where the dust had settled over the ambush site. "Maybe they would share with us?"

Wolf stood grimly, looking at the other hunters. He heard human cries of triumph to the south, now that the thunder of hooves had ceased. He said nothing while he thought.

Heron said, "We are few and weak. If we demand meat from another tribe, they will laugh at us and send us away. They may even—" he looked back in the direction of the tribe's camp "—take our women and our spears. The *good* spears, I mean."

"Mine are good spears!" Boartooth muttered,

but he backed away from the other hunter. Heron, like Wolf, had kept his spear rather than risking its loss on a long throw. He rotated the smooth shaft in his hand as he stared at the would-be spear-maker.

"But we did drive the animals to them," Flash said. "They would not have had easy kills except that the herd fled from us. Besides, if they made many kills, they will have more meat than they can finish themselves before it rots."

What Flash said was true. The other tribe had not so much hunted the horses and camels themselves, as they had simply waited while the panicked herd ran into their spears. Even if the other tribe was very large, two or three adult animals would provide it with much more than its own members could eat.

Unfortunately, what Heron said was true also. When one tribe was very much weaker than another, it was human nature to treat the weak ones as inferior—animals to be preyed upon, not human beings with whom to trade and exchange wives.

Wolf's stomach growled. The sound decided him.

"All right," he said. "All of you search for your spears. We can't help the fact there aren't many of us and we're hungry, but we don't have to meet another tribe while we're unarmed. Boartooth, you go back to the camp and bring everyone here. We will go together, all of us, to greet them."

"I need to search for my spear too, Chief Hunter," Boartooth said with unexpected boldness. "Send Heron back with the message."

"Heron will stay here," Wolf said in his flinty voice. "I know where your spear is. It's in the shoulder of the stallion that cost us our success today!"

Wolf could hear the happy commotion long before he and his own people came in sight of the other tribe. The strangers were butchering out the animals their spears had brought down. The kill was a considerable one—at least half a dozen horses and camels, easily the equivalent in meat of a pair of giant bisons.

The Chief Hunter's plan had been a good one. It just had not worked out for him and his people.

In broad daylight, with a quantity of meat on which to gorge, the other tribe was not keeping a close lookout. Predators would become a problem when the sun went down, but not even the great sabor-tooths would barge openly into a full tribe of humans by daylight in order to hijack a kill.

Wolf led his people openly to the site where the strangers cut up their kill. He didn't want to look to the other—larger—tribe as though he were sneaking up, perhaps with hostile intent. Even though the meadow grass was no more than waist high to Wolf and his adult hunters, none of the strangers noticed them until the newcomers were within easy spear cast.

The strangers must have been very hungry to concentrate so completely on the meat they were bolting raw. Wolf's belly growled in sympathy.

A child carried by a woman in Wolf's tribe began to wail. A girl with a flint knife and a strip of camel tenderloin leaped to her feet. She stared at Wolf, then shouted in surprise. All of the strangers jumped to alertness. The men dropped chunks of meat and seized spears already bloody from the animals they had killed. Women whisked infants to the rear or gathered stones to throw as their part of the common defense.

Wolf pointed his spear to the ground in his left hand and raised his right hand palm outward. "We come in peace," he called. "My name is Wolf."

There were at least forty people in the other tribe, a larger number than in Wolf's even before the troubles of the recent past. Fifteen of the strangers were adult males: hunters during normal times, warriors now if the need to fight arose.

A grizzled, stocky man with eagle feathers in a headband of tanned hide stepped forward from the other tribe. He held his spear in both hands. He was not precisely threatening, but neither was he making a special effort to appear peaceful the way Wolf was doing.

"My name is Bull," he announced. "I am the Chief Hunter of my tribe. This is our kill. Go away and leave us to it."

Wolf continued walking forward. He could see the nearest of the animals brought down in the ambush. It was the roan stallion which Boartooth's spear had wounded. "We come in peace," he repeated. "But it is our kill also, Bull. You and we should share. There is plenty for all."

Several men from the other tribe shouted with anger at the suggestion, though it was obvious to all that there was far more meat than even a large tribe could eat before it spoiled. One of Bull's hunters ran a few steps toward Wolf, bellowing and shaking his spear in the air as if he were about to throw it.

"Get back here, Longshank!" Bull snapped at him. "If you were in such a hurry to bloody your spear, why didn't you manage to do it when the horses ran straight at you?"

Longshank's spear was not one of those which showed signs of a recent kill.

Wolf continued to walk forward. He met the eyes of the other tribe's chief. Boartooth, bolder still, strode past Wolf and pointed to the roan stallion. "Look, Chief Hunter," he said in a loud voice. His hand indicated the chert-bladed weapon. "That is my spear. Without me, you would not have meat. It is right that this meat be shared between your tribe and mine."

Bull and the nearest of his men looked at the stallion in surprise. In their haste and triumph, none of them had noticed that the extra spear in the horse's shoulder was not one of their own. It was obvious to all Bull's men that Boartooth and his Chief Hunter were speaking the truth: Wolf's tribe *had* been an important part of the kill.

"We still don't need to give them part of our meat," Longshank muttered, looking at the horse. "The beasts were running when we killed them."

"There's plenty for all," another hunter pointed out.

The women of the two tribes stood behind the men. As the discussion began and it was clear that there would not be a battle, the women straightened up and began eyeing the other tribe. Some of the unmarried women looked at the strange men with particular concentration; and the single men looked back.

The stallion was partially butchered. Its ribs

showed white on the upper side. The smell of fresh meat was dizzyingly wonderful to Wolf.

A woman stepped up close behind Bull. She was probably a medicine woman, like Elm; and like Elm, she was old and crotchety. "Look at how thin they are, Bull!" she shrilled. "They're unlucky. We should have nothing to do with them."

The hunter who had argued with Longshank now turned to the old woman. "How long has it been since we made such a kill on our own, Troutscale?" he said. "Maybe they have brought us good luck!"

Bull looked over Wolf's hunters with a practiced eye. "With this many men," he mused aloud, "we would be able to hunt even the great mammoths. That would be good."

"We have trouble finding enough meat as it is," Longshank protested. "With more mouths to feed, we will go hungry more nights than not."

"But—" said another hunter.

"Wait!" Bull ordered forcefully. He looked at Wolf. "My tribe and I will discuss these matters in private," Bull said. "You and your people may wait or go, that's up to you. But you do not touch our kills until we have decided."

Wolf nodded at the challenge in the voice of the other Chief Hunter. "We will wait," he said. "Then we will share with you the game that we drove into your spears, as is our right."

Bull's tribe withdrew half a spear cast and huddled together. Their voices buzzed. Both adults and children cast frequent glances toward Wolf and his people. Wolf was not concerned at the delay. He knew that the other tribe was hungry also, and that they would shortly come to a decision.

What that decision would be was more doubtful. It was not traditional for tribes to operate together for more than a brief session of trading, and Wolf well knew that his people had nothing to trade. But it was obvious that the strangers also found it increasingly difficult to hunt bison in traditional fire drives.

Today's accidental pairing of the hunting parties had resulted in a major kill. Bull's comment about mammoth hunting suggested that the other Chief Hunter was thinking still further ahead.

Boartooth walked over to the downed stallion. Several of the other tribe's hunters turned, raising their spears. "Leave the meat alone, you fool!" Wolf snarled.

Boartooth gripped the shaft of his spear and pulled the weapon free. It left a shallow gouge, scarcely even a flesh wound; but, as Boartooth had said to Bull, that was the wound that drove the herd into the other tribe's hunters.

The strangers' discussion became heated. Troutscale raised her shrill voice. The old woman's demands were flattened again and again by Bull, who rumbled like an avalanche. At last, snapping and glowering at one another, Bull's tribe strode back toward Wolf.

"It is right that you should join us," said Bull. "We have decided."

"*Waugh!*" Boartooth shouted in joy. He slapped the flat of his spear across his chest in enthusiasm. The spearhead struck his necklace of tusks with a sharp clack. The chert spearpoint shattered on the hard tooth. The spear suddenly had only a brown nub instead of a true point.

"They are accursed!" Troutscale shrieked in horror, pointing at the omen. Even Bull looked horrified. He stepped back a pace.

"Wait!" cried Wolf. "It is not an omen! We have lost our Chief Spear-Maker!" He stepped forward with his hand out to the other chief.

"Go back!" shouted Bull. He raised his own spear, a well-fashioned weapon whose edges glittered through a film of drying horse blood. "You are accursed! Get away from us or we will kill you all!"

The hunter who had previously argued with Longshank now glowered and thrust his spear at Boartooth. Wolf's would-be spear-maker jumped back, barely avoiding the point.

"It is right that we should share—" Wolf began. A woman from Bull's tribe hurled a rock at him. He dodged, but all the women and children of the other tribe were picking up stones to volley in another moment.

Wolf skipped back around the range, angrily gesturing his people to follow him. They didn't dare fight against such odds.

"What you are doing is not right!" he shouted at Bull.

But as the Chief Hunter fled, he wondered if perhaps the old woman *was* right. Maybe he and his tribe really were accursed.

TAIL FEATHER

The tiger facing Hawk crouched close to the ground, a fierce, tawny menace. Its saber teeth, long upper tusks protruding six inches from either side of its jaw, flashed white in the sunshine. Its short tail was bent in a half curve behind it, and the powerful shoulders rippled as it gathered itself for the attack. It did not snarl, but merely looked with deadly eyes at the two humans it had trapped.

Hawk backed cautiously, keeping Willow behind him and scarcely noticing the puppies. To have an enemy between him and the nearest place of safety was a situation that should never occur. He glanced quickly at the fire, where he had left his spears and throwing-stick. He knew that it was impossible to fight a saber-tooth with just a club alone. But that was all he had, and he clenched his fingers around it desperately.

103

He wasted no time wondering why the tiger was here instead of harassing the camel herd, where he had been sure it would be. Instead, he glanced all around, taking exact note of everything that lay about him. A little to one side was a nest of boulders. If he could get to them before the tiger charged, the boulders would serve as weapons should he lose his club in the fight. They would also supply some slight protection. Hawk began edging toward the boulders.

The tiger followed him, in no hurry. A cat who knew it had a victim trapped, it was taking its time and playing a bit before delivering the final killing blow. The tiger advanced a step at a time, hind quarters near the ground and humped shoulders rising. Hawk gauged the distance to the boulders, and planned his next move.

Men of the early wandering tribes were distinguished from beasts principally by their intelligence, their ability to think. It was a man, and not a tiger or bear, that had first thought of picking up a piece of flint and using it as an axe. It was a man who thought of tying a flint head to a stick and thus having a spear. Man learned that fire could be a servant rather than a terrible master. Man, eternally groping for cause and effect, rather than meekly accepting what offered, had progressed because he was inquisitive. Despite the fact that many had died because man insisted on tampering with things toward which no mere instinct had directed him, those who survived had learned more and more.

A deer or antelope in Hawk's place would have

trembled and awaited the tiger's charge. A wolf might have prepared to fight back, knowing his case was hopeless but fighting by instinct. Hawk sought a means to outwit his foe because he knew that even hopeless situations could be changed. He should have died when he was banished, but he had not. If he died now, it would not be because he had not tried to live and to protect the girl with him. Again he gauged the exact distance to the boulders, and gripped his club a little more tightly.

All in a split second, the tiger made Hawk's decision for him. Stiffening his tail, he padded rapidly forward, snarling. Hawk took two quick steps to the side. As he did so, he shouted as loudly as he could. It was a war cry, and a challenge, meant to focus the enemy's attention upon him and to keep that enemy away from what must, if possible, be protected. He was aware of Willow's breaking away, running toward the pile of boulders. He grasped the club with both hands, ready for the most smashing blow he could deliver.

Without any warning, a new warrior entered the fight. Shrilling his own war cry, the gray puppy flung himself straight at the mighty saber-tooth.

He was small, weighing scarcely a dozen pounds, but every inherited sense and instinct had taught him that, from the time he was old enough to walk, he must help protect his own kind. Accepting Willow and Hawk as such, he was giving everything he had to give.

The tiger stopped, diverted by the attack. When it slapped with its paws, the gray puppy wasn't there. Instead, he was boring in from the side, scoring the saber-tooth's flank with his puppy teeth. The tiger twisted around, spitting its rage at this insignificant tormentor. But now the other puppy had entered the fight on his brother's side. The tiger pounced with both paws and pinned the dun-colored puppy between them. A shrill scream rent the air.

For a split second Hawk hesitated, for he had neither expected nor counted on interference. Then he recovered himself. The tiger had made a kill, and for at least a short time would gloat over its triumph. It would rend and claw the dead puppy before turning to deal with the other one or before again centering its attention on Hawk and Willow. There would be a brief lull, and Hawk took fullest advantage of it.

He wheeled, pushing Willow around. Instantly she fell in beside him, and they raced around the preoccupied saber-tooth. Hawk heard the tiger's angry cough, but did not look back for now it was a question of speed.

As they reached the fire, he heard the gray puppy's shrill battle cry again. Almost without breaking stride Hawk swooped to snatch his spears and throwing-stick. He swung about.

The saber-tooth had come as near the fire as it dared. Having cast the body of the dun puppy aside, it was snarling in enraged frustration at the two humans. The gray puppy continued its valiant attack, and the tiger swung to strike at it. But the puppy was too agile and elusive.

Hawk fitted a spear into his throwing-stick and

purposely advanced. Seeing him, the tiger paid no further attention to the fiercely attacking gray puppy. The little dog was nothing more than a nuisance, now that bigger game was in sight. The saber-tooth crouched and gathered itself to meet the man's attack.

Hawk slowly continued, keeping his eyes on the tiger, on its tense muscles, its jerking tail, and its glaring eyes. At every second he must know exactly what it was going to do next.

Precisely at the right time—in another flick of an eye the saber-tooth would have charged him—he stopped and cast his spear. It sang through the air, glancing along the tiger's neck and burying itself in one of the humped shoulders. Hawk stood his ground, for to run now might prove fatal, and fitted his second spear into the throwing-stick.

The saber-tooth roared in pain and rage, and turned to bite at the protruding spear shaft. Blood ebbed from around the imbedded flint head, and ran down the tawny leg.

Hawk kept his eyes on the tiger, awaiting his second—and last—chance to throw a spear. Fortunately, the saber-tooth was intent on rending the spear shaft, as though that were a live enemy which had hurt it, and had no thought for anything else. Hawk cast his second spear.

This time he struck where he had wanted to, in the neck, and a gush of blood spouted around the shaft. The saber-tooth roared again, and reared on its padded hind feet. With powerful front paws it struck at the spear shaft, fell over backward, twisted to its feet, and came forward with great, leaping bounds.

Hawk stood with his club ready, prepared to fight to a finish. The tiger had been mortally hurt, but was possessed of such strength and vitality that there was no way of telling just when it would collapse. Then it faltered, coughed hoarsely, took three stumbling steps, and sank to the ground.

Still full of fight, the gray puppy charged up, seized a fold of a tawny skin, and strained backward with all his strength. Puppyish growls that foretold the fighting dog to come rolled from its distended throat.

Hawk turned to find Willow, a heavy stone in her hands, at his shoulder. Then he looked back at the puppy.

Bristled, stiff-legged, he was walking around and around the tiger. At last convinced that it was dead, he turned contemptuously to scratch dirt over the fallen enemy. Walking proudly, he came back to join Hawk and Willow.

It was over. They had been attacked by one of the most ferocious of their enemies, and they had defeated it. The fight had left its valuable lessons, too. When the gray puppy brushed Hawk's leg, he reached down to stroke him lightly. The puppy wriggled in delight, and turned to lick his master's hand. From now on his place as a valued member of the camp was secure.

Hawk and Willow grasped the dead tiger by the front paws and dragged it over the grass to the fire. They knelt on opposite sides, flint knives in their hands, while they removed the thick pelt, pulled out the embedded spears, and cut up the meat. And it was Hawk himself who hacked a choice part from one leg and gave it to the dog. The gray puppy lay before the fire, growling softly as he gnawed his portion.

The skinning and dismembering of the tiger and the dead puppy over, and the offal dragged far enough so scavengers would feel safe in coming to feed on it, Willow devoted herself to cooking while Hawk stared into the fire.

It had been a very close call; without the intervention of the two pups he and Willow might have been killed. Obviously they needed better protection than they had, and the answer to that lay in Hawk's ability to strike hard and often at any foe. But how to acquire that ability?

Hawk fondled his six darts, and balanced them in his hands. If only the darts were not deflected by any chance wind! If he could find some way to make them obey him, to hit what he threw them at . . .

He started suddenly, alarmed. Again it was only the bird skin, fluttering in the wind. Irritably Hawk rose, tore it from the bush, and scowled at the rustling feathers. Then he noticed the square-tipped tail. He studied it thoughtfully.

This he had seen before in some connection, but he could not at once remember what it was. Then, suddenly, he had it. The bird, the little bird which proved whether or not a spear was true! The one with which he had tested Short-Leg's first spear had not been able to fly straight when its tail feathers were broken. But the second one *had* flown straight. What did the tail feathers have to do with it? Did the bird with the broken tail lack the same power that his darts did?

Hawk plucked a couple of feathers from the skin and laid them in the palm of his hand. He looked closely at them, but could see no connection between birds and darts. He let a feather drift to earth, closely watching its erratic course. Again and again he let the feather drop.

By nightfall he was no nearer a solution to his problem. He had tried letting the feathers drop from every possible angle and in every possible way, and there was nothing about their descent to indicate how they helped guide a bird or how they might guide a spear. Still puzzled, Hawk brought in more firewood and lay down to sleep.

His problem was there to greet him when he awakened. He was sure that there was something important in the fact that birds could fly straight when they had a whole tail, but couldn't when they did not. But what was it? He stared moodily into the fire. When he finally rose the gray puppy followed him. Hawk paid no attention, but walked directly to a place near the willows and leaned on his spear, studying the birds flitting about the branches.

They were of various kinds, from little insect-eaters to fruit-and-bud eaters, and had different methods of flight. The insect-eaters could bend and twist with unbelievable agility as they pursued their prey. For the most part, the others flew straight. But all seemed to use their tails a great deal, bending them according to the direction in which they wanted to turn or holding them straight if they wished to fly straight.

Hawk's interest heightened. As he watched, a

big predatory bird swooped out of the sky toward the willows, and the little birds scattered frantically. The big bird selected a victim, and banked sharply to cut it off. The little fruit-eater dove close to the ground, so close that the tips of his beating wings almost touched the earth. The baffled attacker spread his wing and tail feathers wide, to avoid striking the ground, and rose sharply into the air.

Hawk wandered slowly back to the fire. He had seen and learned much that he had not known before. With renewed interest he picked up a dart and examined its slender length. He took hold of the butt end and squinted down the shaft, then examined the butt.

A bird's tail was attached to the rear extremity. Always, when the bird wished to fly straight, and apparently they could do so whenever they wished, the tail was straight. Hawk rolled the dart over and over in his hand. Experimentally he laid one of the feathers against the butt, holding it in place with his thumb. He bound it with sinew.

Hawk stood erect, the dart in his throwing stick, and cast at a tuft of grass. Great excitement seized him.

The dart landed to one side, but it was much nearer the target than any he had thrown so far. Also he thought he knew what was wrong. A self-taught master of balance, the Spear-Maker had noticed that the butt of the thrown dart had traveled too low in flight.

He retrieved the dart, unwound the strip of sinew and laid another feather on the butt, on the opposite side. Carefully he rewound them with the sinew, and pulled experimentally to make sure they were tight. He stood up and cast the dart again.

A happy shout of triumph burst from him. The dart had struck the grass tuft squarely, within two inches of the place at which it had been aimed. Hawk bounded high in the air, overcome with elation. He raced happily forward to retrieve his dart, and cast it again. Twenty times he cast at the tuft of grass and every time the dart hit close to where he wanted it to hit.

This was it; he had found the answer. Hawk crouched by the fire, fletching the rest of his darts. Willow, who had been watching with great interest, sat across the fire as he worked. She had buried the dead puppy's skin in the damp ground by the willows, and when it was soaked she had scraped the hair from it. Then she had stretched it out in the sun, with stones on the edges to keep it taut. Now she was working with the cured, parchmentlike skin.

She folded it, forming a long, deep pouch, and pierced the edges at intervals with an awl made of sharpened bone. She laced it with sinew, then cut a long, thin strip of skin which she folded in half. This she attached to serve as a shoulder strap. When Hawk finished fletching his darts Willow gave him the container she had made. Hawk looked at it, puzzled.

"It is for your darts," Willow explained. "You can carry all of them within it."

Hawk grunted his pleasure. The container was

well and strongly made, and was a very practical arrangement. He put his darts in it, heads down and feathered butts protruding. When he slung the filled pouch over his shoulder, he could instantly reach any dart. A new sense of confidence rose within him.

Now, carrying his club, spears and throwing-stick, his darts in the pouch, he was armed as several men. He could strike hard and fast at anything that threatened, and he needn't depend exclusively on the club after he had thrown both spears. Now he could keep on throwing, and though the darts lacked a spear's range and power, he could still hurl them from the throwing-stick farther than the average hunter could throw a hand spear.

The pouch of darts on his shoulder, and the puppy trotting happily beside him, Hawk ranged into the forest. He did not try to drive the puppy back, nor tell Willow to hold it, because he cared little whether or not he found game. There was meat in plenty at the camp. The Spear-Maker was roaming largely because he wanted to try his darts on various targets and under different conditions.

Trotting ahead of him, the puppy stopped suddenly. His ears were alert, and one forepaw was lifted as he remained intent on something. Hawk watched closely. He knew that wild dogs hunted game in this fashion, but had never seen a hunting dog at such close range.

The puppy took a few more steps and dropped his head to the ground. He snuffled audibly, and his tail began to wag. Keeping his nose to the ground, the puppy trotted swiftly away. He did not bark, or make any sound. Hawk advanced to find out what the puppy was hunting.

A deer had passed this way, but to the man the scent was very faint. Hawk had to kneel close to the ground in order to detect it at all. Plainly dogs had an exceptionally keen sense of smell. It was much better than his own, for the puppy had been some distance from the dim trail when he smelled it.

Since the puppy was now out of sight, Hawk began practising with his darts. Time after time he cast them, gaining more and more confidence in his ability to control their feathered flight.

Presently he heard the puppy barking sharply, the sound coming rapidly nearer. A deer appeared among the trees, the puppy almost at its heels. Hawk tensed himself, for here was an opportunity to throw at a moving target. Crouching in the brush, he laid the throwing-stick in position, fitted a dart into it, and waited.

The deer was a bounding shadow in the forest. It appeared, then disappeared, and appeared again. Hawk kept his eyes on a little opening through which the running deer's course would take it, and not until the deer was in that opening did he step from behind the bush.

Seeing the motion, the deer jumped spasmodically, then stood still a moment, head thrown up. Hurrying, but not fumbling, Hawk cast the dart. It flew straight to its mark. The deer gave a single bound, staggered, and fell.

Hawk ran forward. The deer had been pierced just where he wanted to hit it, behind the foreleg, and it had died almost at once. He pulled out the feathered shaft and looked at it proudly. It was good. In the darts he now was master of a weapon with three-fold magic: the hardness of stone, the strength of wood, the flight of birds.

BATTLE

The overcast sky turned twilight to night. Damp, chill air sucked the heat from the bones of the men of Wolf's tribe.

"It's your fault for not apologizing to the spirit of the bison," said Elm querulously. "You hunt other beasts instead, and the bison spirit is angry. This tribe has always hunted bison, back to the memory of my mother's mother."

Kar put another log on the fire. It flared up with enthusiasm and a shower of sparks. At least the tribe had wood, here. The Chief Fire-Maker backed a little. His creation curled the white hairs of his chest and beard.

Fire was good, but it wasn't enough for comfort. The spirit of the fire could only keep men warm on the facing side. A hunter who huddled as close to tonight's blaze as he could stand might still shiver at the touch of cold air on his back. What the tribe needed—

"We need meat, Chief Hunter!" Elm continued. "We will have no luck hunting until the spirit of the bison smiles on us again."

"Bull's tribe hunted horses and camels," Flash replied when Wolf kept silent. "Their luck wasn't bad. Hold your tongue, old woman!"

"They should have shared with us," Boartooth grumbled. He had gone off by himself for a time after Bull's tribe drove them away. When Boartooth returned, he had flaked another chert point to replace the one which shattered at such an unfortunate time. Perhaps the young man hoped that the rest of the tribe would forget what had happened if his spear looked complete again.

"We have fire," said the Chief Hunter wearily. "Tomorrow we will hunt again, and perhaps the bison spirit will send his children to us. For now, we will eat the food the women have found for us."

A child began to cry. "That is no food," said one of the hunters bitterly. "It is dust in our mouths, and it cramps my belly."

Because the women had followed the hunt today, they had not been able to glean as much in the way of roots and berries as they usually would. Besides, the season was too early for the best of the vegetable food; and such crops were never viewed as more than incidentals of diet in a tribe of wandering hunters like Wolf's.

The tribe needed meat. All of them knew that.

"They should have let us share the meat," Wolf

said at last. "It was our meat too. But tomorrow we will hunt game of our own."

Kar stirred up the fire, thinking as he watched the sparks swirl skyward. For an instant he thought he saw the curving tusks of a mammoth in the orange firelight, then the shaggy cape of a bison. Did the spirits of game animals live in the flames, warming the exterior of men as their meat warmed those who ate it?

The talk among the folk of the tribe was merely a pointless wrangle now. Different people, women as well as the hunters, kept saying the same things: that they were hungry, that they needed food, that Bull's tribe should have shared the large kill with the hunters who drove the game into the spears which brought it down.

Magnolia, a nursing mother whose milk had dried up, was particularly shrill. Her loud complaints could not help her infant, though. She held the child to her flaccid breast, but it no longer had the strength to cry. If Magnolia's child was not already dead, it would die soon, and others of the tribe's youngest children would follow it in a few days.

Unless the hunters brought in meat.

"It's because of our spears that we didn't bring down any game in today's hunt!" said Heron angrily. "When the herd ran, we all should have thrown our spears. We would have brought down at least one animal. Anyway, we would have wounded one badly enough that it could not run."

"You didn't throw *your* spear, Heron," said Boartooth, who didn't see where the other hunter's words were leading. "*I* wounded a horse so that it died. Bull stole from me the meat that I had killed!"

"The men who had good spears," Heron snarled in reply, "the spears that Hawk or his father made for us, those hunters did not throw their spears. We were afraid we would lose our good spears and have to use trash that Boartooth made!"

"My spears are good spears!" Boartooth shouted, as though raising his voice would change the facts that everyone in the tribe, even the women, knew.

"Your spears are not good, Boartooth," said Wolf. The Chief Hunter stood up. He held his club. Wolf had been silent during most of the complaints. He knew that because he was the Chief Hunter, the failure to bring in meat was his fault even if no one in the tribe could see anything that he was doing wrong.

Although Wolf kept tight control of his temper, being blamed by everyone—and blaming himself—made him very angry. Kar saw the anger start to come out now, in response to Boartooth's noisy posturing. Kar understood, but he knew also that what the Chief Hunter was doing was very dangerous. While the tribe was having such a difficult time, they needed more than ever to stick together instead of fighting among themselves.

"Your spears do not fly straight, Boartooth," Wolf shouted. "You barely scratched that stallion— and drove the whole herd off, so that none of us have meat. You do not perform the spear-making rites correctly, so your points shatter and bring bad luck on all of us!"

Wolf's club twitched with the strength of the Chief Hunter's grip. All the other hunters were on their feet. They held weapons also. Women snatched their younger children to them. They edged back to keep out of the way of possible violence.

Boartooth realized how serious the situation was. He didn't step away—there were men on every side of him—but his eyes flicked in all directions, looking for a way out of the trouble his arrogant tongue had gotten him into.

The campfire popped loudly. Water which had collected in a knot burst the wood in a puff of steam. Everybody glanced toward the flames. Boartooth slid between two of the hunters and stood among the women at the edge of the firelight.

After a further moment of tension, everyone relaxed. Even Wolf looked relieved. He was a good leader. He knew that it was his job to keep fights within the tribe from occurring, not to start them himself.

Kar stared at the images which formed within his fire. He fed in an additional piece of wood.

"We need better spears," said Flash. He spoke simply and without anger. The hunter held one of the spears Boartooth had made. His fingers ran slowly up the rough, slightly twisted, shaft to the point. The chert was not balanced so that the two sides met along the axis like the halves of a leaf at the stem.

They could all see that the spear would not fly straight if Flash threw it. Worse, there was a chance that the point would break apart if it struck a bone when a hunter ran close to his prey. Even a camel could be dangerous if it lashed out with its blunt-toed feet, driven by the pain of a flesh wound.

Boartooth glowered, but he said nothing.

"Bull's tribe has good spears," suggested Heron. "Maybe their spear-maker would make weapons for us."

"We have nothing to trade," Flash protested. "Besides, they drove us away. If we return, they will attack us to keep our bad luck from harming them too."

"We must pray forgiveness from the spirit of the bison," said Elm. "It doesn't matter what spears we have unless the spirit decides to forgive us for hunting other creatures instead of his children."

Kar stirred the fire. It seemed as though the old, pointless arguments were about to resume. Nothing had changed except that they were all hungrier by the amount of time—he checked the fire—it took to burn a log to ashes.

Usually the fire was necessary to keep predators at bay, but tonight the tribe was not bothered by the usual snaps and snarling of animals which lurked in the darkness. The beasts knew that there was nothing to eat here except the humans themselves . . . and the human were too thin with hunger to make a good meal.

Kar had always thought of the fire as also keeping off the spirit of the dark, a shadowy thing that was separate from all the dangerous animals that hunted within the shelter of the night. As he watched the fire, Kar remembered the previous night when the tribe had been driven away from the bogged mammoth. Many terrifying things had happened—but the spirit of the dark had not attacked them when they fled their camp.

The tigers were tigers. The wolves were wolves. They were dangerous, but they were not usually as dangerous as they had been that night when the smell of the butchered mammoth had inflamed their hunger throughout the day.

Hunger cramped the Chief Fire-Maker's belly and twisted his mind into unfamiliar patterns. Smoke filled his nostrils and formed new shapes of imagination.

Perhaps the spirit of the night did not really exist. Or perhaps there was a spirit of the night, but a tribe was safe from it so long as the Chief Fire-Maker had built a campfire. Men might not have to stay where the fire was to be safe from the spirit.

Kar's fire popped. His eyes flashed open on a wonderful thought.

"We won't have any luck hunting until we have better spears," Flash said for at least the third time. He rubbed his empty stomach.

"Wolf!" the Chief Fire-Maker shouted in delight at his idea. He jumped to his feet. "We will have spears, many spears! We will take the spears from Bull's tribe!"

Wolf looked at Kar in puzzlement. They all knew that sometimes men lost their minds from being out in the sun too long . . . or even from hunger. "They will not give us spears," the Chief Hunter said, speaking simply as if he were talking to a child. "They will attack us if we even go to them to ask."

"We will not ask," said Kar. "We will *take*. They should have shared the meat with us, so it is right that we take from them spears to win our own meat."

"Did you fall on your head, old man?" Boartooth

demanded. "There are too many of them for us to attack. They would kill us all."

Much as the other hunters had come to dislike Boartooth, there was a general chorus of nods and *Waughs* of approval for what the would-be spearmaker had said.

"If we went by day," Kar explained, "they would kill us. Instead we will go now, at night, and surprise them."

Wolf frowned as he tried to understand the idea that the Chief Fire-Maker was proposing. "We will not surprise them, Kar," he said at last. "They will see our torches."

"We will not take torches!" the old man said. "This fire *here* will protect us from the spirit of the night, even when we are far away from it. I have seen this when I watched the flames. Remember when we fled from the mammoth? The fire that I had built earlier still kept the spirit of the night away."

"After the fire went out, it didn't protect us from tigers," said Heron sourly. He rubbed his left arm, still swollen from the claw marks he had received that night. "Or from wolves."

"The wolves and tigers came because the mammoth was there," said the Chief Fire-Maker with a confidence he really felt so long as he was talking. "If we could have carried the meat away, the scavengers would have fought over the remains and left us alone."

"There wasn't time!" said Wolf. He was reacting to what he saw as a complaint about his judgment. "Besides, there was too much meat to carry."

"But Bull's tribe will carry the meat away, to

their camp," Kar explained. "The wolves and tigers will be at the kill site. They will not bother us when we go to Bull's camp."

Flash shook his head slowly. "But there are many hunters in Bull's tribe," he said. "And they have many spears. They will drive us away."

"No," said Wolf. The Chief Hunter had finally understood Kar's wonderful idea. "They will be asleep. They have eaten as much meat as they can hold. We will run in and grab their spears, then run away. They will not chase us in the darkness."

"And besides!" said Boartooth, "we will have their spears! Then we will kill much game!"

Kar looked at the young braggart grimly. If the attempt was successful, Boartooth would probably begin saying that the idea was his.

But if the attempt *was* successful, the only important thing would be that the tribe could hunt properly again. It didn't matter who got credit for that.

Clouds covered what remained of the moon. Kar carried his fire-gourd as well as a club. The hunters would have no need of fire tonight, but the Chief Fire-Maker would have felt unprotected without the slight weight of the gourd jouncing on the end of the thong tied around his waist.

An animal barked in the darkness. A hunter gasped in fear. Kar chuckled. "It is nothing," he said. "Only a fox. Its voice is greater than its jaws."

Kar guided the hunters. There was no tradition governing a night-time expedition to rob another tribe. Such a thing had never happened in the memory of Kar, Kar's father, or Kar's grandfather. That is, so far as the tribe was concerned, such a thing had never happened in the memory of Man.

Hunters never left the circle of fire at night, but sometimes the fire-makers had to go out to get more fuel. Because the Chief Fire-Maker was not quite as nervous as the rest of the men about moving through the night, and because the plan had been his to begin with, he wound up in the lead.

There had not been a vote or a formal assignment. The other men had looked at Kar expectantly. Kar had grunted and taken the first step beyond the fire. The hunters followed him willingly enough.

"How much farther is it, Kar?" Wolf whispered to the Chief Fire-Maker.

"I can smell their fire," Kar replied. "Soon we will see its light. They are not far." Wolf mumbled his approval.

Kar was much less afraid than he should have been. When he left the campfire to drag in more wood to burn, he always carried a torch and shouted loudly to frighten away lurking predators. Now he was tramping through total darkness, as quietly as he could and without an open flame for protection. But because the hunters were so much more frightened than he was, and because they trusted him—with no good reason, Kar knew—he felt a surprising confidence in himself.

What the tribe was doing was new, a thing without traditions. Not exactly *against* tradition, but still a thing that their fathers would never have considered doing. The only reason Wolf and the hunters had accepted the idea—the only reason the idea had occurred to Kar!—was hunger. Hunger was forcing them to do new things.

Kar thought of Hawk, whom they had cast out of the tribe. Hawk had done wrong. Hawk had violated tradition. But—

But the tribe's bad luck at hunting went back moons before Hawk began to use his spear shafts in ways that his father had never done. Elm said that the tribe's luck would not change until their medicine placated the spirit of the bison. Perhaps she was right. Elm was an old woman and very wise.

But Kar was old too, and he had seen, year by year, the herds of bison grow smaller and more wary of men. Wolf and his men performed the hunting rites just as their fathers had done when Kar was a youth. It was hard to see what tradition they had violated to make the spirit of the bison angry.

It might be that the spirit of the bison required a new rite . . . and if the spirit did, perhaps that rite required the Chief Spear-Maker to join in the hunting, or even to use the spirit of the wood in new ways. After all, Kar was Chief Fire-Maker, and he was leading hunters in an action for which the tribe had no tradition.

"We should not have driven Hawk away," Kar muttered under his breath.

"What?" said the Chief Hunter.

"Nothing," said Kar. Then he added, "There is Bull's fire. Now you must creep close. I have led you here, but this next is no business for an old man who is Chief Fire-Maker."

Wolf grunted approval and gathered his men to give them final directions. Kar stared at the fire glittering in the night, ten spear-casts away. No one was moving in Bull's camp. The luscious odor of cooked meat spiced the air.

Kar knew that he and Wolf were creating new traditions because hunger forced them to. Hawk had done new things because he wanted to, because his mind worked in new ways. If the spirits which ruled the tribe's hunting success had decided to demand new rites, then the tribe would have been much better off if Hawk were still a part of it.

The hunters slipped toward the strangers' camp with skills polished in stalking skittish game on the grasslands. Bull's folk were encamped in the open. The fire-maker or one of his assistants nodded by the fire, barely awake. There should have been a hunter on watch also, but he must have laid his head down.

Kar remembered how the folk of Wolf's tribe had been unable to stay awake when they gorged on mammoth after so many days of hunger. Bull's tribe was not in anything like as much danger from animals. The site of the kill, where the tribe left the bones, hides, and offal of the game, was a snarling mass of predators who could be heard far into the distance. As Kar had expected, though, the beasts ignored the fire-protected human encampment since there was plenty of equally-satisfactory food lying in the open.

Kar could see any movement silhouetted against the campfire, but Wolf and his men were invisible. The fire had been allowed to sink low, into a mass of coals. It was not because the tribe was short of fuel. There were plenty of branches piled near the blaze. The watchman was sleepy, and he wasn't adding wood as frequently as he ought to.

The hunters must be very close to the area cleared for the other tribe's camp. Any moment now—

The watchman got up and stirred the fire with another branch. The coals blazed high in a swirl of sparks, doubling the feeble light which the campfire provided a moment before. The sudden flare winked from the eyes of one of the encircling hunters. The watchman shouted in terror and flung his branch, now blazing, into the night.

Wolf, Heron, and Boartooth jumped to their feet and ran toward the fire. Several of Wolf's other men stood up, but they did not follow their chief. Bull's watchman leaped over the campfire to get away.

The hunter who should have been awake with the fire-tender had gone to sleep with his spear in his hands. He woke up as quickly and decisively as a cat. Kar saw firelight wink on the stranger's spearhead of glass-sharp flint as he twisted and plunged his weapon into Heron's belly.

Heron cried out in pain. He dropped his own spear and gripped with both hands the shaft of the weapon whose point now projected from his back. The stranger grabbed another spear. Wolf jumped at him. The guard fled instead of trying to battle the Chief Hunter.

The Chief Spear-Maker of Bull's tribe kept his extra spears, at least a dozen of them, in a sheaf bound together with cords woven from the inner bark of trees. Boartooth grabbed the bundle. Longshank caught the opposite end before Boartooth could flee with his treasure.

The two men tugged against one another. Boartooth thrust awkwardly with his spear. Longshank used the bundled spearshafts as protection, ducking down behind them. He had a club which he swung at Boartooth's knees, but his reach wasn't long enough for the weapon to strike.

The other tribe was fully aroused now. Most of Wolf's men had stopped on the edge of the firelight. They were shouting, but they seemed afraid to venture in to help Wolf and the two hunters who had followed him.

Heron was beyond helping. He was trying to crawl away from the campfire on his hands and knees. The shaft of the spear through his body got in the way, tripping him repeatedly. He might as well lie down where he was and wait for a woman to knock him on the head with a stone. No man wounded the way Heron was could live very long.

"Come on!" Wolf bellowed. "Come on, we've got to get their spears and get out!"

The Chief Hunter had grabbed several loose spears from around the campfire. Some of Bull's men had jumped aside at the first shouts and confusion, leaving their weapons where they lay. There were plenty of hunters who were armed, though.

Wolf was brightly illuminated by the fire. Bull threw a spear at him. Kar saw his Chief Hunter move like a tiger swiping with its paw, raising the spears he had taken as loot. Bull's weapon clacked

on the hardwood shafts and ricocheted out of the
camp. "Come on!" Wolf screamed to his men in
desperation.

Kar suddenly understood why most of Wolf's
men hesitated. They were brave men. They would
have been willing to spear one of the great bison
as it bore down on them. The previous night at
the mammoth's carcase, they had stood until the
wolves had attacked in darkness after the campfire
went out.

But they were afraid to attack another tribe's
fire at night. The folk of Kar's tribe—probably
every tribe in Kar's world—were raised to think
of fire as protection for those who sheltered around
it. Because Wolf's hunters believed deep in their
souls that the campfire was a shield, its flickering
light drove most of them back unexpectedly when
they prepared to attack the other tribe.

Kar had seen a similar reaction sometimes in
the forest when he gathered wood for his fire.
Often he would destroy the web of a spider when
he tore apart a brush pile. Occasionally the displaced creature would be flung into the web of
another spider of the same species.

To the Chief Fire-Maker's surprise, the spider
who had built the web would always drive out the
newcomer, even when the displaced spider was
considerably the larger of the two. The newcomer
seemed tentative as it raised its forelegs and mimed
stabbing motions with its mandibles. The original
owner hopped furiously back and forth, making
the web sway to disconcert its rival still further. At
last the displaced spider scuttled off the floor of

silk and climbed to a new location, where it started to build a small replacement web of its own.

Most of the hunters in Wolf's tribe were almost as tradition-bound as spiders. They lived according to fixed patterns. Even when the world changed drastically around them, they tried to react the way their fathers' fathers had done when times were better. If Kar had realized that sooner, he would not have proposed this plan. It was too late now to change what had happened, though.

Boartooth and Longshank wheezed and grunted in their personal tug of war. The folk of Bull's tribe were also shocked by the new events. They stayed a few paces back from the struggle, across the fire from their attackers.

Bull himself suddenly jumped the campfire. Wolf shouted and pointed a spear at his burly rival. Bull ignored the Chief Hunter and stabbed Boartooth in the throat. The young hunter gurgled and collapsed in a spray of blood.

Wolf backed away. A shower of stones and clubs hit him, far too many to block with his spearshafts. A large rock tore his forehead open. Wolf staggered and dropped the looted weapons.

Bull thrust at the other Chief Hunter. Wolf turned and ran, growling unintelligibly in anger and frustration. The people of the other tribe rushed forward to the edge of the firelight as suddenly as a creek dammed by fallen trees boils forward when one particular log gives way. They hurled a sleet of weapons, spears as well as blunt objects, at the attackers capering nervously in the brush.

Men screamed. Kar thought he recognized two of the voices, Flash and Bigfist. The men who had

been afraid to attack the strangers' camp seemed
to be unwilling to flee from the firelight now that
the plan had obviously failed. Wolf was too badly
injured—or too angry at his hunters' failure—to
give the necessary orders.

"Run away!" Kar shouted from behind the hunters. "Run to me!" This had been his plan, not the
Chief Hunter's, so it was largely his responsibility.
Besides, somebody had to act to save the folk who
could still be saved.

The men standing uselessly outside the hostile
camp suddenly vanished back into the brush and
safety. "Come to me!" the Chief Fire-Maker cried
again. He was safe from thrown spears where he
stood, and surviving hunters would be safe if they
reached him. Brush crackled loudly, reminding
Kar that men were large animals themselves.

Two hunters, then a third, burst out of the dark.
Bull's tribe had built up their fire. The strangers
stood like a wall between the light and their attackers. They flung weapons and screamed their
hatred. Children too young to speak more than a
few words stood between the legs of their mothers, tossing chips of bark while the women cast
rocks and the men aimed spears into the night.

Kar thought of spiders and shivered.

The brush crashed again. Wolf and another
hunter, Redhair, staggered to the group around
the Chief Fire-Maker. Redhair held the Chief Hunter's arm over his shoulders and helped support the
injured man. Neither of them carried spears.

Wolf tossed his head, trying to clear hair blood-
ied by the cut of his forehead from his eyes. He
looked around him. "We must go back for the

others," he muttered. "Flash and Bigfist are not here."

He didn't mention Heron and Boartooth. Wolf *knew* where they were.

There was a terrible cry from the brush just beyond the firelight. It ended with the hollow *thock* of stone hitting bone. The sound was familiar from the evenings after a successful hunt, when the women began cracking the thighs of the prey to get out the delicious marrow. This time it was a skull, not a thighbone, but the principle was the same.

"That was Flash," the Chief Fire-Maker said simply. "Bigfist will be next. We must return to our camp, before Bull leads his hunters out to find the rest of us."

Wolf groaned with a pain that did not come only from the blows his powerful body had received. "Yes," he said. "We must leave before dawn. And we must never return."

Kar led the hunters back the way they had come. Behind them, the triumphant shouting of the other tribe almost hid the sound of Bigfist's screams.

BISON

It had begun to rain before the surviving hunters reached the camp. The women must have suspected what had happened, because they already had the tribe's goods bundled and ready for flight.

The fire made the drizzle glitter like sunlight on an outcrop of mica. For a moment, the women and children remained impassive as the men stumbled into view. When those waiting realized that there were only five survivors, they began to scream and wail.

"I told you!" cried Elm. "I told you what would happen if you ignored the spirit of the bison!"

"We didn't ignore anything, old woman," said Wolf. He was trying to remember what had happened at the other tribe's camp. Kar had brought the Chief Hunter a wad of wet grass with which Wolf mopped the blood from his forehead. His

135

mind still moved in flashes rather than a connected trail. He remembered a spear coming at his face—and Boartooth spraying blood like a horse whose throat has been cut to finish it quickly. "I perform the rites as my father did. We needed good spears to take game."

Elm stood with her hands and her hips and her elbows out, shrieking at the hunters with a voice as raucous as a crow's. "You should have—" she began.

Redhair knocked the medicine woman down with his hand. She squawked in surprise. Redhair had lost his spear, but he still carried a club. He drew the weapon from beneath his waist thong and started for Elm again.

Wolf grabbed him from behind. "No!" the Chief Hunter shouted. "We are a tribe! We do not harm one another!"

Redhair turned away angrily. "Tell her to keep her mouth shut, then," he snarled. "If she speaks again tonight, I'll treat her as Flash was treated. Flash was my friend."

"Come," said Wolf to the others. "We must leave at once. Bull will not follow us any distance, but if we meet his hunting parties on the plain they will surely attack."

"It's night," said Grassblade, one of the women. "How will we . . . ?"

Wolf opened his mouth to reply, but his vision suddenly blurred. He saw two of everything, fuzzy images which were no more material than wisps of fog. He swayed and would have fallen except that old Kar put an arm around his shoulders.

"We will carry torches," said the Chief Fire-

Maker. "The animals will not harm us. They don't hunt in the rain either."

Wolf felt his vision clear and his balance return. "The rain will put our torches out," said a young boy—Heron's son, the Chief Hunter thought. He was too young to have the right to argue with one of the chiefs, but all discipline was breaking down under the crushing weight of hunger and catastrophe.

"Soon it will be dawn," said Kar. "Besides, the night is less dangerous than being here at dawn when Bull's hunters come."

He spoke mildly instead of slapping the child to assert adult authority. Perhaps the Chief Fire-Maker wanted to avoid additional violence on a night in which violence had proved disastrous for the tribe . . . but perhaps Kar, like Wolf himself, had doubts about the traditional rules which had brought them to this state.

"Quickly," said Wolf. He felt another spasm of dizziness when he bent to snatch a branch from the fire to use as a torch. While the hunters were gone, the women had built the blaze high so that its heat would prevent it from being extinguished by the slow rain.

Wolf led his tribe into the chill darkness. They were not going anywhere, just away from Bull and his angry tribe. Old Elm stumbled along near the end of the column, bent under the weight of her herbs and magical equipment. She muttered under her breath, but she was wise enough to believe Redhair. She did not raise her voice loud enough to be heard by others.

*   *   *

It continued to rain all day. The only change was that long periods of pelting, hammering downpour interspersed the drizzle. In a way the rain was a good thing, since Bull's tribe certainly wouldn't bother struggling out in it to look for their beaten enemies.

But if the rain kept up, Wolf feared that it would wash him and his tribe completely away.

The Chief Hunter had never felt as miserable before in his life. The cut on his forehead bled severely, which left him weaker than usual. The blow had done him other injury as well, he knew, because he suffered several attacks of dizziness and double vision.

Once Wolf fell down because of the spell of dizziness. The rest of the tribe was so dulled by hunger and fatigue that most of them ignored their fallen chief. They continued plodding onward, stepping around Wolf's legs as he thrashed in the mud, trying to rise.

Kar helped the Chief Hunter to his feet. The Chief Fire-Maker was old but wiry, well familiar with awkward weights from his experience in dragging loads of timber into camp through the clinging undergrowth.

"I'm all right," Wolf whispered. He moved his arms to prove that he could. His whole side was smeared with gray mud almost the consistency of the tar which oozed from pits on a hot day.

His vision cleared as suddenly as it had blurred. There was nothing to see but a bleak expanse of meadow pounded down by the rain. It was past noon, but the light which filtered through the heavy clouds was too weak to awaken any colors from the grass.

As if to mock the humans, the whitened skull of a giant bison lay beside the trail the tribe was taking. All traces of flesh and hair had been cleaned away by scavengers. Field mice had even begun to nibble the bone.

The black, smoothly curved horns were still attached to the skull, though they had begun to weather loose on their bony cores. They were immense. Tip to tip, they spanned almost twice the height of a woman. To the Chief Hunter in his present state, the curve of the horns was a sneering smile.

There were no living animals in sight, and there was no hope of food for the tribe.

"I can walk," Wolf repeated.

"Yes," said Kar. "We will walk together, Chief Hunter." Most of the tribe had trudged past them by now. Kar put his arm around Wolf's waist as the two chiefs resumed their trek. A stranger would not have realized that the small fire-maker was helping the burly hunter instead of the reverse, but Wolf was glad of the older man's touch.

The Chief Hunter had several more spasms of double vision and dizziness. Because the Chief Fire-Maker was beside him, he did not fall again.

They set up a camp of sorts at night. A long limestone outcrop a little taller than a man provided some shelter from the weather.

The rain continued.

There was no food at all. The women had not been able to forage while need for escape drove the tribe on at the best speed it could manage. When Wolf finally called a halt, a few of the women went out with digging sticks to see what they could find. They were tired to the bone, and it was almost impossible to see anything in the rain-swept darkness anyway.

Magnolia still carried her infant. The child had died of hunger before dawn. When two of the other women, crooning their sympathy, tried to remove the tiny corpse, Magnolia snarled and slashed at them with a digging stake of sharpened antler. After that, the rest of the tribe stayed a cautious distance away from the grief-maddened mother.

Kar seated Wolf as comfortably as possible with his back to the outcrop. The blow to the head had drained away Wolf's strength. The Chief Hunter watched dull-eyed as Kar stretched a piece of deer hide between short poles and began to build a fire-set of punk and dried moss beneath it.

"You can't get a fire to burn in this weather," Wolf said. The remainder of the tribe huddled together, watching the Chief Fire-Maker without enthusiasm. They had nothing better to do.

"I will build a fire," Kar said calmly. He shaved at a dead branch with his hand axe. When he got through the rain-soaked outer layers of the wood, he began to add the dry chips to the fire-set.

"Chief Hunter!" cried Elm in her normal shrill voice. She had just reached the camp. She must have been far behind the rest of the tribe. In the darkness and general feeling of misery, no one else had noticed that the old woman was missing —or had cared.

Besides her previous load of herbs and magical apparatus, Elm carried a horn from the bison skull the tribe had passed. It was almost as tall as the stooped old woman.

"Why did you bring that?" demanded Redhair. "Did you think we could eat horn?"

Wolf saw that Redhair's thigh had been badly bruised by a club flung from Bull's camp. The pain caused by having to walk for so long on an injured leg made the young hunter even more sullenly angry than he had been when the men first returned in defeat from the other tribe. He was too tired to get up to strike Elm as he had threatened.

"Chief Hunter!" the medicine woman repeated, ignoring Redhair's gibes. "Since you have not sufficiently apologized to the spirit of the bison, I will talk to him on behalf of the tribe. We are not all to blame for you! The spirit of the bison will relent and send his children back to us."

Everyone except Kar was staring at Elm. The expressions of the tribes-people ranged from the fury of Redhair's face as he tried to stagger to his feet, to agreement—even admiration—on the part of some of the women and starving children.

The Chief Fire-Maker kept on at his task. He had completed his fire-set and was striking flints together with exquisite care under the shelter of the deer hide. The coals in his gourd had gone out while he helped Wolf walk. A pair of sparks touched the cushion of dry moss. A gust blew a single droplet of rain sideways beneath the hide. It extinguished the sparks before they could turn into a true fire.

Kar continued striking his flints together with a rhythmic *tik! tik! tik!*

"Get away from us, woman!" Wolf snarled. He didn't think he was strong enough at the moment to prevent Redhair from killing Elm, and he wasn't sure he even wanted to save her again. "We have enough trouble now without your foolishness."

"Yes, I will go off by myself with my magic!" the old woman replied. She shook the long horn as though it were a curving spear. "I will bring bison to the tribe when you could not, Chief Hunter!"

Elm scuttled off into the rain. Wolf relaxed. Even Redhair looked thankful as he lay back down, rubbing his thigh. No one had enough energy for trouble. Besides, trouble would come to the tribe whether or not they made trouble for themselves.

The Chief Hunter thought about Hawk. Surely they had been right to drive the young man away. Hawk had violated tradition. But . . . Wolf and the rest of the tribe were performing all their rites in perfect harmony with tradition—and they were dying, either from sudden disaster or by cold and starvation.

The wind was gusting. When it was in the right direction, Wolf could hear Elm's voice worn thin by the distance it traveled. The medicine woman was chanting something. Wolf could not understand the words. They might not have been words at all, just a wail of rhythmic wretchedness to call the spirit of the bison's attention to her.

Wolf wondered if cold and hunger had driven Elm mad. Even if the old woman did manage to fashion a medicine that brought game to the tribe, it would do them no good on a night like this. The hunters had only two spears remaining. They would need to run animals over a high cliff or into a bog with a traditional fire drive in order to kill them. It would be impossible to light the grass in such rain, much less keep it burning with an intensity that would make animals panic and ignore the terrain.

Kar had his moss and punk alight. A wisp of flame lifted toward the deer-hide cover. The Chief Fire-Maker fed chips of dry wood into the tiny blaze. All eyes in the tribe were focused on him. Despite their hunger and general misery, the folk were thrilled to see one of their number achieving a sort of success.

The rain hammered down. It seemed to be growing colder. Lightning flashed in the near distance. "Bring me wood!" shouted the Chief Fire-Maker. "Small branches, and crack them open so that the dry wood shows!"

People moved with the jerky stiffness of cripples. Most of the men had been wounded in the battle with Bull's tribe. Now that they had let their muscles cool, the injured limbs cramped and bound them. The women, carrying burdens for so many hours without food, were almost as badly off. The children had less fat and muscle to live off than the adults. They were on the verge of starvation.

The Chief Hunter tried to get up. His legs would not obey him. He was seeing double again, two orange-red glowing fires being fed by a pair of Kars who were so pale that they looked transparent. Thunder rumbled across the sky, drowning out the sound of Elm chanting. Lightning flashed and rippled again.

"Quickly!" screamed the Chief Fire-Maker. "Bring me wood!"

Kar's store of chips was almost exhausted, and the miniature fire was not hot enough to sustain itself with damp wood. A woman handed the old man a gnarled branch. Kar began chopping at it furiously to get through the wet layers in time to preserve his creation.

Thunder boomed. It continued to roll without letup. Even the ground trembled. The folk of the tribe clustered instinctively around their Chief Fire-Maker, trying to block the threatening gusts before one of them blew out the infant fire.

Kar slid a long sliver into the glow. People gasped as the fire took the fresh fuel and changed it into a livid tongue fiercer and more vibrant than any the Chief Fire-Maker had coaxed from his fire-set thus far.

Old Elm ran up to the back of the circle, screeching and swinging the bison horn like a club in both hands. People cried and jumped aside at the unexpected attack. Wind surged through the sudden gap in the human wall, putting out the fire as the thunder rumbled onward.

"Run!" the medicine woman shrieked.

"I warned you!" shouted Redhair. He lunged forward, swinging his club in a long downward arc.

Elm raised the horn in an attempt to defend herself. The thin material shattered into a shower of black splinters which the wind tossed. The club struck Elm's forehead with a hollow sound. The weapon crunched the old woman's skull almost as completely as it had done the bison horn. She toppled backward, her mouth still open to scream.

Wolf looked out into the night, past Redhair and over the fallen body of the medicine woman. Lightning flashed again. The fire from the heavens glittered on the eyes of hundreds of giant bison, charging straight toward the huddling tribe. The herd had been stampeded by the lightning. It was their hooves, not the thunder, which had been shaking the ground.

"Run!" cried someone.

Wolf jumped to his feet. He was fully himself again. In this crisis, all the Chief Hunter's wounds and fatigue were forgotten. "Up the cliff!" he bellowed. "We can't outrun them, but they won't jump the cliff!"

Kar was blinking in surprise. He had been so focused on his fire-set that he seemed to have forgotten the outer world. Wolf grabbed the old man by the shoulder and half-lifted, half-threw him upward to safety on top of the limestone outcrop. Shrieking in the wind, the rest of the tribe tried to follow.

The same lightning flash that displayed the herd to the humans warned the leading bison of the existence of the ledge of rock. The beasts tried to swerve away, but the weight of their fellows to either side and behind them made that impossible.

Wolf clambered to the top of the outcrop. The weather-rotted stone had easy hand- and foot-holds, even in the dim light, but there was no time to choose them. The Chief Hunter used the strength of his powerful shoulders to lift him up. Twice he kicked his legs as if he were swimming instead of climbing rock.

He reached down. A woman was trying to climb one-handed. Wolf caught her by the upper arm and jerked her brutally to safety. The woman was Magnolia. The dead baby fell from the crook of her other arm and bounced downward just as the first of the giant bison thundered over the ground where the tribe had been sheltering a moment before.

The Chief Hunter saw a great bull hunch its shaggy shoulders and lift them. Redhair's body was impaled on one of its horns. The hunter was still screaming, though he could not live much longer. Wolf wondered if Elm watched the events from somewhere in spirit land. If so, she must be laughing shrilly.

Other members of the tribe had climbed the limestone, but not very many. Perhaps there were more, hidden by the rain-swept darkness. The bison's hooves made an unimaginable thunder, but over the sound came an occasional squeal of final pain as a human's life was stamped out against the soil.

The herd somehow managed to divide at the outcrop. For a moment, Wolf had imagined the great beasts crushing themselves into a ramp of flesh up which bison farther back in the throng would climb to tred down the surviving handful of Wolf's tribe.

Not quite. But the stampede continued for longer than the Chief Hunter dreamed was possible. Even in his boyhood he had never seen a herd of such immense size. He was quite sure, though, that when dawn broke and the rain stopped—if the rain ever stopped—that the bison would have vanished with only trampled sod to mark their passing. Another tribe might find a lone beast in a mud hole, or a bison that had broken its neck when it pitched over a gully in the darkness. There would be no such good luck for Wolf and his pitifully few fellows.

Kar was weeping. Wolf heard the word, "Hawk," between the old man's sobs. The Chief Fire-Maker seemed to be begging Hawk's forgiveness.

The herd thundered on.

NAMING A DOG

No longer a puppy but not yet full-grown, the gray dog had grown unbelievably. The large gray dog sat by the fire... his tail ... rested his head ...

... in the months they ... learned both to trust ... him better. In return ... thened loyalty to the hunter ... made him to leave the ... Willow or Hawk went out ... fully accompanied them.

As time went on, Hawk ... daily experimenting ...

MAMMOTH HERD

No longer a puppy, but a strong, agile beast who had grown unbelievably in a very few months, the gray dog sat by the fire, staring into the forest. His tail was straight behind him, his pointed ears alert, and his head slightly turned as he sought stronger evidence of some scent or sound that must have come very faintly to him. On the other side of the fire, Hawk watched intently.

In the months they had been together he had learned both to trust the dog and to understand him better. In return, the dog had given whole-hearted loyalty to the humans. Nothing could persuade him to leave the camp for very long unless Willow or Hawk went too. Then the dog cheerfully accompanied them.

As time went on, Hawk had also perfected his darts, experimenting ceaselessly until he found just what he wanted. He had discovered that, by using the broad parts of wing feathers instead of tail feathers about the butt of the dart, he could get better distance without sacrificing any accuracy, and he had made a new and better throwing-stick. By using a different wood for the shafts, and shaping the flint heads narrower, he could carry nine darts instead of six in his pouch. Continual practice had made him an expert marksman. He knew just what he could do with his darts, exactly how to throw them, and as a consequence he seldom missed.

He was surer of his ability to protect himself, Willow, and their camp from any beast that threatened, even saber-tooths. While remaining prudent, and never going out of his way to seek trouble with the larger beasts, he was no longer in such fear of them. But now a new factor had entered.

He had hunted incessantly; he had to hunt most of the time if he and Willow were to have enough to eat. First the darts and then the dog had increased his hunting ability, so that he could consistently get many kinds of game which the tribe's hunters had almost never been able to bring down. The consequence was that game within easy striking distance of their camp was becoming scarce and wary. The less alert had fallen first; most of what was left had learned to avoid him.

So Hawk now watched the dog very carefully to know just what had attracted his attention. If it was game he could bring down, he would go get it. The dog turned to look at him, whined, and took a few forward steps.

Hawk shouldered his pouch of darts and picked up his throwing-stick and spear. He had learned that the dog reacted differently to different game. If a saber-tooth, a pack of dire wolves, a cave bear, or any other formidable thing were out there in the forest, the dog would be bristled and fearful. For small game he would be eagerly impatient. Now he was questing, anxious but uncertain. Therefore he smelled large game which he thought the two of them together might handle.

The dog waited a moment, and again glanced over his shoulder to see what the man was going to do. When Hawk followed him, the dog headed toward the forest, holding his head high the better to catch the elusive scent.

He did not travel fast because as yet he did not have a sure lead. Born to parents that had always had to find their own food, there was within the dog an instinctive and finely developed hunting sense. He knew when to go fast, and when it was better to travel slowly. Only when they were well within the great trees did he increase his pace.

Hawk trotted after him. He stayed alert to the scents, sounds, and sights of the forest, but he need not be as cautious as he once would have been. Experience had taught him that the dog's nose was much keener than his, and that he reacted faster to any possible threat. Hawk centered most of his attention on keeping the dog in sight.

The dog turned to look questioningly at him, and Hawk correctly interpreted the look. He and the dog lived under the same conditions, and faced the same problems. Though one was human and the other animal, they were not so far apart but that each was able to understand the other. Now the dog wanted to know whether they should go on or abandon the hunt.

Hawk stood still, concentrating all his faculties on a strained, intense investigation of whatever lay in the wind. He detected and rejected the scents of various rodents and tree-dwelling beasts. Finally, and faintly, he got the scent which was now very plain to the dog.

It was a giant elk, a monstrous beast with an antler spread so big and clumsy that it frequently troubled its owner in heavy brush or thick forest. This very unwieldiness, coupled with its lack of offensive ability, was its undoing, for already the great elk were very scarce. In his whole life Hawk had seen no more than a dozen of them.

He fitted a dart to his throwing-stick, and at this signal the dog whisked into the forest and disappeared. Hawk trotted easily toward a place he had in mind. The elk would try to escape the dog, but it would not seek deep thickets for a refuge. The elk knew better than to go there.

Hawk soon reached a hillside he knew, a slope where tress with slender branches grew in scattered clumps. He tested the wind, and took a stand where his scent would not betray him.

This was the way he hunted with the dog. The dog's function was to find game and trail it. No pursued beast ran in a straight line. Sooner or later it would circle, and Hawk used his knowledge of animals to determine the place where he might intercept any quarry. He poised a dart in his throwing-stick and waited.

He was a little more tense than usual. This was

no deer or antelope he awaited but a monster the size of a bison. It would be a real test of his darts, for until now he had attacked nothing as big as this. A half hour later, he saw the elk.

It came through the trees on the lower slope of the hill, almost exactly where he had expected it to come. Its head was up, massive antlers laid along its back, as it raced swiftly ahead of the pursuing dog. Hawk gauged the distance between the elk and himself and drew his arm a little farther back as he made ready to throw. Just at that instant the elk swerved.

Having seen or scented him, it turned toward the far side of the sparsely forested hill. Hawk ran toward it, trying to lessen the distance, then stopped and cast.

It was a mighty throw, a determined attempt to get the food represented by this huge beast, but the distance was too great for much penetration. He saw the dart pierce the elk's side, and the mottled feathers of the butt trembled from the impact. The elk faltered. Then, regaining its stride, it raced swiftly away.

Hawk took up the trail at a dead run. It was easy to find because a blood spoor marked it, and could be followed by the eye alone. The elk was badly wounded. Though it might run a long way, it would weaken as it ran and could be eventually overtaken. When it was caught, it should be easy prey.

The dog overtook and passed Hawk, flying along the trail as if he knew exactly what to expect. The man pressed along as fast as he could, sure of success.

This had happened once before. He had wounded a buck, and it had run away with his dart. He had tried and been unable to stop the dog from following, but when he had reached the buck the dog was holding it at bay, preventing further flight. The kill had been an easy one, and so Hawk had learned to let the dog run along on the trail of wounded game.

He came suddenly upon the dog, which was bristled and snarling. When Hawk stopped, the dog came back to stand against his knee. He looked inquiringly up, willing to go on but wishing first to know his master's decision.

Hawk considered.

The wind brought him plain scent of a pack of dire wolves. They had evidently intercepted the elk, dragged it down, and were probably feeding on it already. Anger flared in Hawk's eyes. He thought of the dart in the elk, and of the eight darts remaining in his pouch.

There were undoubtedly more than eight wolves in the pack, and they would fight savagely to defend their kill. It would be folly to attack; he had no chance of winning the fight if he started it. Glumly Hawk changed direction and went on in search of other game.

After a time he passed the home of the great cave bear, and swerved to examine it again. The bear was not in its cave, but some distance down the valley, crushing its ponderous way through a tangle of sweet berries. It bent the bushes to the ground, licked up their fruit, and trampled on over the crushed bushes. Hawk swerved and went on. Only a foolish or very desperate lone hunter would try to kill such a beast.

The dog started off on a deer's trail. Hopefully Hawk took a stand where he thought the deer would run, but after an hour the wind brought no scent or sound of the chase. Obviously the deer was a wise one, aware of possible ambushes and with no intention of being trapped. Discouraged, Hawk gave up his stand and returned to the fire. The dog would come in after the deer had outdistanced him.

Grinding seeds in her hollow stone, Willow looked expectantly up. Hawk unslung his pouch, put his throwing-stick beside it, and leaned his spear against a log of wood. Listlessly he bit into one of the cakes Willow brought him, then took another, bigger bite. The cakes were not tasteless, but had a flavor such as he had never known before. He looked inquiringly at Willow.

"There was a little meat left," the girl explained. "I cut it into small pieces and cooked it with the seeds."

"It is good."

Hawk ate his fill of the cakes, and sat staring into the fire, as though he expected to find something there. But there was no answer in the dancing flames and he knew it. There was only one solution to the problem facing them—the age-old remedy his tribe had always sought when faced with the scarcity of food. When there was little game, they must move to some place where there was a chance of finding more.

"We go tomorrow," Hawk said sullenly.

Willow said nothing, but resigned disappointment showed in her face. The life of a wandering hunter was a hard one, with danger at every turn and privation likely. Not soon again would they know the settled comforts of this camp.

The panting dog came back and threw himself wearily down beside the fire. Hawk inspected his darts, looking to the heads, shafts, and the bindings that tied the one to the other. He made a new dart to replace the one carried away by the giant elk, and collected more flints for additional heads. There was no telling where their travels would lead them or what they would encounter on the way. He might be too busy fighting or hunting to have any time for spear and dart making.

Willow was busy with her own preparations. She had gathered and dried a quantity of seeds, berries, and roots, and was packing them into skin containers, which were easier to carry than her open baskets. She, too, realized that neither of them knew where, how far, or for how long they would travel. They could carry with them only the simple necessities of their way of life: Hawk's weapons and materials for making more, dried food, and the all-important fire stones.

Sleeping by the fire that night, the hungry dog growled and twitched his paws as he dreamed of game he had hunted and eaten or game he would like to hunt and eat. He awoke and sniffed the air, then settled himself in a more comfortable position and went back to sleep. This was his life, too, and had been the life of his ancestors. When they killed game, all could eat. Otherwise, all went hungry.

The next morning, Hawk leading, Willow following, and the dog ranging from side to side, they began their uncertain trek toward better hunting grounds. Because they were the logical places to find game quickly, Hawk started toward the lush river bottoms. He might find a herd of bison there, or camels, or horses. Possibly there would be deer and antelope. But just what he would find, or exactly where he would find it, he did not know.

As they walked, the dog ranged farther and stayed away for longer intervals. He, too, knew that the object was to seek game, but even he could find none. They seemed to have left the camp, and its scarcity of wild life, for a place where it was even scarcer. Save for an occasional bird, they saw nothing.

The humans trudged stolidly on. They had been through this before. There was food here for grass-eaters, and the meat-eaters always followed them, but for some inexplicable reason, at various times, all the game deserted certain areas. They had no choice but to seek further.

Then, far in the distance, Hawk heard the dog bark.

It was a shrill sound, a far-carrying one that left faint echoes rolling in the distance. The dog had found game too big and too fierce for him to attack, and he had bayed it. The bark was to summon his mates, his pack. The dog barked again and again. There was a faint snarling and growling.

For a few seconds, Hawk stood perfectly still. Then, having located the dog's exact whereabouts, he trotted swiftly toward it, Willow at his heels. The dog's continuous barking and snarling became louder, fiercer. Then Hawk caught a glimpse of a giant sloth.

He slowed down, knowing now what he had to deal with. The great sloths were powerful creatures and therefore dangerous, but they were neither swift nor intelligent. Soon they came upon the dog and his cornered quarry.

The sloth was in a grove of trees, and all about a litter of stripped and broken branches attested to the fact that it had been feeding there for some time. Now it was backed against a tree, a solid, massive mountain of flesh. The dog swept swiftly in front of it, and the monster struck out with its front paws.

It missed completely; the dog was far too quick to be trapped by anything so slow. But when it struck at the dog it turned, and Hawk saw something he had not noticed before. The sloth was protecting a quarter-grown calf that huddled at its side. Hawk calculated his chances.

He might kill the mother sloth, but it would take most of his darts to do so and then what if the sloth waddled off, wounded? His darts would be gone, and he and Willow might be attacked by something before he could make new ones. But perhaps he could kill the young one.

He circled cautiously, a dart ready in his throwing-stick. Working its mouth nervously, the giant sloth wheeled with him. Hawk feinted in the opposite direction, and the sloth turned to meet this new thrust. It was slow and stupid, but determined when the defense of its own young was involved. Always it managed to shield the calf with its own ponderous body.

Hawk kept moving, awaiting a chance to hurl his dart. Then the dog attacked.

He flung himself in with a rush, leaping high as he grasped a mouthful of the sloth's coarse hair. As swiftly as he had attacked, the dog retreated, escaping the blow of a massive claw-tipped paw by a hair's breadth. But in wheeling to repel the dog, the sloth exposed its calf.

Hawk hurled his dart, and saw it bury itself to the feathers in the calf's chest. The calf groped at it with both front paws, and started to waddle away. Hawk cast another dart, that pierced the back of the neck and severed a vital nerve. The calf slowly tumbled to the ground.

Still the mother sloth refused to leave. Flicking its long tongue in and out, it stood protectingly by the calf's body. The dog snarled furiously in, and out again. The sloth struck at him and stood her ground, refusing to leave the calf.

Hawk pondered. He had killed the calf, but could not get at his prize unless he could drive the mother away. Deliberately he danced in front of her, teasing her to strike. When the giant sloth tried to crush him he leaped backward. The dog barked furiously. The sloth pursued them a few feet, looked back at her calf, and returned to it.

"Fire! Try fire!" Willow cried.

Hawk looked appreciatively at her. Fire had driven the giant bison, and it might work on this great beast. Going into the grove of trees, he sought among the lower branches for twigs covered with dry bark. He shredded this into the finest of tinder and made a little heap on the ground exactly to windward of the sloth. Keeping dry sticks ready, he struck a spark into the tinder.

It caught, making a tiny glow that might live or might die out. Hawk got down on his hands and knees to blow into it. The newborn spark glowed more hotly, then a tiny flame spread through the tinder. Hawk laid a few twigs on the little fire, then added more. In a moment a plume of smoke blew about the giant sloth's head.

It snorted, shook its head, and stared nervously. Then the smoke increased. At a lumbering trot, the sloth started away. A hundred yards from the fire it stopped, looked around, then at a slow walk it started toward another grove of trees. Its own personal tragedy was already forgotten in the pressing need to get more food to keep its massive body alive.

As Willow bent over the dead sloth, a stone knife in her hand, Hawk gathered more wood for his fire. They had started out to seek food and now had much more than they could possibly carry. Therefore, their camp would automatically be right here until the meat was gone.

While Willow tended the new camp, Hawk and the dog ranged into the surrounding country scouting for game signs. The sloth would not last forever; they must locate more game for the future.

But in ten days the dog found and ran only one deer at which Hawk could get a fair shot. But the wounded animal escaped, and they could find nothing else. They must move again.

The rich river bottoms, the best grazing lands, were still the logical place to go. Of course, if they attracted herds of grazing animals, the grass-eaters, in turn, would draw more dangerous beasts. There would be saber-tooths in plenty, packs of dire wolves and wild dogs, and the whole range of meat-eaters, big and small. There might be men, too, the fiercest hunters of all, and they might or might not be friendly. Though different tribes could live amiably together, in times of hunger any tribe that found a good hunting place would defend it. But that chance they had to take.

Cautiously, his own senses always alert and keeping his eyes on the dog, Hawk led Willow over the small hillocks, toward the river bottoms. Three days later, they looked down on the meadow where the unsuccessful fire drive had been attempted. All scars of the fire were gone, and a rich carpet of green grass covered the meadow. A herd of mammoths fed there.

There were twenty in the herd, ranging from immense, heavy-tusked bulls to calves at their mother's side. As Hawk watched, a bull circled cautiously. He faced into the wind, his trunk extended. The Spear-Maker took interested note.

The hairy elephants were so big, and so strong, that almost nothing dared attack a herd. But obviously this one had known danger and was expecting it again. Although the bull could not have scented them, he seemed to have some premonition of their presence. Hawk drew Willow back into the sheltering forest.

Evidently there were, or had been, human hunters ranging the river meadows. If so, they were desperate hunters. Failing to find giant bison, camels, or other game which they could kill with comparative safety, they had been attacking the mammoth herds. As a result, the mammoths were alerted. Whoever went into the river bottoms now did so at the risk of his own life. To be seen meant to be attacked. Unlike the sloths, the mammoths were intelligent beasts and despite their bulk they could whirl and twist like cats.

The dog sat down, ears pricked up as he studied the herd of mammoths. He looked questioningly at Hawk, and fell in beside him as the two lone humans started up the series of forested hills that rose out of the flat river meadows.

The meadows had been flooded by a veritable inundation of mammoths. The lumbering beasts were everywhere, and all seemed aroused and belligerently ready for whatever danger might come. But Hawk saw no humans, only a few saber-tooths that probably hoped to catch a calf separated from its mother, and a pack of dire wolves. Though he continued to study the situation, Hawk did not dare go down into the meadows. He would have to find his food on the forested slopes.

But there was nothing, and that night they made a hungry camp in the hills. The next morning they went on.

Ranging ahead, the dog bristled and came to a sudden halt at the edge of a little clearing. Lips curled back from long fangs, he backed against Hawk's legs. Hawk fitted a dart into his throwing-stick and intently sniffed the various winds. He looked all around, then centered his attention on the clearing.

There was a trampled place in the center of the valley. All about were smashed bushes, and a few broken tree limbs. Faintly dominating all was the scent of mammoths.

The dog snarled, and pressed closely against Hawk's legs as he went forward, Willow following fearfully.

He stooped, attracted by an object that met his eye, and picked up a spearhead. As he examined it, he realized that it was one he himself had made. Near it, smashed into splinters, was the broken shaft. The spear was one he had made for a hunter of his own tribe. Then he knew.

Some of his former tribesmen had died here, but what had killed them? There were no tracks in the trampled earth save those of mammoths, and rains had obliterated most of those. There were no bones, but of course anything left to eat had already been devoured by starving beasts, and bones might have been dragged away. Nothing whatever remained except the broken spear. Had the tribesmen, driven by desperation, attacked and been trapped by a herd of mammoths? Had they been overwhelmed by a pack of dire wolves? Or had hunters of some other tribe killed them? Perhaps his whole tribe had been wiped out here in a grim, determined battle for food, without which they could not live.

Shuddering, Hawk left the place. He led Willow up the opposite hill and looked again into the river bottoms. His interest quickened.

Far out, near the river's edge, a herd of a hundred or more mammoths was dozing in the sun. But just beneath the hillock, a single cow and her calf had detached themselves from the herd and were wandering alone. Hawk remembered the young sloth. If he could somehow manage to kill the calf, then wait until the rest departed, he and Willow would have meat. Hawk turned to the girl.

"Hold the dog," he directed, "and wait for me."

Quietly he slipped down the slope. This would be the ultimate test of his hunter's skill and ability. He must get near the mammoth and her calf without being detected, then cast his dart and escape before he could be overtaken.

Hawk hid himself in the tall grass and crept forward, careful to stay downwind. Carefully he raised himself just far enough so he could see his intended quarry.

The cow, suspicious, shuffled nervous feet, spread her ears, and snaked her trunk in various directions. The calf, too young to be aware of any danger, squealed happily. It ran a few steps, intrigued by something it heard or saw, and the cow promptly followed. She whacked it with her trunk, grunted, and shepherded her baby toward the river.

Hawk followed, knowing that he had to get his shot before she neared the rest of the herd. He ran swiftly along, maneuvering for position.

Suddenly, without any warning whatever, a thrown spear came so close to his head that he felt a little wind brush him as it passed. Hawk spun around.

Coming through the grass, spread out to cut him off, were more than fifteen strange hunters. There was no escape; the hunters were too well dispersed and coming too fast. Nor was there any doubt about their purpose; for whatever reason, they were deadly intent on killing him.

Without hesitation Hawk ran straight toward the cow. He hurled his dart, not at the calf, but at its mother. The cow bellowed for help.

Answering bellows and angry trumpetings came from the herd at the river's edge. They wheeled, and at top speed stampeded to the aid of their wounded comrade.

ESCAPE

The dart was sticking in the cow mammoth's neck, just behind her flaring ear, and a little blood dribbled down her hairy side. She bellowed again, high and shrill, and waved her trunk. Wheeling on her huge pads, she examined her calf to make sure it was safe. Then she whirled and launched herself straight at Hawk. Behind her appeared the charging herd, literally shaking the earth as it pounded along. In another few seconds everything in the meadow would be overwhelmed.

But Hawk was poised for instant action, another dart ready in his throwing-stick. When the cow swerved toward him, he cast his dart straight at the calf.

It skidded across the baby's back, plowing a bloody furrow with its flint head. The calf squealed its alarm. Instantly the cow pivoted and returned to it. She stood protectingly over her baby, rumbling threats while she awaited the rest of the herd. Hawk turned and ran, straight toward the enemy tribesmen.

At the best he had only a very few seconds, and two kinds of enemies to avoid. He had purposely aroused the mammoth herd, hoping by so doing to divert the human hunters on his trail. But now he had to run back toward the enemy tribesmen, to escape the greater danger of the thundering mammoths.

His ruse had worked. The hunters were running, too, most of them scrambling toward a high pinnacle of rock that reared from the base of a nearby hill. Seeing the many hunters, the approaching herd bulls roared their defiance and led the herd toward the pinnacle. Hawk stooped, so that the waving grass reached over his head, and veered toward the left, away from the rock pinnacle. He swung far out, making a wide circle, and when he thought he had run far enough he changed his course to take him back into the forest where he had left Willow. Not until he was well within the trees did he stop to catch his breath.

He tried to look back, but the trees obstructed his vision and he could not see what the angry mammoths were doing. The roaring and trumpeting of the enraged herd filled the air. They were, Hawk guessed, milling around the base of the pinnacle where the hunters had found safety. High above the mingled sounds, there came the angry squeal of a cow.

Hawk shivered. This was undoubtedly the cow

at which he had cast his dart to bring on the stampede, the mother of the calf he had wounded. She had probably assured herself that he was not among the hunters on the pinnacle, and now was seeking him. The cow knew her real enemy. Again she squealed, and Hawk decided that she had detached herself from the herd and was casting about for his scent. He started running again.

He had no plan beyond finding Willow and taking her to some safe place, but he knew they would have to move fast. The enemy tribesmen would know, from the action of the cow, that he had not been killed in the stampede. Therefore they would trail him at the first opportunity, and human hunters were far more deadly than any other kind. Judging by their first actions, these tribesmen would not be contented until they had caught and killed him.

Without any warning another spear sailed out of the brush, flicked into a tree a few inches from his shoulder, and quivered jerkily.

Hawk realized that he had made a mistake in assuming that all the hunters had fled to the pinnacle of rock. And in that confidence, and his haste to return to Willow, he had become careless. He had run with the wind instead of against it, and therefore had been unable to scent whatever might lie ahead of him. Now he dodged behind a tree, fitted a dart to his throwing-stick, and made ready to defend himself.

There were three hunters after him, savage, hairy men with bison-skin girdles flapping about their waists. Hawk noted with relief that none of them carried throwing-sticks; he had that much advantage, at least.

As soon as he saw them, Hawk cast his dart and struck the first hunter squarely in the throat. The wounded man dropped his spear, clutched at the dart with both hands, and took two backward steps. Then he fell, dead or dying.

The two remaining hunters screeched their rage, and melted into the brush. Hawk waited, knowing that he could do nothing else, for now he could see neither of his enemies. He tried to locate them by their scent, but the eddying wind came in fitful gusts and he could detect only occasional snatches of either man's odor. They were working around him, one to either side, until such time as one or the other, or both, were in position to throw another spear.

Again there came the squeal of the enraged cow. She was very near the forest now, working out the way Hawk had taken and still on his trail. He tensed himself.

In the deep brush at the left he caught the faintest sound. His back to the tree, Hawk stood perfectly still, trying to pierce the brush with his eyes but unable to do so. The two men hunting him had worked out a cunning strategy. He could be seen. They were in brush where they were hidden, and they knew it. When both had maneuvered themselves into position, they would attack.

Faintly the sound came again, and Hawk saw a slight motion in the brush. With lightning swiftness he cast another dart. The man in the brush rolled into sight, clawing at the dart in his chest, and Hawk pivoted.

The other man was closing in, club held high. Hawk snatched at a dart, but knew that he could not possibly shoot in time. The man was almost upon him, and coming fast. Hawk grabbed for his club and stepped forward to meet the attack. As he did so, his toe caught under an unseen vine and sent him sprawling. Hawk threw himself sideways.

Then, as though he had appeared by magic, the dog hurled himself out of the brush, straight upon the hunter. The man whirled to meet his new attack. He half-swung his club at the dog, but before he could complete the blow, a rock struck him squarely on the side of the head. He dropped in his tracks, and Willow stood framed in the brush.

"Hurry!" she panted.

Hawk leaped to join her, and the dog bounded alongside. From behind they heard the smashing of trees and brush, and the angry trumpeting of the cow mammoth. She had body scent now and was coming fast.

Willow plunged deliberately into the thickest brush, a tangle of vines and small trees, and threaded an agile way through it. Hawk followed, silently approving her strategy as he did so. There was no place in the forest they could go where the mammoth would be unable to follow, but at least the brush would slow her. In open forest again, Willow swerved sharply to the right.

A moment later Hawk saw why she had turned. Some of the small hills were separated by gentle valleys, others by deep gorges, and they were now approaching such a gorge. About forty feet wide at the top, its sides dropped sharply down in uneven layers of rock. Scrambling from ledge to ledge, they worked their way down one side and up the other. Hawk turned to lift the dog over the last high ledge, and they clambered to the top. Willow turned breathlessly.

"The mammoth cannot cross here!"

"No," Hawk agreed, "she cannot."

He sat down, panting heavily while he regained his spent breath. The dog, tongue lolling, whirled to look back in the direction from which they had come. He did not bark, or make any sound, for the value of silence had been born within him. A few seconds later the cow mammoth appeared on the opposite side of the gorge.

Somewhere she had brushed against a tree or ledge of rock and broken the dart; its ragged end still protruded from her neck. She stamped angry feet, extended her trunk to its full length, and screamed her hatred of the two humans. Cautiously she tested a ledge with her front feet, seeking a safe way down, and when she could not find it she beat a restless patrol back and forth on top of the ledge.

Hawk watched her calmly, no longer concerned about her or the herd. That danger had been passed. But there was another, vastly greater peril to worry about.

The hunters trapped on the rocky pinnacle would be likely to remain there for a considerable length of time; the herd of mammoths would see to that. But the mammoths would eventually go away to feed, and when they did the men could escape.

Their first thought would be the man they had tried to trap, and when they took the trail they would find out that Willow was with him. Whatever had been their original reason for attacking Hawk, they would be doubly determined to catch him when they found the men he had killed.

Somehow they would have to be thrown off the trail, and that would be a very difficult feat; all men who lived by hunting were past masters in the art of tracking. A broken twig, or a bent or broken blade of grass, were usually enough. Hawk turned to Willow.

"We must escape the hunters who are sure to follow," he said. "Even without them, the situation here is not good. There are only mammoths to hunt, and they are too dangerous. There was not much game around our old camp, but it could be hunted. We must return."

Hawk led off, still following the hillocks that flanked the river meadows. The pursuit, certain to follow, would be patient and relentless. To throw it off, they would need all the guile and craft at their command. By traveling away from their old camp instead of toward it, the pursuers might be deceived into thinking they were going to continue in that direction.

They walked carefully, choosing each place to put their feet down. They avoided grass or brush whose broken or trampled appearance might betray them, and walked on stones or stone ledges where they were available. Often Hawk circled to cut back on their trail and brush out some real or fancied mark.

It was midafternoon before Hawk swerved away from the hills, making the first arc of a great circle that would carry them back to the camp they had left. When he turned, he walked down a rock ledge that sloped in the direction he wished to travel. They stopped at the end of the ledge.

Beyond was nothing but sand, a great area of white sand in which sparse tufts of grass grew at scattered intervals. Hawk looked worriedly back toward the hills. He doubted if the hunters would escape from the mammoths in time to see them crossing the sand, but he and Willow would leave plain tracks. Still, there was no guarantee that they would not run into more sand if they returned and sought a new way, and they had to travel in this direction if they would reach their old camp.

A strong breeze blew down the ledge and plucked at the sand. Its surface ruffled gently.

Stooping, Hawk gathered the dog in his arms and held him tightly. He started across the sand. Behind him, Willow stepped exactly in his tracks. On the other side of the sand-covered area at last, Hawk stopped and looked back.

Their tracks were still plain, but the wind was filling them; before the hunters came along it might cover them completely. They would have to trust the wind.

An hour later Hawk turned toward a grove of trees. Night was coming, and any human foolish enough to travel at night did so at the risk of almost certain death. But at least the hunters would not travel at night either. He and Willow had eluded their pursuers so far, and were safe from them until morning.

The trees were chunky forest giants with tough vines dangling thickly from huge limbs. Hawk stopped beneath one and looked up into its interlaced twigs and branches. If they were to hide their trail, a fire was out of the question. Therefore they must spend the night in a tree. Hawk grasped the trailing end of a vine and put his weight on it. The vine held. It would not come tumbling down, or break and let them fall. Hawk motioned Willow to climb up.

She went up hand over hand. Halfway to the first limb she twined her legs around the vine and rested. Then she resumed her climb and drew herself up on the great limb. Leaving all his weapons except his knife behind him, Hawk followed. Once on the limb, he turned around to examine their night's bed.

The limb itself was so large that they might have lain on it without too much danger of falling, but the crotch at the trunk was much safer. They walked down the limb, and settled themselves in the massive spread of branches that rose from the crotch. The space was large enough so they could sleep comfortably and safely.

At the foot of the tree, the dog was curled in a furry ball, his bushy tail over his leathery black nose. The dog got up, padded restlessly about, and returned to his bed at the foot of the tree. He knew how to take care of himself at night, and there was no need to worry about him.

When Hawk awakened sometime during the

night, a bright moon had risen and was shedding a soft brilliance that almost matched the light of day. He stirred uneasily. He had been awakened by a sensation of danger, a premonition of something that was not as it should be, and was troubled because he could not locate what had caused it.

Then there was a distinct, alarmed snarl. It came from the dog, and Willow awakened quietly. She sat up, looking questioningly at Hawk but making no noise. Hawk walked up the limb and stopped at the vine they had used to climb the tree.

He looked down, but could see nothing. There was another snarl, then a series of them, and the dog came out of the moon-painted shadows to bristle at the base of the tree. He was facing the brush, snarling, and Hawk swung out on the vine.

A moment later a dire wolf came out of the brush and circled the dog. The dog was big, but the wolf dwarfed him. For a second it continued to circle, then closed in. The dog leaped aside, and feinted at his enemy.

Unhesitatingly Hawk scrambled down the vine. The dog had helped him when he was hard-pressed by the enemy hunters, therefore he must not let the dog fight alone. Hawk leaped lightly from the vine, catching himself on the balls of his feet, and snatched up his spear.

The wolf, aware of the fact that a new enemy was entering the fight, left the dog and sprang forward. Hawk hurled his spear, and knew he had made a hit. But the wolf scarcely paused. Hawk groped for his club.

As he found it, the dog closed in from the rear. Savagely, aroused to the very peak of fury, he sliced at the wolf's haunch, leaped away, and sprang in again. The wolf doubled to deal with him, and when it did Hawk swung his club. It struck home, in a vital spot, but the wolf was too big and too full of life to die easily. It growled throatily, and dragged itself forward to close with the man.

Club swinging, Hawk sprang to meet him. He sidestepped the wolf's vicious lunge, and struck with his club. It smashed solidly down on the wolf's head, but still the monster came on. Hawk struck again and again, beating the wolf with bone-crushing blows. Finally the wolf lay still.

For a moment the dog worried the wolf, then stood quietly while Hawk knelt beside him. He ran his hands over the dog, and brought them away sticky with blood. Certainly the dog had been hurt, but he did not seem to be crippled and could move freely. A wild thing, and powerful, the dog could survive anything except a crippling wound. Hawk considered.

He did not want to leave any evidence of a fight along their escape route. There would certainly be blood stains at the base of the tree and they would not be easy to erase. However, now that they had meat, they should certainly take advantage of it, even though they could not build a fire. With his knife Hawk hacked off both hind quarters from the wolf and had Willow pull them up into the tree by the vine. Safe in their retreat, the humans ate raw meat, while at the base of the tree the dog satisfied his hunger on the remains of the wolf.

The next morning, packing such meat as they could carry, they went on. As they left, Hawk looked back at the tree. Vultures were already circling it; they would soon devour whatever was left of the wolf. But that would not be enough to throw the pursuing hunters off. Only a man or a saber-tooth could kill a dire wolf, and there would be no evidence of tigers around the tree. Should the hunters come this far, they would have all the proof they needed that Hawk and Willow had fled this way.

On the second day, after spending another night in a tree, they completed their great circle and came back to their former camp.

The ashes of their fire were a cold, damp mass, and already green grass was laying a fresh new carpet over the trampled, bare earth. A herd of antelope, grazing in the meadow, danced away. At this evidence that grass-eating creatures had come back to the clearing, Hawk grunted in satisfaction. They had found no game except mammoths elsewhere, but apparently some animals which had moved out of the rest of the country had come back here. He and Willow had done well to return.

But there was still something lacking. Hawk had proved that he could defend their camp against any animal that dared attack it. They were not dealing with animals now, but with men, and should the enemy hunters come they would do so craftily. They would surround the camp, and strike from all sides. Even though Hawk might kill two or three with his superior weapons, he could not destroy them all. If a determined group of humans attacked the camp, they could take it and kill its defenders. He paced nervously back and forth.

There were many places to which he might take Willow, but moving had not proved a happy experience. Food they must have, and as long as they stayed here he could get food. Furthermore, if they moved again they would probably run into other hunters and just as likely they would be hostile. They would stay here, then, and try to strengthen their defenses. But first came the more immediate needs of fire, food and weapons.

Hawk rebuilt the fire, gathered wood, and with the dog at his side ranged into familiar hunting country. The dog found a track which Hawk identified as that of a deer, and he took a stand where he thought the deer would pass. After a short interval he saw it coming and killed it with the first dart.

Now they had meat, and he could attend to the next most important matter. On their ill-fated venture to the river he had lost half his darts, and must make more at once. Hawk busied himself chipping flint heads, and fashioning dart shafts. On the other side of the fire, while she waited for meat to cook, Willow was contentedly weaving another basket.

Hawk worked on his darts until night, then lay down to sleep. With morning he finished them and went out to hunt again.

Certainly there was more game than there had been. Apparently animals needed only a few days of security to make them bold again; creatures which had formerly fled to hide from him were no longer so wary. Hawk considered the significance of that. While the dog ranged into the forest he squatted on a stone, waiting, trying to bring some orderly arrangement out of this new thing he had learned.

Hitherto he had hunted all parts of the country which he could easily reach, which meant all the country within striking distance of the fire, indiscriminately. He had been guided only by the game itself, and had hunted where he thought he would find the most.

Perhaps it would be wise to do things differently, to divide his hunting range into sections and leave one alone while he hunted another intensively. When game grew too scarce wherever he was hunting, he could go into one of the other sections. That way he might assure a constant supply of meat.

After a while the dog came back and sat down at the base of the rock. He had failed to find any game, and let Hawk know it by whining. Hawk leaped from his rock and went on.

Presently bear scent came very strongly to his nostrils and Hawk remembered that, very close to this place, the great cave bear had its home. He circled to go around the cave, then changed his mind and swung closer to it. He had remembered something else. Although in recent years his tribe had traveled mostly in open country, following game herds, it had at times taken shelter in caves when attacked.

That might be his answer, too. If he could get

possession of the bear's cave, and the hunters came, he would not have to meet them on all sides. They could reach him only from the cave's entrance, and would have to come singly. Hawk crept cautiously down until he could see the cave.

As quietly as he had approached, he slipped away and returned to his fire. He thrust a knotty club into the fire until it blazed, and held it high.

"Come with me," he told Willow. "We are going to drive the great cave bear from its home."

DOGS

A vulture flapped slowly into the air as Wolf's tribe approached. The big bird did not seem particularly frightened. It had no important business to perform on this stretch of plain any longer, so it left as the human staggered in its general direction.

Kar walked at the end of the line of march. Wolf was in the front, but the Chief Hunter could not really be said to be leading the tribe any more. Wolf was simply walking forward. The tribe had not had any real direction since it left the camp where so many of its members were trampled into bloody muck by the bison herd.

The vulture had no reason to fear them, the Chief Fire-Maker thought dismally. In the shape the humans were now, they would have been hard put to drive the bird off if it had not wanted to go.

Well, the tribe was a little better off than that,

183

but they were not doing well. Only three of the
eleven survivors were adult males. Most of the
hunters who had not been killed in the attack on
the other tribe's encampment had at least received
wounds. Normally the men of the tribe were best
able to run and jump to safety when a fresh disaster threatened. Because of the stiffening injuries,
many of the hunters were caught by the horns and
hooves of the bison while women and children had
managed to escape.

Wolf's tribe now consisted of four women, two
juvenile boys, two girls—and Bearpaw, in addition
to Wolf and Kar himself. Bearpaw had the only
spear. They carried only a few tools instead of
bundles of their belongings. Virtually all the tribe's
possessions had been lost in the bison stampede,
and the folk were too weak for burdens anyway.

It seemed a lifetime ago that the tribe had abandoned Willow in accordance with long tradition,
because her injured leg prevented her from keeping up with healthy people. Now, because of hunger, fatigue, and injuries, scarcely any of the
survivors were in better condition than Willow
had been when they left her.

The tribe had exiled Hawk at the same time,
also because of tradition. Kar wondered if tradition
was going to kill them all.

It had stopped raining just before dawn. The
sun blazed down with all its fury, sucking water
from the sopping soil and vegetation. Walking felt
like a bath in springs heated by the fires of the
earth. Despite the drenching heat, the Chief Fire-
Maker was wracked with occasional bouts of shiv-

ering as his tortured body protested at the abuse it had received.

Wolf halted and raised his hand with a flash of his old leadership as Chief Hunter. Kar rose to his full height, peering over the grass heads. He saw nothing, but perhaps Wolf's keener eyesight had spotted game that the tribe could kill even in its present condition.

"Food!" cried Grassblade from just behind the two hunters at the front of the line. She trotted forward jerkily. Everyone else—even Wolf himself —lunged into the swiftest motion they could manage in their present condition. Kar found himself running like a leaf blown by the wind. His head wobbled from side to side. Tears of exhaustion dribbled from the corners of his eyes.

The others were already bent over the source of the excitement when the Chief Fire-Maker reached them. It was a horse, or at least the barren remains of a horse. Tigers had killed the beast so long ago that the corpse scarcely stank any more. After the saber-toothed cats gorged their fill for two or three days, they had abandoned the kill.

The saber-tooths' jaws were not well adapted to picking bones, so quite a lot of meat must have remained on the carcass. The jackals and vultures had taken over then. The scavengers pecked and nibbled. The vultures used their long beaks and featherless necks to reach deep into the body cavity, plucking out hard-to-reach scraps. The jackals gnawed at the stiffening tendons and dragged the skeleton apart in their determined efforts to clean every bit of the edible material.

When the humans arrived, the horse had been

reduced to scattered bones and a swatch of horse-hide lying hair-side down at the site of the kill. Flies buzzed at the tribe's approach, but even the insects seemed to have stayed in the area out of habit instead of hoping for sustenance. No wonder the vulture had lifted high in the air and disappeared rather than perch nearby in case the humans left.

Three of the women slashed at the hide with hand-axes, worrying it into bits that would fit in their mouths. Cracked and dust-caked though it was, the raw leather could provide the protein that starving bodies demanded. Some of the half-grown children tried to snatch bits from the women. Others pounded at the horsehide with ill-chipped stones of their own.

The fourth woman was Magnolia. She had not been right in the head since her baby starved to death at her breast. Now she kept at one corner of the horsehide and chewed at it. Magnolia held her digging tool, a deer's cast antler ground to a single sharp tine. Whenever another member of the tribe came too close to her, Magnolia growled deep in her throat and jabbed with the antler.

The two grown men smashed the horse's big leg bones to get at the tasty, nutritious marrow within. Bearpaw slammed the end of a thighbone against a rock, bellowing with his concentration. Bone splinters flew in all directions.

The Chief Hunter proceeded with more deliberation. Wolf had set the shaft of the other thigh across a head-sized lump of quartz. He struck the bone expertly with his club. The thigh chipped but did not break open. Wolf rotated the shaft a quarter-turn and hit it again. This time the bone tube shattered. Most of the thigh remained in the Chief Hunter's hands, but the knob flew straight at Kar who managed to catch it.

Wolf snarled and started to rise, like a wolf whose kill has been snatched by a jackal. He lifted his club. Kar bleated in surprise and stumbled back, still clutching the chunk of bone. The Chief Hunter hunched to lunge after the old man. Then the madness of hunger left Wolf's eyes and he sat down. "No," he said heavily. "There is enough for both of us, Kar. You should eat also."

The Chief Fire-Maker sucked at the salty, incredibly delicious, marrow. He did not recall ever before having eaten something that tasted so good. There were other bones besides, too sturdy for the jackals to break apart and filled with the same wonderful nourishment.

Soon Kar would have enough energy to gather wood and build a fire which would protect the tribe during the night. But first he would suck his belly full of marrow and luxuriate in the feeling that he was not starving to death—for the moment.

Kar smiled in contentment, listening to the pop and crackle of the campfire. Those warm sounds comforted the humans even more than did the flickering light which brightened the sky's last glow. The constant rain of the previous moon-phase had washed the air clean of dust, so that the scents of earth and growing vegetation were strong and pure.

Because the humans had fallen so far, the scraps of horse carrion provided a feast beyond imagining. The folk of Wolf's tribe were still hungry, but they were a tribe again. Mothers and children had ignored one another for the past several days in a rivalry of starvation. Now they resumed mutual grooming. People combed through one another's hair with fingers and bits of bone, straightening tangles and cracking lice between their teeth and fingernails. Magnolia sat apart from the rest, but even she seemed to have relaxed slightly.

Bearpaw sucked thoughtfully at a rib bone cracked lengthwise. Wolf chipped at a hand-axe, trying to convert it into a spearpoint. The flint axe was flawed by a grayish streak of shale, but it was the best stone available for the purpose just now.

Kar knew the Chief Hunter was no spear-maker. Wolf's big, calloused hands were strong, but they lacked the delicacy necessary to pressure-flake flint into a well-shaped weapon. The important thing was that Wolf was *trying* to improve the tribe's condition instead of grimly stumbling from disaster to disaster the way he had done for so long.

Stumbling was all the tribe had done since they cast Hawk out of their community. Kar's lips pursed in concern as he settled another branch carefully on the fire. Throwing wood only scattered the coals. A properly made fire burned clean and bright. It did not shower sparks that threatened the hair of the folk the fire was intended to protect.

Perhaps the tribe's luck had turned. Perhaps matters now would improve to where they had been before Hawk's exile—or even better, to the way they had been when Kar was a child and bison were easy to hunt!

They heard the pack clucking and growling among themselves before they saw the beasts. They were plundering dogs, not true dogs but similar enough in appearance. There were six of them, and they were ambling through the grass in the last twilight.

One of the women wailed in frustration and misery. Bearpaw blinked in surprise. He gathered his spear as the Chief Fire-Maker added more wood to the fire. Wolf drew his club from beneath his waist thong and jumped to his feet.

Wolf snarled. The leader of the plundering dogs snarled back at him. The pack spread out. The animals crouched with their powerful chests close to the ground.

The plundering dogs had short, tawny fur. Their necks and chests were thick-muscled, but their hindquarters were relatively weak. The beasts were not able to run fast enough to capture game of their own—but they didn't need to. Their huge, bone-crushing jaws enabled them to break up the skeletons that even the much larger dire wolves left at their kill sites.

Under normal circumstances, plundering dogs were not a danger to tribes of human hunters. The beasts were not quick enough to attack a properly-armed tribe; and anyway, the bones and hides that attracted the dogs were waste beneath the concern of humans to protect.

Here, though, the remains of the long-dead horse provided the tribe's first hope of survival in days. Kar's face scrunched up in frustration like that which had driven the woman to tears. They couldn't leave this food!

But the Chief Fire-Maker knew they had to leave. The pack would begin snarling over scattered bones and the portions of horsehide at the edge of the firelight. Then they would move closer. As Kar used up the fuel piled within easy reach, the fire would die back to coals—and the humans would face a repetition of the disaster which had occurred the night they slept close to the bogged mammoth.

This time the disaster would be worse and probably final. The plundering dogs were less dangerous enemies than the dire wolves had been, but for all practical purposes the tribe was without weapons. Jaws that could smash a bison thigh bone would rend human flesh with ease. If the tribe had a sufficiency of weapons, a volley of spears would kill or maim most of the small pack before the animals could close.

One thrown spear would only infuriate the remaining dogs, even if it killed; and the tribe's sole spear was too valuable to throw.

Wolf's face bore a beastlike expression of its own as he glared at the plundering dogs. All the folk of the tribe were on their feet, clutching anything that could be used as a weapon if the pack rushed them. The tribe's arsenal was pitifully slight. The women hefted hand-axes, digging tools, and clubs, while the half-grown children hunched with stones and jagged bone splinters in their hands.

The Chief Hunter had his club. Bearpaw held his spear ready. He edged sideways to face a big male dog creeping closer from the edge of the pack's arc. Kar sighed and dragged out a branch with which he had fed the fire some minutes before. The upper half of the wood blazed brightly, but there was still a comfortable unburned length by which the Chief Fire-Maker could hold his weapon.

The torch *looked* like a dangerous threat. Kar knew well that if a dog had the courage to leap at him despite the torch, the beast would bring down its prey and suffer only minor burns in the process.

The plundering dogs snarled and slunk closer. The sky was still light enough to show the animals as shapes in the grass instead of merely cruel, glinting eyes. Kar glanced at Wolf. In a moment, it was going to be too late for the tribe to attempt to flee—as they *must* do.

The Chief Hunter must have felt the same thing, because he suddenly sagged. "We will leave the rest of the horse to them," he said loudly. "There's nothing left anyway."

Wolf began to back away, staying between the advancing pack and the folk for whom he was responsible. Kar waved his torch furiously and backed also. A big bitch with black markings jumped to her feet. She circled, snarling, to avoid the light and sparks of the torch.

The campfire was now between the Chief Fire-Maker and Wolf. Bearpaw was near the Chief Hunter, facing outward to prevent the pack from closing in from that side. The women and children obeyed Wolf's order with relief, although they knew that the remaining scraps of carrion were still more meat than they had had for days until they stumbled onto the horse.

One of the boys darted ahead of the tight group. The swift movement drew the attention of the dog which Kar's torch had driven wide. The boy's weapon was a sliver of the horse's foreleg, broken into a dangerous point when one of the tribe searched it for marrow. The bitch may have been more interested in the bone than the youth holding it. Whatever the reason, she rushed in with her huge jaws open.

Kar shouted and hurled his torch at the big dog. He knew as soon as the wood left his hand that he had made a mistake. He was now unarmed, and the campfire separated both the other adult males from the immediate threat.

The burning branch slammed into the bitch's shoulder, rocking her onto her side with its weight. Her fur ignited in pale, stinking flames. The boy threw up one hand to protect his face and stabbed with the other. The plundering dog rolled to her feet and slammed powerful jaws closed on the boy's hand and weapon together. There was a black, singed patch on the animal's hide, but the short fur could not sustain a fire by itself.

The boy screamed as the dog started to drag him away. A woman ran from the tight throng of humans with her hand-axe raised high to rescue her son. The whole pack of plundering dogs moved toward the prey with the speed and grace of water tumbling over a cliff. The leader snapped at Kar. The Chief Fire-Maker shrieked and jumped away, barely avoiding jaws that reeked of carrion and death. Two more of the dogs grasped the mother by the opposite ankle and arm before she could even strike the bitch which held her boy.

The two humans disappeared in a mass of tawny, snarling bodies. It seemed incredible that only six dogs could have so many legs. The screaming stopped almost immediately, but the sound of cracking bones continued.

Wolf had leaped the campfire in an attempt to help the victims. There was obviously nothing more to be done.

"Come!" shouted the Chief Hunter. "We must leave this place."

Kar grabbed another burning branch to light their escape. The tribe moved quickly away from the kill site.

The plundering dogs ignored the surviving humans. The beasts' present prey was ample for this night.

CAVE BEAR

The great cave bears were large and powerful, and as ferocious as saber-tooths when aroused. If a dozen hunters attacked one they could kill it, but somebody was almost sure to be hurt. For one man to attack a bear deliberately was unthinkable.

But Hawk had learned a valuable lesson from his encounter with the giant sloth. They were larger than bears, and though slow and stupid, they had enormous vitality. Since the dull-witted sloth had been disconcerted when smoke blew about its head, Hawk thought it might be possible to smoke the great cave bear out of its cave.

That would not be the end of it, he realized. The monster bear would not willingly relinquish its home and would get back in if it were possible. Such a beast, always lurking about and awaiting an opportunity to reenter, would be far too dangerous to leave around the cave. Therefore the bear would have to be killed.

Hawk reviewed his plan, in his mind going over and over each tiny detail. He knew that he must have everything right beforehand, because once the fight was started there would be no stopping it and even a minor slip could spell disaster.

As they approached the cave, Hawk gave Willow his torch, and told her to hold the dog. Then he went on alone.

He advanced cautiously, carefully staying downwind, until he could see the bear. It was outside the cave, busy ripping the lower branches off a tree laden so heavily with purple, meaty berries that some of the branches were already broken from the weight of the fruit alone. Hawk parted a leafy branch so he could see better.

The bear was about forty feet from the door of its cave, eating berries from a branch it had broken. It licked furry chops with a berry-stained tongue, and looked all around. Then it reared on its hind paws, braced its body against the tree, and ripped another branch down.

Hawk shivered, partly from excitement and partly from nervous fear. The bear was a monstrous beast, three-quarters of a ton of sheer brute strength. It would not be an easy thing to overcome.

The bear turned, silently and swiftly for all its bulk, and gazed steadily at the tree behind which Hawk lay. Some eddying breeze had carried an alien scent to it, or perhaps some deep-seated instinct had merely made it suspicious. At any rate it was alert, without being sure of just what might be trespassing on its domain.

Hawk slipped away. He moved slowly, always careful to place his feet so that he would make no noise and traveling with the wind. Conditions were as he had hoped to find them, and now he could put the rest of his plan into effect.

When there was sufficient distance between himself and the bear, Hawk ran swiftly back to Willow and the dog. He looked to his supply of darts, picked up his hand spear and throwing-stick, but left Willow with the torch. She fell in behind him when he started back toward the bear.

The dog trotted tensely by his side, sensing that they were after game which the man had already located. Furthermore, since the man kept the dog beside him, it would be dangerous game. Hawk stopped, and the dog stopped beside him, quivering with excitement.

The blazing torch in her hand, Willow waited questioningly. She, too, had a part in this or she would not have been brought along. But, like the dog, she did not as yet clearly understand what that part was. Hawk turned to her.

"The dog and I will drive the bear into the cave," he explained. "Stay here with the torch until you hear me call. Then come as fast as you can and give the torch to me."

"I understand."

The dog at his side, Hawk slipped away. They came within the area where the bear's scent could be detected, and the dog looked inquiringly at Hawk. The man did not turn aside and the dog moved two steps ahead of him, sure now of their quarry. Ordinarily they avoided creatures as powerful as this, but the dog was willing to fight anything as long as the man thought it should be fought.

Making no attempt at concealment, Hawk walked openly into the clearing in front of the cave.

Having scented or heard him, the bear was waiting. It stood at the foot of the tree from which it had been ripping branches, feet braced and tensely alert. Its ears were flicked forward, its eyes questioning, and its snout moving slowly from side to side. The bear took an uncertain step, and reared on its hind legs the better to see. Dropping to the ground, it stood still a moment more and then snarled, its jaws gaping wide. Hawk fitted a dart into his throwing-stick, shouted and bounded forward.

He stopped suddenly, for this was part of his plan. To wound the bear where it was, and to lack a place of refuge, would mean disaster. The bear must be driven into the cave and forced to take a temporary stand there. Hawk had started a false attack to incite the dog; he wanted him to go after the bear on his own initiative.

The dog snarled forward. Hawk halted, and stepped back with the dart still poised in his throwing-stick. If his plan went wrong now he would have to go in anyway and help the dog. He watched tensely.

The bear remained beneath the tree, snarling at the onrushing dog. Then, when less than twenty feet separated them, the bear wheeled and lumbered into its cave. It turned about in the entrance, knowing that it could defend itself there.

Hawk breathed easier. This was the way he had hoped it would work out. The bear would not run from a man, but it had been assaulted by at least one pack of wolves and, presumably, by wild dogs as well. It knew that it could stand them off if protected on three sides by the mouth of the cave.

The bear's enormous head and front shoulders protruded from the cave. The dog leaped in and out again, never going near enough to be hit by one of those sledgehammer paws.

Keeping his throwing-stick beside him, and a dart ready, Hawk grasped a handful of dry grass, wrenched it loose, and laid it on the ground about twenty feet from the cave's opening. A gust of wind scattered the little pile, and Hawk laid a dart on it to hold it. He gathered more dry grass, and more, until he had a great pile. Then he raced to a bit of nearby marshland, pulled up some swamp roots and damp muck, and laid them on top of the grass. Then he called Willow.

At the cave, the dog continued to harass the bear. He feinted, growling and barking, and leaped in to snap whenever an opportunity offered. But at no time did he put himself within reach of the bear's paws, which would have broken his back as easily as a stone breaks an egg.

The blazing torch in her hand, Willow broke out of the forest and ran lightly into the clearing. Handing the torch to Hawk, she stepped back, cast about until she found two rocks, and held one in each hand while she awaited whatever came.

"Stay near the fire," Hawk cautioned Willow. "Don't leave it no matter what happens."

He touched the torch to the great heap of dried grass he had gathered, and threw the torch on top of the pile. The sun-dried grass exploded in a roar of flame, and for a moment blazed high. Then, the readily combustible portion having burned out, thick yellow smoke rose from the wet swamp refuse. Hawk stepped back, his darts ready.

So far everything had worked well, even the wind's direction and force. What happened now depended on whether or not he had been able to guess how a cave bear would react to smoke.

Like a large, elongated feather, yellow smoke curled toward the cave. It paused there, as though not quite knowing where to go, then sent an exploring finger into the cave. The bear backed up. In a moment it was almost hidden by smoke; only its furious snarls showed it was still there. Suddenly the bear came out.

Every hair on its body was erect, lending it an appearance of being much bigger than it was. Coughing, snapping its jaws continuously, roaring mad, it ran to one side of the fire, out of the smoke, whirled about, and faced the two humans. The dog bored in from the side, and the bear swung to slap ineffectively at him.

A dart ready, Hawk advanced. The crucial test had come; from now on it was up to him and the dog. Hawk hurled his dart with all his strength. It sang through the air, and buried half its length in the bear's shaggy side.

The bear stood erect, a mountain of flesh that for a moment walked on its legs like a man. Dropping to all fours, it exploded its fury in a mighty, snarling roar, and charged.

Hawk retreated back toward the smoldering fire. In attacking the great cave bear, he had counted on the fire as a safe retreat. Now his reckoning was to endure the acid test; would fire stop a wounded, enraged bear?

A thick plume of smoke enveloped the oncoming bear. It stopped, shifting its forepaws uneasily, and backed up. The dog threw himself furiously upon it.

Another dart fixed in his throwing-stick, Hawk walked out of the smoke to where he could have a clear view. The bear, safely away from the smoke, was sparring with the dog. Hawk loped toward them, and when he was near enough he threw the dart. The bear turned, bawling its rage, and bit at the shaft protruding from its side. Then it threw itself at the dog.

Hawk readied another dart, and circled to get in good throwing position. Careful not to let the bear between himself and the smoke blanket, he threw the third dart.

The bear grunted, spun in an erratic circle, and struck with blind fury at a nearby clump of grass. As though that were its real foe, and the thing that had hurt it, it hit again and again until the grass was ripped to shreds. It lumbered to another grass tuft and destroyed that. When the dog came near it bellowed at him and in a series of insane hops tried to pin him between its front paws.

Hawk followed, ready to shoot another dart. But since he could not tell which way the wounded bear would leap or what it would attack, he dared not get too near.

The bear broke suddenly. Racing across the clearing in long leaps, it headed straight for the sheltering trees. Running, it was a terrifying sight. Blocky legs worked like swiftly moving pistons, carrying the bear's huge body along so fast that even the pursuing dog was hard put to keep up.

Although the dog was barking and snarling continuously, the sounds of the running pursuit faded deeper and deeper into the forest. Hawk followed, confident now that his battle was won. The bear would run for a long way, probably, but the darts were sunken deeply and eventually they must take their toll of even such strength as the bear's. It could not run on forever.

For as long as he could hear him, Hawk guided himself by the barking dog. When the noise faded in the distance, he ran along the plainly marked trail. Bright spots of blood showed on the leaves, with here and there a patch of coarse hair. Faintly, he heard the barking dog again.

He ran easily, fast enough to cover distance swiftly but not so fast that he would tire himself out. Five minutes after he was again within hearing of the dog, he came upon his quarry.

The great cave bear was backed against a tree, swaying from side to side, its front feet braced. When it saw the man it left the tree and lurched forward, growling hoarsely. Hawk stood still and fitted another dart. He could take his time now; the bear's pace was a mere crawl. Hawk cast his dart.

Straight and true, it sailed to its mark. Still the bear tried to come forward. It had lived all its life by brute strength, and would fight as long as that life remained. The bear made one more valiant effort to crawl forward, then lay still.

Hawk remained where he was, troubled by an emotion he had never felt before. He lived in a world whose basic rule was kill or be killed, eat or be eaten, and he hunted and killed as much as he could because, if he did not, he could not continue to live. But he felt a strange sympathy for the bear, a stout and lonely creature like himself, which had given up only when there was nothing left with which to fight.

Solemnly Hawk approached the inert monster and intently studied the curving claws, that were polished to ivory whiteness by almost constant digging for roots and small animals. He would keep those claws, he decided, and from now on would conduct himself as the bear had. When the time came, he too would fight with all his heart and strength.

But he had no time for further contemplation of the bear's might; the grim business of simply staying alive was too pressing. The bear represented a great deal of value in both fur and food, and scavengers must not have it. Also, Willow was alone in the clearing and save for the fire she was defenseless. He must secure the bear and see to her safety.

He shredded tinder, adding kindling to it, struck a spark, and when the fire blazed he arranged green sticks on it. He piled them high, to arrange here a fire that would last until such time as he was able to return. While the fire burned, nothing would dare come near his prize. Then he called the dog to his side and trotted back to the cave.

Willow, who had built her own fire into a roaring blaze, waited expectantly beside it.

"The bear is dead," Hawk told her. "It lies in the forest, well-guarded by fire."

He went eagerly to the cave, the real prize for which he had dared challenge a great cave bear. Hesitantly he entered, and when the dog would have backed out Hawk pulled him roughly to his side and made him stay there. At the same time, he fought a growing desire to escape from the place himself. He had been born under a tree, and except for scattered occasions when his tribe had taken shelter in caves or under ledges, he had lived his whole life in the open. The cave made him nervous because he was confined. Still, the real purpose for which he had wanted it remained foremost in his thoughts.

Dimly illumined by the little daylight that filtered through the opening, the cave was roughly circular in shape and about thirty feet in diameter. Spear-shaped stalactites depended from the roof, but there was no evidence of dampness or water. To one side was the bed of leaves and sticks where the bear had slept.

Willow came in behind him. At first hesitantly, then eagerly, she explored the cave. Already she could foresee some of its possibilities as a home. More interested in its offer of safety, Hawk swung to look at the entrance.

The cave's opening was somewhat taller than a man, and just wide enough so that anyone standing in it would have plenty of freedom for action. Any enemy would have to come through the entrance, and if there were more than one, only one at a time could attack. The place could easily be defended. A man on the inside could not possibly be overwhelmed from the sides or rear. It was a snug retreat, ideal for their purposes.

While Willow remained inside to complete her examination of their new home, Hawk went out, crossed the clearing into the forest, and gathered wood. He arranged a fire in the middle of the cave's floor, and lighted it with a burning brand from the still-smoldering fire with which he had driven the bear out.

Almost instantly they were coughing and sputtering. Instead of a cheerfully crackling blaze, the fire was nothing but a smoking pile of assorted sticks. There was no place for the smoke to go, and no draft to fan the fire. This was something Hawk had not counted on. As the cave filled with smoke, he ran out the entrance, Willow at his heels. They looked back into the cave.

"The fire will have to be built nearer the entrance," Hawk said. "It does not like to be shut in the cave."

Willow said nothing, but her face was thoughtful. Hawk took a deep breath, stumbled back into the cave, and knocked the fire apart. He stumbled out again, coughing smoke from his lungs. After a few moments he peered cautiously into the cave.

The smoke had lifted, and was hanging near the ceiling, most of it in a cleft that seemed to extend up into the roof. Hawk reentered the cave, gathered his scattered sticks, and moved them to a new place just inside the entrance. He lighted his fire again and stood back to await results.

They were infinitely better insofar as most of the smoke could now escape through the entrance. Some still went back into the cave and left a foggy wreath, but at least the cave could be entered without danger of choking. Hawk grimaced. From a fighting man's viewpoint the cave was the answer to his needs, but he already knew that he was not going to like living in it.

"Stay here," he told Willow. "I am going back to the bear."

The dog accompanied him when he set off toward the place where he had left the bear. Once he was back in the forest Hawk felt better. He had done what he wanted to do, and assured himself of a place from which he could fight almost any number of men who dared to come against him, but he was still uncomfortably aware of the cave's restrictions and of its sense of confinement. It was much better to be free, and in the open, than in any cave. But there remained the grim necessity of having a place he could defend; they needed the cave.

When Hawk returned with the bear's shaggy skin, Willow was in the cave. She had carried two boulders inside, and built a platform of sticks on top of them. Standing on this platform, she was digging at the cleft in the cave's roof with a sharpened stick. A shower of dirt and pebbles fell about her, and gathered in a growing pile at her feet.

Hawk looked at her, puzzled, but said nothing. Women were always busy, and much of what they did made little sense to him, so there was no point in questioning her. Going back to the bear, he brought an ample supply of the meat, laying it on ledges near the top of the cave. He stood doubtfully back because a heavy pall of smoke swirled there. Still, smoke shouldn't spoil the meat and certainly it was safer inside the cave than it would be anywhere else.

Then he returned to their old camp to bring up Willow's baskets and an additional supply of shafts for making new darts.

That night he built up the fire and slept on the grass outside the cave, the dog beside him. He liked it better there, for the wind carried most of the smoke away. Rising at intervals to replenish his fire, and to scout the winds, Hawk spent a comfortable night.

The next morning he again took up the seldom-absent problem of renewing his stock of weapons. Willow, who had refused to sleep outside the cave, was again on her platform deepening the hole she was making in the roof. She had already dug so far that she had had to use a longer stick, but there was still no explanation as to what she was doing. Hawk grunted and left the cave.

The dog at his side, he started toward the ledge of rock where he found the best flints for dart heads. As they started up the slope, the dog roamed ahead, nose to the ground.

A hare leaped out of the grass ahead of them and scooted swiftly away. The dog gave half-hearted chase, then returned when Hawk called him. The hare ran to the top of the ledge and turned to look back. As it sat up, it was clearly silhouetted against the skyline.

Then something like the swiftly moving branch of a tree rose near the hare. It flashed toward the little animal, then disappeared. The hare leaped high, stiffened convulsively, and fell back.

It had been struck by a big, deadly grass serpent whose bite meant instant death.

GRASS SERPENT

The dog trod warily, the hackles on the back of his neck raised. He knew that when they wished to lay an ambush, the deadly grass serpents were able to conceal their odor, but the scent was very plain now. It was a musty smell, and strong, faintly reminiscent of crushed, pungent leaves. The dog started a wide circle that would bring him to a little rise from which he could see the snake but at the same time would keep him from going too near.

Hawk stooped to pick up a rock. It was a woman's weapon, but very effective for fighting snakes. He had met such serpents before, but luckily there was not a great abundance of them. When they wanted to feed, the few that existed haunted grassy trails along which hares and other small game were apt to run. The serpents were vicious crea-

tures, so sure of themselves and their own power
that they refused to move aside for anything. An-
gered, they would freely attack whatever provoked
them. Once they had fed, they sought sunny ledges
and lay on them almost unmoving, until they were
ready to feed again.

Hawk kept his eyes on the place where he had
seen the serpent. He knew how they fed. After
they had killed their victim, which invariably died
on the spot, they opened their jaws and literally
crawled around it until the meal was in their belly.
But this snake seemed to have sensed the presence of an intruder, and was apparently waiting to
see whether or not the trespasser would have to
be routed before it fed.

The dog, having sighted the serpent, was stretching his nose forward while at the same time he
remained tense, ready to leap aside should the
snake slither toward him. Again, like a violently
snapping limb of a tree, the serpent rose and
struck. The dog jumped, but the strike would
have fallen short anyway. Never lacking in good
judgment, the dog knew which creatures he could
approach closely and which he could not. A grass
serpent was one of the latter. The dog began an
excited barking.

Hawk walked forward calmly, unafraid because
he now knew exactly where the serpent was. It
was only when one blundered upon them unaware, as the hare had, that the serpents were
dangerous. They could strike with lightning-swift
speed, but when they had to move from one place
to another they were almost sluggish. A man could
easily avoid them if he knew where they were.

From a little rise, Hawk looked down at the serpent and the dead hare. He was mystified. The hare was a small thing, but it was hardy and not too easily killed. There were no marks on it and no blood on the grass, yet the hare had died almost in its tracks. It had given only a few convulsive leaps after the snake had struck it.

Therefore the snake had some mysterious power. Hawk did not know what it was, but it must be as strong a magic as fire, which he could now control, and the flight of birds, which his darts now possessed. His curiosity grew, and he went to step nearer.

The serpent raised its squat, ugly head, its neck bent in a graceful curve, and pounded the earth with a warning tail. When it slithered a few feet forward, Hawk stepped back.

He remembered that he had once seen a bison calf step on such a serpent, and been bitten by it. The calf had been able to take only a few stumbling steps before it, too, had died. At the time he had given the incident only a passing thought because he had been still a member of the tribe and the tribe was strong. Since he had been banished from the tribe, and entirely dependent on his own resources, he had learned that he must neglect nothing which might add to his own strength. Now he wanted to understand the snake's secret.

He threw his stone, deliberately making a false cast so that the stone rolled beside the serpent instead of hitting it. Instantly the snake struck, and a thin liquid streaked the stone.

Hawk shook his head, having learning nothing. He did not know how snakes killed their prey because he had never thought them worth studying; they were merely bad things to be avoided. But obviously they possessed few brains, or this one never would have been teased to strike at a stone. Hawk circled the snake, to examine it more closely.

It was longer than a man, pale green in color, with rough, overlapping scales. But there was little to be learned from examining its body. Plainly the serpent's lethal qualities lay in its head, for it always struck with its head. Just as plainly, it inflicted death by some method other than a serious bite, for the hare had no visible wound.

He sought and found another rock, and when he threw it he did so accurately. It struck and broke the snake's back, and the serpent thrashed its mighty body about. In its struggles it crushed grass and knocked bushes down, then turned over and over. Overhead, a vulture was already soaring.

The dog at his side, Hawk turned away. Snakes could be eaten, but belonged in that category of foods which were to be eaten only if nothing else offered. Hawk did not like the taste of the flesh, and anyway he had all the meat they could possibly use. Replenishing his supply of weapons was the important thing now.

At a frightened, throttled squawk from the vulture, he whirled about. The big scavenging bird was in the air, its ten-foot wings spread wide, the snake clutched in its talons. Even as Hawk watched, the vulture's wings fluttered and it dropped limply to the ground. Hawk turned and trotted back.

Though the serpent was dead, its reflexes remained vital. When the vulture alighted upon it, the snake's head had snapped back and its fangs had penetrated the bird's breast. They were still there, entangled in the feathers. Hawk squatted and looked very closely.

The snake's curved fangs, about an inch and a half long, protruded from its mouth and into the vulture. Hawk looked at them in bewilderment. The fangs were tiny things, no bigger than needles, and within themselves they were surely incapable of inflicting a mortal wound. There was something else here, some secret power which he had not fathomed.

When he touched the snake, its body twitched but the fangs did not loosen themselves. Venom had spilled onto the feathers, and Hawk poked at it with a dart, remembering that the stone the snake had struck had been streaked with the same fluid. It was colorless, and looked harmless, but surely it had some direct connection with the serpent's magic power to kill. There just was no other answer.

Replacing the dart in his throwing-stick, he left the serpent and vulture still entangled and walked thoughtfully away. There were many things in this world of his that would bear the closest possible inspection. He was increasingly aware of forces and powers which were all about, but which he did not understand. He must learn their secrets, for he and Willow could continue to live only if they remained stronger and shrewder than the many things that would kill them. His thoughts remained with the serpent. It had a marvelous power, a magic ability to strike things dead almost instantly, but just what was the source of such magic and how was it used?

Hawk neared the ledge of rock he wanted, and turned to climb to it. The dog fell in behind him, and while the man selected the stones he desired, the dog rested in the sun. Hawk filled his pouch with choice pieces of flint and they started back.

A herd of deer had drifted across their trail and were feeding in one of the many open meadows. When Hawk approached, the deer stared curiously at him, and when he was as near as they thought he should get they skipped away. He glanced disinterestedly at them; there was plenty of meat in the cave and they could not possibly use any more now. But the dog gave enthusiastic chase.

As the deer raced into the forest the dog came to a sudden stop and an angry snarl rippled from him. He gave voice to his battle roar.

A puma-like beast, a short-fanged cat whose size was midway between the saber-tooth and the wild cat, had been lying on a limb of a tree. When the deer herd passed beneath, the puma dropped on one and for a few seconds had a wild, plunging ride. Then the cat's probing teeth met through the deer's spine, and brought the quarry down.

It crouched on its victim, fangs bared and tail jerking angrily. The dog made a furious attack which he halted just short of the crouching cat. When the puma made a short rush at him, the dog dodged warily. He was no match for the puma, but the big cat was unwilling to leave its game and give chase. Meat abandoned, even for a moment, was frequently meat lost.

Hawk sprang into action. Game was none too plentiful as it was, and every meat-eater raiding the stock of game meant less for Hawk and Willow. A puma such as this one might well make a kill every other day, and such a toll mounted terrifically. In many areas there was little or no game solely because a preponderance of meat-eaters had cleaned it out.

The dart in his throwing-stick, Hawk stalked the crouching puma. It was a dangerous antagonist, well able to put up a good fight, but Hawk had fought bigger and more savage creatures. He had killed a saber-tooth and a great cave bear, and he felt sure of his ability to kill the puma. If he did not, he would have to share the game with it.

He came nearer and nearer. The puma, eyes fixed on Hawk, tensed its muscles for the spring that would carry it upon the man. The dog, awaiting this moment, attacked furiously and the puma wheeled to spar with him. Hawk cast his dart.

Instantly he reached for another, for just as he threw the first dart, the puma moved. Instead of piercing the throat, its intended target, the dart had merely skimmed across the big cat's neck and sliced through the skin. It was scarcely more than a scratch, enough to infuriate the cat, and Hawk backed rapidly away. He laid the dart in his throwing-stick, and awaited another opportunity. But the puma was behaving strangely. Instead of attacking the man, it crouched where it was. At last the puma rose, stiffening all four feet and arching its back. Its tail became very stiff. It reared on its hind paws, while it lashed the air with its front ones. Then it fell to the ground, retched convulsively, and was still.

For a moment Hawk remained rooted in his tracks, overcome with amazement. Slowly he walked forward. The dog, as surprised as the man, was stretching his nose as far as he could, snuffling the dead cat.

Still incredulous, Hawk looked down at the slain puma. In his whole memory nothing else like this had ever happened. Even severely wounded pumas were capable of putting up a terrific fight, and this one had been scarcely scratched.

Suddenly Hawk was overcome by a hot surge of excitement. The puma had been killed by the serpent's magic power!

This, then, was the secret. He was master of a new and mighty power, almost unbelievable strength, for he remembered now that he had shot the puma with the same dart which he had dipped into the strange fluid that came from the snake's deadly head. It was the fluid and not any wound that killed the snake's victims. Hawk stood still, shaken to the core by this new thing he had learned. A dart dipped into a serpent's venom was indeed a mighty weapon. Equipped with such a thing, he might well walk safely anywhere at all.

Awed and fearful, trembling with what he had learned, Hawk shouldered the deer and made his way back to the cave. The big grass serpents were scarce and therefore hard to find, but he must hunt some more at the earliest opportunity.

He came in sight of the cave and stopped, while a feeling of alarm rose within him. He had left Willow safe, protected by a fire at the cave's entrance, but now the fire was only smoldering ashes. He tested the winds, which carried nothing except an odor of smoke. But he could see no smoke. Hawk dropped the deer, fixed a dart, and stalked forward.

He peered cautiously into the cave. Inside, a cheerful fire leaped high and beside it was Willow, working on another basket. Hawk followed with his eye the course of the ascending smoke, and saw it rising through the hole Willow had poked in the cave's roof. Thus her mysterious actions with the stick were explained at last. She had been making an opening where the smoke might escape. With a grunt of admiration, Hawk went back for the deer.

When the deer had been cut up and stored in the cave, Hawk sat down to work on his dart heads. He had practiced so much and made so many that he knew almost by instinct whether or not he could make a good one from any piece of flint. He also knew exactly how the stones were going to split, and often, by striking a good-sized stone in exactly the right place, he could break it into a dozen fragments, all of which were already partly shaped. It was work to which he was so accustomed that he could do it with his hands and part of his mind; the rest of his thoughts wandered elsewhere.

The serpent's venom was very powerful magic; a mere touch of it had killed the puma. If he could transfer the snake-magic to his own dart heads, would it not be possible to use even smaller darts? It would no longer be necessary to inflict a mortal wound, and if he could make his darts smaller he could certainly carry many more of them. The more he could carry, the better he could hunt and defend himself.

But how could he make small darts fly any distance? The heavy darts he was now using depended on their own weight, their feathers, and the power of the throwing-stick. It would be impossible, even with the throwing-stick, to hurl a small dart a long way.

Willow had finished her basket and was stretching sinew which she would later use in sewing skins. She stretched it by tying one end to a slender green stick, bowing the stick, and then tying the sinew to the other end. The stick itself, slowly straightening, kept the sinew taut. Hawk was annoyed because a strip of sinew had broken with a loud snap, and disturbed his thoughts.

"Bring me water," he said.

Willow rose to get the two skin pouches which they used for water containers and started out of the cave with them. Hawk watched her impatiently.

Cave life had positive advantages, but it was not without its disadvantages. When they had lived in the open they had been within a few feet of a clear-flowing spring where they could quench their thirst any time they wished. But there was no water at all in the cave. The nearest spring was across the valley and up the opposite slope. All their water had to be carried from there, and there was never enough of it. Neither of the pouches held more than a thirsty man could drink, and water left in them for any length of time had a bad taste. At night they dared get no water at all.

Willow came back with two filled pouches and

Hawk drank. The dog looked expectantly up, and when no water was forthcoming for him he drifted out of the cave to go get his own drink.

Hawk laid down the empty container thoughtfully. Until now it had not occurred to him that lack of water could be a very serious thing. He had wanted the cave largely because it was a safe place, and one he could defend if they were attacked by alien hunters. But now he realized that if the hunters came, they could block Hawk and Willow from their source of water, and that would be fatal. He turned to Willow.

"You must make more containers, many more, and keep them filled so that we will always have water."

"We do not need them," Willow replied.

"What do you mean?"

"Let me show you."

Willow brought the basket she had woven. It was wide and deep, and so finely woven that when she held it up, no light showed between the supple sticks of which the basket was made.

"It is strong and tight," Hawk said, "but it will not hold water."

"No," Willow admitted, "but if the holes between the sticks were filled in, it might."

"Filled with what?" Hawk asked, his interest aroused.

"The sticky black mud you use to catch little birds," Willow replied. "I watched you the day you made the new spear for Short-Leg. There was a little pool of water on the black mud. If water did not sink through the mud there, it might stay in a basket coated with the mud."

Hawk remembered the tar pit and grinned delightedly. It was an excellent idea and might work. It would be much easier to fill and carry a tar-coated basket than several skin containers, and the basket would hold more water.

"We'll try it," he said, snatching up his spear and throwing-stick. "Bring the basket."

Together they left the cave. The dog, sunning himself in the warm grass, looked lazily up and thumped his tail at them. He rose to follow as they made their way to the tar pit.

Hawk dug into the sticky surface with his fingers. He brought out a handful and examined it closely. The tar formed a firm but pliable ball, and when he squeezed it, it spread out readily. It did not disintegrate as a handful of mud would have done. He handed the tar to Willow, who began pressing it against the inside of the basket. Hawk dug out more tar.

An hour later their work was done. The basket had a smooth, sticky lining of tar, which Willow had carefully worked into each tiny crack. Returning to the spring, they lowered the basket into the icy water, and breathlessly lifted it out again. It was brimful of clear, sweet water, and only a few drops seeped through here and there. Willow patiently began to work the tar in tighter at such places.

As pleased as though it had been his own idea, Hawk squatted beside the spring, watching her.

"Why did the women of the tribe not make these lined baskets before?" he asked.

"I do not know," Willow replied. "Perhaps it

was because we were always moving, and skin containers are easier to carry."

As she carefully lifted the basket and carried it back to the cave, Hawk walked beside her, greatly pleased. Back in the cave, he took a long drink. He smacked his lips, while a vast sense of well-being filled him. Nobody else had ever been as well-off, he was sure. There was meat in the cave, and dried seeds and berries, and plenty of water, and a good supply of darts. Hawk awakened to the startling fact that he need not devote every waking minute to the grim business of just getting enough to eat or protecting himself and Willow. Luxuriously he stretched out beside the fire and slept while Willow began cooking bear meat.

The dog's low growl brought Hawk back to reality.

Darkness had fallen while he slept, and the dog was lying in the cave's mouth rumbling at a prowling tiger. Hawk felt a sudden little panic.

Again the cave seemed small and close, a prison of a place. The only light was that cast by the fire. Hawk went to the entrance and peered out. He had intended to sleep outside, but there was no way now he could do so, for it was unsafe to go out at night and attempt to build a fire. Disgusted, he ate in silence, then threw himself down on the bearskin and went to sleep again.

He did not sleep heavily, and as usual was ready to awaken in a second, but there were no alarms during the night. With morning's first light, Hawk rose and stretched. He threw wood on the low-burning fire and looked at the basket, which was still nearly full.

It was good, very good, and they should have

more of these tar-lined baskets. Willow started weaving one while Hawk went out to gather more dart shafts. He knew where the best ones grew, in a thicket of small trees in a nearby valley. There were so many that they crowded each other, and their limbless trunks were of a uniform size, free of branches. Hawk entered the thicket and started cutting sticks. Suddenly he was aware of the dog's warning growl.

Hawk peered out cautiously, to see the first of a long line of strange hunters swing down a slope and disappear into a gully. A moment later the head and shoulders of a man, with the lower body still concealed by the slope, reappeared. Hawk faded silently into the thicket, the dog beside him.

Beyond any doubt, the hunters were on his trail.

BEAVER

Wolf's tribe camped on the edge of a marshy lake. Halted would have been a better word than camped. Kar made an effort to build a fire, but he could find no dry wood in the darkness, and none of the others were willing to help.

In the morning, the women began to grub up cattail roots to grind into a bitter flour, and the Chief Fire-Maker got a small blaze going to ease his conscience. Kar avoided the eyes of his surviving fellows. In Kar's own mind, it was his failure to drive the bitch away that had caused the death of the boy and his mother.

Nobody else seemed to care—about those deaths, or about anything else. The cattails would keep the tribe alive for a few days more, but the women who dug in the marsh went about their task with less animation than the reeds twitching in the light wind.

Dawn displayed a stand of willow saplings which a blight had killed. They made poor firewood, but they were the best available. Kar fed in another billet of wood cut to length with a borrowed hand-axe. He thought grimly about the previous night. Even with a proper spear, he could not have been expected to drive away the pack when it rushed his side of the camp. He was old and the Chief Fire-Maker, not a hunter.

Willow bark hissed as it peeled back in the fire. Wolf sat nearby and stared at his hands. Bearpaw glared at the Chief Hunter as if expecting him to change events which had already occurred. Bearpaw was a good hunter—strong and fast—but he did not have a quick mind. He couldn't understand why everything was going wrong.

If last night's disaster wasn't Kar's fault, then who *was* responsible? Wolf, because the Chief Hunter should have ordered the tribe to flee as soon as the plundering dogs appeared? Perhaps that was so, but the tribe had been desperately glad to find food of any sort. *None* of them had been willing to accept the need to run away from what would otherwise provide at least one more meal. Wolf was no more to blame than any of the rest of them.

Grassblade, bent over in the muddy water, suddenly straightened and stared at the low bank partway around the lake. The reeds near the bank were all young growth, short and colored a brighter green than those in the far distance. A few cut-off stems poked up above the lake's surface, yellowing in the sunlight. Had another tribe been harvesting cattails recently?

The thought turned Kar's mind back to Hawk. The Chief Fire-Maker knew with vivid certainty what was responsible for the tribe's recent cycle of catastrophes. They had been following tradition, as their fathers and fathers' fathers had done, but the spirits which ruled all aspects of life wished to *change* tradition. The spirits had shown Hawk the new ways that they wanted the tribe to adopt— and the tribe had exiled Hawk, instead of listening to the spirits who spoke in the voice of the Chief Spear-Maker.

Kar couldn't imagine *why* the spirits had decided to change the traditions which had been followed throughout all the generations of men, but Kar was only a man himself. The spirits did as the spirits chose. Men could only obey the spirits' decisions.

Or disobey, and find themselves driven across the face of the world—starving and at the mercy even of scavengers like the plundering dogs.

Kar jumped to his feet. "Wolf!" he cried. "We—"

"Chief Hunter!" shouted Grassblade from the marsh. In her excitement, she dropped the bundle of cattails she had laboriously gathered. "I've found a beaver den! We will have meat!"

Wolf and Bearpaw roused instantly and peered in the direction in which Grassblade was pointing. The children and the other women also stopped their business of chopping and grinding the bitter roots.

"Wolf!" the Chief Fire-Maker repeated. "We must find Hawk and take him back into the tribe if we are to survive!"

"Hawk is dead," Wolf said flatly. He picked up his club from the ground. "Come, all of you!" he continued, "but don't make any noise. If the beaver is in its burrow, then we'll catch it at once. Otherwise, we'll wait till it returns."

"Fresh meat at last!" Bearpaw rumbled as he trotted in the direction of the beaver den beside his chief hunter.

Kar, carrying a willow sapling which he had shaped to a point, followed the rest of the tribe. He was behind everyone except Grassblade, who had to wade out of the muck before she could join them.

The willow stake was a poor weapon. The wood had burned to ash when Kar tried to harden it in the fire, so the point was splintery. It was better than nothing; that was all he could say about it.

The rest of the tribe was enthusiastic. The Chief Fire-Maker was not. He felt sick. He was sure that the tribe was still refusing to obey the spirits' decree. The only thing which could come of that was what had come to the tribe ever since they drove Hawk away: disaster.

Wolf waved the others to halt while he mounted the bank. A track, more easily spotted from above than at the lake's surface, wove through the freshly-sprouted reeds.

Kar watched the Chief Hunter snuffle the air through his broad, highly-sensitive nostrils. Even the Chief Fire-Maker, whose sense of smell had been blunted by decades of kneeling over smoky fires, scented the musk which the beasts used to mark their territory. Wolf was searching for the hole which ventilated the den. The actual entrance was beneath the surface of the lake, safe from most dry-land predators.

These were giant beavers, not the smaller variety which cut down trees for food and dammed creeks into ponds in which they built covered nests of sticks and mud. The biggest of the giants were the size of a large black bear, larger than any two men together. The beavers dug into the muddy banks of lakes and ate reeds which they cropped with front teeth as long as the fingers of a big man. They spent almost all their time in the water through which they drove themselves with oversized hind feet.

Out in the lake, the giant beavers were too large to snare and too swift for a hunter balanced on a floating log to catch. Trapped in their den, though, the rodents could be killed as easily as rabbits dug out of their burrows.

Wolf located the vent which marked the living chamber of the den. It was hidden in lush vegetation at a distance back from the bank, but the animal odors rising from the opening displayed it to the Chief Hunter. He broke a reed and set it in the edge of the hole as a marker.

The women moved toward Wolf. He waved them back. Magnolia ignored the order. Grassblade and Moonflower grabbed the other woman's arms and pulled her forcibly to a halt. Magnolia's eyes were wide and staring with the prospect of food. Her mouth opened. Kar feared she would shout and warn their prey, but at the last instant Magnolia's eyes glazed and her body slumped into disinterest.

Kar had hoped that when Magnolia lost the corpse of her baby in the bison stampede, the young woman's mind would return to normal. That had not happened.

The Chief Hunter bent down and put his ear against the ventilation opening. What he heard must have pleased him, because he smiled as he got up again and moved to the bank. There he gestured Bearpaw and Kar to join him.

The Chief Fire-Maker followed Bearpaw cautiously, trying not to snag the vegetation with his sharpened pole. He stared into the water. The lake was less than Kar's own height beneath the top of the bank. The track which the beavers' slick bodies had worn across the bottom mud was obvious from this angle, though the water was dark with silt and decaying vegetation.

"I can hear them breathing," Wolf whispered to the other men. "They're inside, and we're going to trap them."

We, thought the Chief Fire-Maker. Kar was not a hunter, but Wolf clearly expected his Chief Fire-Maker to act like a hunter while hunger demanded it. They had cast out Hawk for violating tradition, but now they were all ignoring tradition. . . .

"Kar," the Chief Hunter ordered, "you will jump into the water and wedge your pole across the mouth of the opening."

"The beavers will push me out of the way, Wolf," the old man protested. His skin crawled at the notion of standing waist deep in cold water, but he knew better than to object on those grounds.

Wolf glared. "Bearpaw will stand with you," he said. "Your pole will hold the leading beaver for a moment. Bearpaw will spear it. Meanwhile, the women and children will dig down through the vent. If the beavers turn back in their tunnel when they see the way is blocked, I will club them through the hole we dig in the roof of their den."

Bearpaw nodded. "When do we start?" he muttered. "I'm hungry."

"Kar?" Wolf asked sharply. "Do you understand?"

Kar sighed. It seemed like a good plan. "Yes, Chief Hunter," he said. "I will do my part."

Wolf nodded. "Then do it now," he ordered.

Kar jumped off the bank. The cold water was a shock. It rose almost to his chin by the time the old man's feet came to rest in the soupy mud of the bottom. He felt for the tunnel mouth with his toes and rammed the willow pole down across the opening as hard as age and hunger permitted him to do. Shouting with haste and hope, the tribe's women and children joined the Chief Hunter at the vent. They began to dig furiously.

Bearpaw hunched beside Kar. He held his spear slanted in the water so that its point crossed the pole and protruded into the tunnel. If one of the beavers slithered down the underwater ramp to escape, the beast would impale itself on the spear. Nothing could go wrong.

The Chief Fire-Maker shivered. The water was cold. He told himself that was the only reason he was trembling. Through his skin, Kar could feel the high-pitched shrilling of the animals trapped

within the burrow, but nothing tried to force its
way past the pole and spear.

"Hurry!" Kar shouted, though he knew the others were digging as fast as their crude tools permitted them. The soil here was soft, and the lakeside
vegetation did not have thick roots. By looking up
at the bank, Kar could see dirt flung high by the
hands after digging sticks had loosened it.

The squealing from the burrow continued. Why
didn't the beavers try to escape?

The realization struck Kar like a blow. The squeals
came from beaver kits afraid to leave the den on
their own. That meant their mother was somewhere close by in the lake. Beavers were not
normally dangerous, but a mother with her off-
spring to protect—

Kar looked over his shoulder. A ripple as straight
as a spearshaft raced toward him and Bearpaw.
"Behind us!" the Chief Fire-Maker screamed.

Bearpaw looked at Kar in surprise. Kar thrashed
sideways to get out of the way. The mother beaver's head lifted just as she crashed into Bearpaw
with the force of a boulder dropping from a cliff.
The hunter cried out in terror. The beaver did not
eat meat, but she was willing to use her curving
teeth to save her young. Her great chisels sheared
through Bearpaw's shoulderblades and backbone.

Kar sobbed and tried to scramble up the bank.
He kept slipping back on the wet earth. Behind
him, Bearpaw thrashed in convulsions. The hunter
was face down in the water. His flailing arms had
no strength. His spear had sunk. A spray of blood
brightened the muddy water.

Wolf grasped the Chief Fire-Maker's hands and pulled the old man to safety. "What happened?" Wolf shouted. "What happened?"

Kar wept uncontrollably. He looked back. Further ripples streaked the lake as the mother beaver led her kits out of the threatened den. Their bodies did not show above the surface.

Bearpaw had ceased to thrash. His corpse bobbed in the beavers' wake.

"Hawk," said the Chief Fire-Maker. "We must find Hawk and appease the spirits!"

BESIEGERS

Hawk quietly faded farther into the thicket. The dog stayed right beside him, making no noise and ready for whatever came. As the dog had fitted his hunting to meet the needs of his master, so he now fitted his other talents. He would do whatever was required, always looking to Hawk as a guide. Born to be a part of a pack, the adaptable dog had blended himself perfectly into the life of a human being.

Beyond the thicket, Hawk broke into a swift run. He had no idea how the strange hunters had at last found him. It might have been chance, but more likely they had sought him endlessly, following every tiny clue and as patient as wild beasts while they traced the man and woman who had eluded them once. It mattered little how they had come here. It was important only that they were here, and that they had undoubtedly come to kill.

When he reached the next thicket, a tangle of small trees and brush wherein visibility was limited to a few feet in any direction, Hawk slowed his pace again. He got down to crawl, staying on rock ledges wherever that was possible and leaving no more traces than he could help. The dog left his tracks freely, but Hawk could do nothing about that. He could only hope that the invading hunters would not connect the dog with the quarry they sought. Dogs were common wild creatures, and their tracks might be anywhere.

Deliberately Hawk entangled his trail, crossing and recrossing the thicket and leaving a maze of signs that would be very difficult to unravel. Still, he had no real hope of baffling his enemies for more than a few hours at the most. They might not be able to see where he had gone, but they could ferret out his tracks. By trying to throw them off at this point, Hawk hoped only to gain time.

When he reached the end of the second thicket, he grasped a trailing vine, climbed to the crotch of a great tree, and walked out on a limb to another vine several feet from the first. He slid down this, struck the ground with running feet, and dodged into the trees ahead of him.

He stopped to reconnoiter, looking over his back trail. But in his haste to escape the men who pursued him, he had run with the wind instead of against it, and now the soft breeze brought him no evidence at all of the enemy. Hawk circled cautiously.

The dog detected the first fresh sign of the

invaders. He stopped, bristling. Hawk squatted beside him, trying hard to read the message which was already very plain to the dog. Then he caught it.

The hostile hunters were evidently trying to work out the trail he had left in the thicket. Hawk guessed that there were more than ten of them and not as many as twenty; but certainly they were in formidable strength.

Hawk ran to a clear-flowing stream he knew. He stepped in and, unmindful of the dog, who ran along the bank beside him, waded down the stream. Two hundred yards down he stepped out of the water on the bank opposite the one he had entered.

The hostile hunters had come a long way, and they had worked out a very difficult trail to do so. They were not to be thrown off lightly; even if he got Willow and ran again, the hunters would find them. The battle had to come, and it might as well be at the cave. But first there were things to be done. Hawk stepped out of the stream and gave a precious moment to a long backward look.

The invaders were not in sight; evidently they were still trying to work out the trail he had left in the thicket. It would be some time before they got this far, and he had a little time. The dog loped beside him as he set a direct course for the cave.

He stopped in a clearing where deer usually browsed. The fight was close at hand. During it, he would be a virtual prisoner in the cave, until he had either defeated the hunters or they had killed him and Willow. They would need food to last out the siege that was sure to come, and the only food they had was some bear meat, the deer the puma had killed, and such dried food as Willow had ground. Meat spoiled quickly in weather like this and they should have some fresh-killed game.

The dog cast back and forth, nose to the ground while he sought a scent fresh enough to hunt. Hawk watched anxiously, impatient to find game and be on his way. Willow was alone and should the hunters find the cave they would have little difficulty in killing her.

After the dog had cast for ten minutes, and failed to rouse any game, Hawk abandoned the hunt; they would have to make out the best way they could. At a fast trot, he returned to the cave. Willow met him at the entrance.

"Give me the water basket!" Hawk panted. "The hunters have come, and we will have to fight."

Willow brought him the basket without a word. Hawk ran to the spring, filled the basket, and returned to the cave. During his absence, Willow had been carrying rocks and boulders into the cave, and was now storing them in strategic places. Hawk waited at the entrance. Had there been time, he would have again tried to find game. But there was no way of telling just where the invaders were or what they were doing. They might arrive at any moment, and Hawk had no wish to be caught outside the cave or to have the enemy trap Willow alone. He must stay, and hope they had enough food.

The dog slunk out, padded restlessly back and forth across the meadow, then returned to Hawk's side. He stood still, close to his master, and waited tensely. The dog knew that something was going to happen without knowing what it might be. He remained in the mouth of the cave, bristled and alert, while Hawk went back to inspect his store of weapons.

He was glad now that he had made additional darts; there were nine in the quiver and sixteen in his reserve stock. In addition there were the two spears and his club, but lately he had seldom used these. They would be useful only in a close-quarter fight, when and if the invaders tried to rush the cave. Hawk laid both spears at the cave's entrance, far enough back so that they could not be seized from the outside, and put his club beside them. Restlessly he prowled outside, and mounted the bluff above the cave to look all around.

There was nothing in sight; evidently he had hidden his trail well and the hunters were having difficulty unraveling it. But they would come. They had come too far already to turn back now. Sooner or later they were sure to find the cave.

Hawk considered their stock of firewood. He had carried much into the cave and Willow had brought more, but fire was their strongest weapon and their stoutest defense against constantly prowling beasts. Without fire, another bear, or a tiger, or a pack of wolves, might try to enter the cave. They needed fire all the time.

The dog padded close to his side as Hawk started across the valley and into the forest on the other side of the clearing. Willow took a stand in the cave's mouth, standing guard and ready to call a warning should anything appear. Hawk found a dead tree, dragged it across the valley, and into the cave. He went back for another, and a third.

About to start a fourth time, he was halted by

the dog's warning snarl. Hawk stood quietly in the entrance, testing the winds. They brought no news to his nose, but obviously they had carried a message to the dog's much keener senses. Something was coming. Silently Hawk retreated to the cave, and warned Willow.

Two by two, she was bringing up her store of rocks and placing them near Hawk's spears and club. Fear showed in her eyes, but she said nothing. Hawk appreciated her strength and courage; it was good to have her beside him in this crisis, even though she was only a woman.

A moment later he caught a glimpse of the enemy through the trees.

They were coming fast, on a clear trail. Hawk moved about, assuring himself that he had plenty of room, and fitted a dart into his throwing-stick.

They came out of the forest, sixteen shaggy, hairy men with fur girdles flapping about their waists. The dog rose and stood ready, growling, but at a word from Hawk he subsided. The dog waited, uncertain what his master would do.

The oncoming warriors halted in the clearing, and milled about uncertainly. While they stood still, Hawk appraised them.

They were strange men, he saw, but doubtless of the same tribe as the three he had fought back near the river meadows. Their foreheads receded, and they lacked the firm chins which characterized the people of his own tribe. Their spears were also of a primitive type; a full half of the warriors carried only sharpened sticks that had been hardened by scorching them in a fire.

The leader of the warriors looked directly across

the valley and saw Hawk. He stood a moment, as though unable to avert his eyes, then leaped furiously up and down. His bare feet rapped a sharp tattoo on the earth, and he swung his arms wildly. Then an unearthly shriek rolled from his throat. The rest followed his glance and they, too, began a concerted shrieking, and all leaped up and down. Hawk braced himself to meet the attack.

They came in a body, still yelling and waving their spears. Hawk forced himself to remain calm. He had already planned how he would meet such an attack if it came, and he knew the exact range of his darts. He could fling a dart twice as far as they could throw a spear, and certainly could kill some of the hunters before they were able to get within their spear range.

The hunters pressed on, howling at the tops of their voices and brandishing their spears. Inflamed with the lust to kill, they ran recklessly, each inspiring the other.

The dog was tense and ready to spring, but Hawk remained relaxed. He was afraid of this howling mob, but experience had taught him that he could not shoot straight when his muscles were tense. He must be relaxed and easy, and he had faced danger a sufficient number of times so he could force himself to be that way.

The howling was fierce, but Hawk knew that there was nothing in that which was able to hurt him. It was only meant to strike fear into the heart of an enemy. There was no indication that the hunters intended, at once, to press right up to the cave's mouth. Perhaps they would break and run, and launch half a dozen of these screaming attacks before they drove one home.

However, they had ventured into dart range, so Hawk stepped out of the cave and shot. Before the first dart had reached its target, he shot again and reached for another dart.

The foremost hunter stopped, a look of disbelief on his face as the first dart pierced his chest. He grasped it with both hands, tried to pull it out, then collapsed where he stood. The second dart struck another hunter squarely in the neck. He went to his knees, and fell limply backward, blood gushing from his jugular vein. The rest of the hunters turned and ran.

Hawk took his time with his third dart. Carefully he gauged the distance between himself and the leader, knowing that he would have to shoot very well to kill the man at such a distance.

Instead of shrieking, the hunters were now yelling in fear as they scrambled to get out of range. Hawk shot, purposely aiming high because the distance was so great. As the dart flew toward the fleeing men, Hawk caught his breath. He had aimed well, and if the dart kept on course it would strike the leader in the middle of his back.

However, at the last moment, a gust of wind deflected the dart. It curved to one side and went past the leader. A shout of mingled fear and rage broke from the man.

A moment later they were all safely out of range. Hawk did not pursue them. He had killed two and just missed a third in the first mad rush, but one man did not have even a faint chance of overcoming fourteen unless every advantage was on his side. To leave the cave would mean to give up his strong position and his only chance of meeting his enemies on something remotely like even terms.

The enemy tribesmen assembled at the point from which they had launched their charge, and swung to look back. Bewilderment was plain on their faces, and fear. They had come expecting to kill a man armed with a spear and a club, the only weapons they knew. Instead, they had run into something utterly beyond their comprehension. Not one of them should have been in danger at the distance this cave-dwelling man was able to kill. For a few minutes they stared stupidly at the cave. Then the leader spoke to them, gesturing violently.

Presently they came again, shrieking as before but spread in a thin line instead of grouped together. Again Hawk stepped out to meet them.

Instead of rushing forward, in an attempt to overwhelm the cave's defender by sheer weight of numbers, the hunters halted. They danced up and down, yelling, and made little dashes back and forth. Hawk tried desperately to reach them with a dart. He shot again, and again. Each time the dart fell short. Then Hawk stopped shooting, realizing what had happened.

The hunters had once made the mistake of coming within range of his darts, but they could not be tricked a second time. They were dancing and weaving just out of range, knowing that Hawk must have a limited supply of darts and tempting him to shoot what he had. They might be primitive, but they were crafty.

Hawk took stock of the darts remaining in his

quiver and turned quickly to speak to Willow. Immediately she was there, handing him six darts to replace the six he had expended. Never taking his eyes from the enemy, Hawk maintained his stand just outside the cave's entrance.

He waited, watching carefully for someone to make a break and come a little farther toward the cave. When an unwary hunter did so, Hawk shot again. But his target was a leaping, writhing one, and he missed. Instantly the hunter bounded out of range, and Hawk resolved not to throw another dart until he was reasonably sure of hitting his target.

Soon after, one of the men went into the forest and returned with wood and tinder. He knelt to arrange his fire, and added wood to it when it began to blaze. Two others busied themselves gathering a great quantity of wood.

Hawk's heart sank. The hunters had been defeated in two initial skirmishes, but obviously they had no intention of leaving. Instead, they were going to besiege the cave.

Three hunters started into the forest, probably to look for game. The rest gathered about the fire, and Hawk watched them closely. There seemed to be no immediate danger of another attack, but neither was there any indication that the enemy intended to leave.

Hawk ventured outside the cave, and all leaped to their feet and stood with spears ready. Hawk understood now why only three had gone hunting. With their quarry cornered, the rest had no intention of permitting it to escape. They would attack again, but next time they would not rush forward foolishly, or give any advantages. As he retreated back into the cave, Willow questioned him.

"What are they doing?"

"Waiting. Either they have some plan, or they wish us to make a foolish move."

"Then they will attack again?"

"I am sure of it."

Hawk sat down at the cave's mouth, patiently waiting for his enemies to make a move. They did not, and an hour before dark the hunters returned with two deer. Their fire leaped higher, brighter, and the smell of roasting meat filled the air. Hawk came back into the cave.

He and Willow were safe, at least until morning. Meat-eating beasts might not attack the hunters lying about their fire, but the odor of cooking meat would attract them to the vicinity. Already one saber-tooth was in evidence. The tiger had come, as usual, to patrol the camp in the hope that somebody would stray from it. In consequence, the hunters would be anchored to their own fire until morning.

Furtive rustlings in the grass told of wild dogs that had come to tear at the slain warriors. Then came the hoarse cough of the saber-tooth, and the sound of the wild dogs disappeared. In the darkness, Hawk heard bones cracking and knew that, with morning, there would be nothing left of the hunters he had killed. Already they were filling the lean belly of the big cat. Hawk lay down to sleep fitfully.

He was awakened by the dog's warning growl, and sprang instantly to his feet. The first faint, wan streaks of daylight filtered dismally through the cave's opening, and the mournful twitter of an early-waking bird was borne to his ears. Snatching up his darts, he went to the opening and looked out.

Morning mists swirled lightly over the clearing, and smoke from the enemy fire curled lazily up through them. Three of the hunters squatted on their haunches, just out of dart range, looking steadily at the cave. Others dawdled about the fire, but not all were accounted for. They could not have gone hunting, for it was too early to hunt. Suspicious, Hawk peered out of the mouth of the cave to see what had happened to the rest.

A pebble fell behind him, and a little chunk of earth dropped to the floor of the cave. The dog snarled fiercely and trotted back into the cave. He stood still, muscles tense and head alert, then nervously padded back to Hawk. Another clod of dirt dropped from the cave's roof, and another. Again the dog returned to the cave, as though he wanted to locate something that should be there. He bristled.

Hawk jerked about, startled. There were faint scrapings and pawings on the roof of the cave, and dirt sifted down steadily. Now he knew where the missing hunters were. They were on top of the cave, trying to dig their way through the smoke hole. After they had an opening through which a man could drop, doubtless they would attack from two sides at once. But until the hole was big enough, there would probably be no further attacks.

Fear touched Hawk's spine with icy fingers. He could defend the door, but this was a situation which he had not anticipated. Obviously it was impossible to be in two places at once, and Willow was no match for even one hunter. She could help little if some came through the door while others dropped through the hole in the roof. Hawk squatted in the entrance, considering the new danger.

Willow brought him a chunk of roasted meat, and Hawk grimaced as he took it. The weather had been warm, and meat did not keep well in warm weather. When it started to spoil it was both distasteful and apt to induce a sick stomach. They should have had fresh meat today, but there would be none until he dared leave the cave.

Gingerly Hawk smelled of the meat, then sniffed again, more deeply. It should be spoiled but certainly it did not smell that way. Rather it had a smoky odor, not unpleasant. Hawk nibbled a bit, then took a bigger portion. It was not spoiled at all, but good, with a smoky taste as pleasant as its odor. Hawk looked up at the ledges where the rest of the meat lay.

Most of the smoke went out the smoke hole, but some always lingered near the top of the cave, so that the stored meat lay constantly in a thin pall of smoke. Evidently the smoke was responsible for keeping the meat from spoiling.

Hawk stored this discovery in his brain with all the others he had made. It was most useful. If meat could be preserved, for even a little while, it meant that they could have that many more meals out of any large game animal, instead of eating just a little and throwing the rest away. That was something for the future—if there was any future.

From overhead came a muffled pounding, and the scraping of rock on rock. The diggers, Hawk guessed, had struck a ledge of rock and were tying to break through it. The scraping and pounding continued. Hawk picked up the water basket, and drank. He put the basket down and listened intently.

The diggers on top of the cave had abandoned their first hole and were starting a new one in a different place. Hawk breathed a little easier; perhaps the entire cave was roofed with rock and could not be broken. The smoke hole might go through a crack in the rock too narrow for a man. Or maybe it was too difficult to dig there; the smoke emerged in a grove of trees, and digging a hole large enough to admit a man, through interlaced roots, could be almost as difficult as digging through rock.

Suddenly a boulder, dislodged from the roof, bounded against the rim of the water basket and tipped it over.

Both Willow and Hawk sprang instantly to right the basket, but they were too late. Their precious water flowed in a spreading, dark stain on the floor of the cave.

MARMOT

Wolf's eyes caught the flash of motion against the grass of the distant hillside. Not even the Chief Hunter's keen vision could make out the shape of the small animal moving there, but he knew what it must be from the location.

"Marmot," Wolf said aloud. He spoke to reassure himself that he was still a hunter capable of leading the tribe rather than because he needed to inform the others of what he had spotted.

Wolf's ears no longer rang in memory of the blow he had taken in Bull's camp, but sometimes the Chief Hunter had waking dreams of the way the world had been when he first led the tribe many years before. Then they had meat regularly. Old men said it had been better in former days, but to Wolf's memory that time was a paradise in which he and his folk gorged on bison and never worried about the next day's hunt.

Then, suddenly, the memory of the past would vanish. Wolf would see the haggard faces of those he led and feel hunger claw his belly. He was embarrassed to dream of the good days which had been. It made him fear that he was losing his mind, the way Elm had gone mad shortly before her death.

The marmot on the far hillside barked a quick preliminary warning when the little animal realized a human was staring in its direction. The marmot was the lookout for a tribe of dozens of its fellows.

Thought of numbers forced the Chief Hunter to consider the draggled remnants of the tribe which followed him. Kar was at the end of the line. The old man carried a crude spear which was the best Wolf could fashion. It was mostly for protection. A party of two adult males and a young boy could not even pretend to be able to hunt real game.

The three women—Grassblade, Moonflower, and Magnolia—and two girls gathered the roots and berries on which the tribe had been forced to subsist. It was not a satisfying diet to a tribe of nomadic hunters, nor was even vegetable food ample in quantity.

Magnolia often went off with her deer-antler digging stick. She bolted whatever edibles she found instead of bringing the food back to share with the others. No one commented on her behavior. Magnolia sat sullenly by herself at the campfire, crooning as though the infant which had died so long ago could hear.

The marmot realized that the humans were not coming closer. It clucked reassuringly to its fellows. They went back to cropping grass or simply lolling in the warm sunlight. If the lookout had given its shrill call of immediate danger, the upland pasture would quiver for an instant while all the creatures leaped to the safety of their interconnected burrows on the rocky slope.

Magnolia suddenly left the line of the tribe and strode toward the opposite slope. She made no attempt to conceal herself, though the sharp-eyed marmots were almost impossible for even cats to stalk successfully. The lookout whistled in alarm. The speck that was the little animal's body disappeared from the outcrop which it had taken as its watchtower.

"Magnolia, where are you going?" Wolf demanded. "We can't hunt marmots!"

Magnolia ignored him. The young woman had borne a charmed life since she started going out alone to gather food. No predator had harmed her, though a woman armed only with a digging stick should have been easy prey. Perhaps the spirits chose to spare those who had lost their minds.

Wolf had been spared, while most of those he led had died. He shivered at the thought.

"We might be able to dig them out of their holes," suggested Moonflower as she watched the other woman walking stolidly across the valley.

"Of course we can't do that!" Wolf snapped. "The ground is rocky and all the burrows join under the ground. We'd just be wasting our time!"

"What meat will *you* be bringing us tonight, Chief Hunter?" Grassblade asked in a bitter voice.

Wolf's head jerked back at the insult. He raised his hand to strike the woman. She glared at him, too angry and frustrated to be afraid. Wolf lowered his hand.

Grassblade dropped the load she was carrying and set off after Magnolia, carrying only a pointed branch for digging. Moonflower looked at the children and said, "Come along," before following the other women.

The women and children did not look back as they walked across the valley on a hopeless quest. Wolf stared at them. He did not attempt to shout orders which he knew the others would ignore.

"It is not right," said Kar sadly.

The Chief Hunter looked at him. "Perhaps they *are* right," he said. "What have I brought them except misfortune? Go on, Kar. Join them. They will need a Chief Fire-Maker."

"We did wrong to send Hawk away," said the old man firmly. "That was not your fault, it was the fault of all of us together. The spirits will not bring back the tribe's good luck until we apologize to Hawk."

Wolf looked at the clumsy spears he had made for Kar and himself. He sighed. "Hawk is dead," he said at last. He nodded toward the women and children, who were beginning to climb the far side of the valley. The tribe of marmots had vanished utterly from the grassy slope above.

Kar took the Chief Hunter's arm. "Come," he said. "Perhaps we can dig out a marmot. Anyway, the sun is bright. It will feel good on my old bones."

*　　　*　　　*

The women and young were hard at work, digging the earth away from several burrow entrances, when the two men joined them. The holes were easy to find, since the marmots had worn trails across the meadow to them. Wolf could see half a dozen entrances besides the three at which the humans were working.

The wind keened around the humans, coursing up the slope of the valley and whistling through the bare rocks of the ridge line above them. It was strong enough to feel cool, despite the sunlight on which Kar had remarked.

Magnolia was digging particularly fast. She kept her deer-antler implement sharp, and she worked as steadily as a force of nature. Watching her was like seeing grass sway in the wind, or a stream gurgle downhill without ever stopping or slowing. Despite Magnolia's mindless concentration, her efforts were as vain as those of the other diggers.

The marmot burrows began with a drop shaft which plunged straight down for the length of a man's hand and forearm. It was this design which permitted the little creatures to disappear so suddenly when danger threatened. From the base of the drop shaft, the burrow extended sideways in a runway along which the marmots could move swiftly. Grassblade and the two girls had excavated a runway far enough to find the first of its many branchings.

It was as Wolf had said: digging out the marmots was an impossible task. Despite that, the Chief Hunter sighed and began to tear at the earth around another entrance. His awkwardly-fashioned spear made a better digging stick than it did a weapon with which to hunt big game.

Instead of digging, Kar stared with an expression of wonder on his face at the holes thus far excavated. Wolf grunted to catch the old man's attention. "Come," he whispered to his Chief Fire-Maker. "Help me. If we are to stay together as a tribe, we must act as a tribe . . . even if what we do is a waste of time."

Grassblade had sharp ears. She looked over from where she was levering a rock out of the soil with her digging stake. "What you have done for the past months has been a waste of time, Chief Hunter," she said sharply. "Otherwise we would have had meat to eat, as is proper."

Wolf pursed his lips. He concentrated on thrusting his spear into the ground and twisting the earth loose to shower down the drop shaft. He did not reply.

"No," said Kar. "There is a better way!" The Chief Fire-Maker's face became suddenly lively. He bent and began to fumble with the implements of his profession, the tinder and flints with which he lighted his fires. "Help me, everyone!" Kar ordered. "Bring bundles of grass. Quickly!"

The three children willingly stopped what they were doing and clutched handfuls of the long, coarse grass that carpeted the meadow. The women were doubtful and hostile. Because of the long succession of catastrophes, they had lost the habit of obedience to the chiefs of the tribe. "You can't drive marmots with fire," Moonflower objected. "They're underground, can't you see?"

"Yes, and we *can* drive them!" said Kar. The old

man drew himself up to his full height. At times like this when he spoke with assurance, the Chief Fire-Maker projected the authority which Wolf believed he himself had lost.

Kar pointed to the hole Magnolia was excavating, the entrance farthest down the slope. "The wind comes up the valley," the old man explained. "I will build a grass fire in the mouth of that tunnel and the wind will blow it through all the burrows."

Grassblade shook her head uncertainly. "But—" she said, no longer hostile. "The tunnels will not burn . . . will they, Chief Fire-Maker?"

"The tunnels will not burn," said Kar, "but the wind will blow the smoke through them and drive the marmots out of other holes. We will wait and catch them when they come out."

"What if they don't—" Moonflower began with a frown on her face as she tried to understand the new idea. Wolf was frowning also, but he had learned that old Kar's mind was quicker at establishing new concepts than his own was.

"Do as I say, woman!" snapped the Chief Fire-Maker. "Do you want to starve?"

The grass was long and green rather than dry. Wolf knew that it would not burn well, but for this purpose it was better that the fuel give off billows of smoke. He had to remember that they were not trying to drive a herd of bison into a trap with bright, swift-spreading flames.

The Chief Hunter helped crop the grass, cutting the stems with the edge of his spearpoint. The task was familiar. All his conscious life he had sawn grass and twisted it into torches with which to drive the herds. Maybe that was what the tribe needed: not new traditions, exactly, but rather traditions changed slightly to accommodate new circumstances.

What Hawk had done, for instance—training the spirit of the wood to throw spears by itself. That did not seem so unreasonable any more. Why had they thought they must drive their Chief Spear-Maker away for doing a valuable thing like that?

Wolf stacked his armload of grass on the pile the women and children had harvested. Kar had his fire burning already, an orange gleam turned pale by the sun. The Chief Fire-Maker fed a twist of grass to the tendril of flame reaching from his set of punk and shavings. Yellow-white smoke curled up and streamed along with the breeze. Kar dropped the twist into the lowest excavation and added more grass to it.

Wolf came to life. "Everyone go to another hole and wait!" he ordered sharply. He was again the tribe's Chief Hunter, even though this was an unfamiliar form of hunting. "When the marmots show themselves, strike quickly! Otherwise we will miss them."

Wolf ran to a hole to the side of the one where Kar was generating smoke. The women and children scattered to other openings, clutching clubs and rocks. They were scattered over fifty yards. Magnolia stopped digging, but she remained poised where she was with her sharpened antler in her hand. The expression on her face would have been more fitting on a beast of prey.

A wisp of haze drifted out of the tunnel by

which Wolf was watching. It was scarcely visible, but the Chief Hunter could smell the sharp tang of the smoke when he bent close to the opening. He drew his head away quickly, afraid that he would frighten back a marmot which would otherwise have bolted from cover.

Wolf raised his spear to stab if he got the chance. The marmots whistled shrilly within their tunnels. The sounds were thinned and deepened by echoing through the burrows.

The women and children poised with greater or lesser expertise. Grassblade was farthest up the slope, but there were burrow entrances even higher than she was. It was while glancing at Grassblade that Wolf saw a marmot unexpectedly pop from a hole behind her.

"There!" screamed the Chief Hunter, pointing. Grassblade and the marmot were equally surprised. The plump animal jumped toward her just as the woman turned around. Grassblade dropped her digging stake and grabbed at the beast with both hands. All the tribe were running toward her.

Though the marmot squealed and thrashed its stubby legs, it did not attempt to bite Grassblade. It was a strong, healthy animal which weighed almost twenty pounds. Its body fat and smooth, russet fur made it difficult to hold, but the woman clung to it desperately.

Magnolia elbowed past the others converging on the struggle. "Meat!" she shrieked. "Give it to me!" She clawed at Grassblade's face with her left hand in a furious attempt to make the other woman give up her prize.

"No, it's mine!" Grassblade shouted. She twisted

away and kicked out at Magnolia. Wolf reached the melee and caught Magnolia by the shoulder. The young woman gave an insane scream and stabbed Grassblade in the stomach with the sharp-pointed antler she carried.

Wolf gasped and stepped back. The whole tribe froze. Grassblade's face went gray. Half the length of the digging implement was buried in her body. She did not collapse at once, but the marmot leaped from her nerveless fingers and disappeared back down its burrow before anyone thought to act.

Magnolia threw her hands over her mouth. For the first time since her baby died, Magnolia's expression was that of a normal human being—a human wracked with horror at what she saw, at what she had done. "Oh, Grassblade!" she cried. "Oh, Grassblade, it wasn't *me* who . . ."

Her voice trailed off. The murdered woman stumbled to her knees, then fell on her face across the marmot burrow.

Smoke continued to rise from some of the entrances, but no more marmots appeared.

"Come," muttered Wolf. "We must leave this place. It is unclean."

BENT BOW

The dog, padding over, bent his head to the spilled water and licked up as much as he could. Then he ran a pink tongue over his furry upper jaw and sat back on his haunches, looking expectantly up at Hawk.

Hawk brushed a hand across his shaggy mop of hair and dangled the empty water basket while the enormity of this tragedy sank in. They could live, for days if need be, without food. But not without water, and their entire reserve stock had been in the basket.

Almost automatically he swung to look at the cave's entrance. Under no conditions must the enemy learn of this disaster. If they knew, or found it out, they could get both Hawk and Willow with no risk at all to themselves. It would be necessary only to wait until thirst drove the two mad, and kill them when they came out. He must get more water before their situation became desperate, but the only water near the cave lay in the spring across the valley.

Hawk's throat and tongue were dry, and already he felt thirsty. Having water, he had used it sparingly. Now, lacking anything with which to quench his thirst, he had a sudden strong desire for something to drink.

Willow's eyes were haunted, desperate, and she licked her lips. She, too, was suddenly thirsty. Her eyes were riveted on the damp floor of the cave, as the dog scratched inquisitively at the place where the water had spilled.

Dirt and small stones continued to patter into the cave, a monotonous dribble like rain, as the diggers on top strove to enlarge their hole.

Hawk went to the entrance, carefully choosing his way over the tumbled dirt and stones, and looked out. As usual, excepting for those who were trying to dig through the top of the cave, the hunters were merely sitting well out of dart range. Their only purpose seemed to be to prevent the escape of the people trapped in the cave. They apparently had no wish to attack again, or to make any more, until there was all possible chance for success. The digging went on.

Again Hawk licked dry lips. It was cool inside the cave, but outside the hot sun beat mercilessly down and even the birds were not moving. Instead they had sought the forest's shade, and were lingering in it until such time as the sun started to sink so they could move about comfortably.

The panting dog came to sit beside Hawk. In his own way the dog considered the situation, too, although he did not see the complete picture. The people outside the cave were enemies and must be regarded as such, but the siege had become an accepted thing and nothing special was happening. The besiegers had not broken in, and until they did those inside the cave were in no danger. Therefore there was no use in remaining constantly excited. The dog returned to the cool cave, and lay down facing the entrance. The monotonous thud of the diggers' tools still sounded on top of the cave but that, too, had become a customary thing, almost an accepted part of living.

Suddenly the dog leaped backward. A large crack had opened in the roof, just behind the doorway, and stones and dirt poured in a steady stream through it. The dislodged earth piled unevenly on the cave's floor, so that there were two narrow alleys running to the entrance and a pile of debris in the center. The dog scurried toward an overhanging ledge at one side of the cave, and hovered uncertainly near it.

The two humans looked worriedly at the disturbance. Hawk listened intently to the sound of the diggers, while he tried to think of something he might do. The falling earth had left a thin cloud of dust behind it, so that breathing was difficult. Dust gritted between his teeth, and when he swallowed it added to the torment of thirst.

When the digging finally ceased, so accustomed had they grown to it, both looked questioningly up. Now that the sounds had stopped, they missed them. The fire leaped higher and brighter, painting the inside of the cave with its yellow glow, and they realized that twilight had come again. The diggers had to leave and return to their fire because of the dangers night brought with it. They would be easy prey for any prowling beast if they remained on top of the cave.

Hawk dug thoughtfully in the cave's floor with his bare toes. Tomorrow would be another hot day, from all signs, and already thirst was hard to bear. Before the night ended it would be harder, and by tomorrow it would be torture.

Hawk went again to the mouth of the cave, careful not to stir up any of the piled earth, and peered out. The sun had gone down, and with it the day's heat had gone too. In the valley, the besieging tribesmen were dark shadows beside their leaping fire. There was no smell of roasting meat; evidently the hunters had failed to get any. Tomorrow the enemy camp would be a hungry one.

Dim light still lingered, and familiar things had become night-haunted shadows. Like such a shadow, the same saber-tooth that had been at the enemy camp last night drifted within thirty feet of the cave's entrance. Ordinarily Hawk would have thrown a dart at it, and tried to kill the tiger, but now he welcomed it. It would keep the enemy from attacking at night. There was a chance that one of the hunters would stray from the fire, and that the tiger would kill him. In that happy event, Hawk would have one less to deal with.

The darkness deepened, and as it did the fire

across the valley became very bright. Back in
the forest a dire wolf sounded its lonesome wait,
and at a distant point another wolf replied. They
must have fed recently; wolves never gave away
their positions by making noise when they were
hungry.

The tiger, again on its regular patrol around the
camp fire, came back, and when it passed the cave
it stopped to look searchingly at the entrance. It
did not come any nearer because the tiger had
already investigated the cave thoroughly. It knew
there was fire within, and fire it dared not approach. The tiger went on its way around the
enemy camp.

Hawk timed its beat, and it was a regular one.
The saber-tooth appeared in the same places at
about the same time. After a while it failed to pass
the cave and Hawk knew it had become discouraged and gone to seek other game.

A night breeze stirred, blowing from the hunter's camp to the cave, and Hawk tested the scents
it carried. There were none save those of the usual
timid creatures which had found what they hoped
were safe places for the night and were staying in
them.

Willow was roasting meat, but Hawk had no
appetite for it. His lips were dry, his tongue a
twisted piece of grass in his mouth, and he felt
very warm. His need was for water, not food, and
he must drink before he could eat. Hawk walked
back to the fire.

Willow's lips were cracked and dry, and her
eyes seemed abnormally bright as she looked up at

him. Suffering more than he, she wanted nothing to eat either. Hawk came to a sudden decision.

"I am going to get water," he said.

Willow's eyes filled with fear. "It is night."

"We must have water, and I cannot get it by day. I think the saber-tooth has gone, and that I can be back before it returns."

Willow offered no further protest, as Hawk picked up the water basket and a spear and went to the mouth of the cave. When the dog would have followed him, he told Willow to restrain it. For a few moments he remained quietly in the cave's mouth.

It was an unheard-of-thing that he was about to do. Night was a time of terror both real and imagined. The darkness was always alive with fierce creatures that did exist and fantastic things that lived only in the mind. No sane person ever voluntarily left the fire's safety at night, but Hawk was desperate. Spear in one hand, water basket in the other, he slipped quietly into the darkness.

He walked fast and erect, making no attempt to hide, but he was careful to stay on soft grass where his padding feet would make no noise. Away from the cave, he broke into a trot. The spring was a long way off, and though the tiger was gone there was no guarantee that it would not return.

When he neared the enemy fire, Hawk slowed to a walk. The hunters were lying about, sleeping, but Hawk knew how lightly they slept. If they suspected his presence, they could tell as easily as he had that there were no tigers or other dangerous beasts close by, and would be after him.

Past the camp, Hawk breathed more easily. He reached the spring, faintly illumined by glowing fox fire, and dipped his basket. Hastily he yanked the half-filled basket out, while cold fright made his heart pound. The camp was alert!

He himself had made no noise, but he had forgotten that water gurgled when it poured into the empty basket. Now, every hunter was on his feet, spear and club ready. All were staring toward the spring. They knew that there was plenty of water all around, and no reason to suppose that any beast would drink so close to a camp. Besides, drinking beasts did not make that kind of a noise.

The half-filled basket in one hand, and his spear in the other, Hawk remained rooted in his tracks while he sought some plan of escape. He could not stay here, but the alerted camp was between him and the cave. Pursing his lips, he brought the growl of an angry tiger from the very depths of his chest. Then he started circling away from the fire on a course that would take him back toward the cave.

For a moment the watching hunters were silent. Then the wind veered sharply from Hawk to the fire, and at once the hunters began their insane leaping and their weird, animal screaming. Following their noses, they rushed toward the place where they knew their enemy, and not a saber-tooth, waited.

Clinging to the basket of water, Hawk ran desperately. He had been discovered, and there was no more need of subterfuge. Even as he ran he made ready to hurl his spear, for the enemy was between him and the cave. He would have to fight, but he would do it in his own way. As soon as he could see the first hunter outlined against the glow of the fire, Hawk stopped suddenly and hurled his spear.

He missed; in the dim light he had been unable to see the man clearly. Then, as he turned to run again, there was a sudden interruption.

Another snarl, a real one, sounded in the night, and was followed by a wild shriek. The hunters scrambled desperately to return to their fire and Hawk ran faster. The tiger had come back, and just in time. There was no immediate danger because the tiger had its victim, and would not leave it. Hawk sprinted into the cave, still clutching the basket with its precious contents.

When he and Willow had satisfied their thirst, Hawk lay down to sleep. It was a peaceful sleep; tomorrow would bring its problems but he had solved the most immediate one.

During the night he awakened, and went to the mouth of the cave to test the winds and to listen. The hunters apparently remained about their fire, and anyway the dog was lying close to the cave's entrance. Hawk looked gratefully at him. More and more he was coming to rely on the dog. The animal always alerted him when anything was about, and never gave a false warning. He would be sure to create some disturbance if the hunters were foolish enough to leave their fire and try to attack the cave by night.

It was most unlikely that they would. They had

already gone out once and learned that night was no time to venture away from their fire. But another day was soon to come, and sooner or later the diggers on the roof would find a way to break through. When they did, and if they came through the entrance at the same time, he could not repel them. Even if the dog and Willow helped, there were too many to beat back.

Hawk came back to throw more wood on the fire, and the flames leaped halfway to the cave's roof. Hawk fretfully paced about.

He must do something, but what could it be? The hostile hunters knew how far he could shoot his darts; they would not again come within range. If he went out to meet them he would certainly be killed. Hawk looked at his darts, particularly the special one whose tip carried the mysterious power of the serpent's deadly ability to kill. If he could reach his enemies with it, if he could enlist the serpent's magic in his defense, he might yet win this battle.

The dog got up to sit expectantly beside him, as though he thought something was about to happen. Hawk paid no attention. The dog was valuable in his own way, but Hawk could see no use for him in the present problem.

Hawk looked up at the roof of the cave, where the firelight made dancing shadows. The diggers had tried to break through in half a dozen places, and had as yet succeeded nowhere. But sooner or later they were sure to find a soft place, one that would yield to their efforts. Hawk paced about, looking from the roof to the fire, and back again. If he knew where the enemy would finally enter, and had a great fire underneath that place, the flame might drive them back.

But where was his fire to be built? The cave was rooted with dirt, broken here and there by a layer of stone. Looking at the roof from the inside, there was no way to tell exactly where those digging from the outside might finally gain an entrance. It took time to build up a roaring fire, and if it was even a few feet away from the right spot, the hunters could attack anyway.

His eyes on the roof, Hawk stepped backward, and trod on something that snapped against his foot. He looked down, and saw that he had thrust his foot between the sinew on one of Willow's drying sticks and the stick itself. With an annoyed grunt, he bent down to free himself, but the stick caught on his toe and only bent when he tugged at the sinew. The sinew slipped from his hand and snapped against his foot as the stick tried to straighten itself. Hawk squatted down, looking more closely.

As a spear-maker, he had always been intrigued by the magic life in a supple green stick. That magic was still evident in the drying stick, but now it seemed to be controlled in some way by the sinew tied to it. Fascinated, Hawk carefully disengaged his foot and picked the stick up. Experimentally he pulled at the sinew, and when he did the stick bent. As soon as he released it, the stick straightened. The quivering sinew seemed to sing softly to him.

Hawk forgot everything else. He took the drying

stick in his left hand and, with his right, pulled back the sinew. The stick bent, but when he released the sinew, the stick immediately straightened and the sinew became taut. Again it sang its humming song.

A green stick itself had great power, a mysterious force that belonged to things that grew, but did not move freely by themselves. And animal sinew, Hawk reasoned, so useful to both beasts and men, who could move as they pleased, must contain some magical elements of its own. Combined, the two seemed to possess a power greater than either alone. Hawk drew the sinew again, and again, and let the stick snap itself back to its former shape.

The cave, the dog, the hostile hunters, even Willow, who had awakened and was quietly watching him, faded into insignificance. For years he had tried to master the strength and life in the green wood, and now he knew that he was on the verge of finding what he had been seeking. Wood alone was not the answer. He must pair wood with sinew; the strength of trees with agility of animals.

Sitting beside the fire, he drew the sinew taut and flexed his fingers across it. It sang pleasantly to him, a happy song of triumph, a promise of great strength. With fingers that trembled from excitement, Hawk took one of the darts from its quiver. He fitted it against the sinew, pushed against the bent stick with his feet, and let the sinew go. The dart wobbled weakly across the cave, and bounced against the far wall with scarcely enough force to make a mark.

Hawk looked down at the stick, baffled. He almost had the answer he had been seeking; it was almost in his grasp. But something was lacking; what was it? A moment later he knew what that was. In three great bounds Hawk sprang across the cave.

A spear shaft! It had been a supple spear shaft that had first awakened him to the life in wood! Feverishly he sought among his bundle of shafts, and plucked out the greenest and most limber. He grasped it by both hands and bent it. A happy smile lighted his face.

This was what he needed! Sinew-drying sticks were green, and as such they had strength, but they were not strong enough to propel a dart. The spear shaft was stronger, thicker, and had the needed power. Hawk tied a length of sinew to one end of the shaft, braced that end against the cave's floor, and bowed the shaft. Making a loop in the free end of the sinew, he tied it over the other end of the shaft. Very carefully, a little awed, knowing he held magic in his grasp, he pulled the sinew and bent the shaft more. He released the string and the shaft snapped back.

The breaking sinew snapped with a sharp report, and Hawk winced as one end struck him smartly across the cheek. Unmindful of the sinew's sting, he looked in bewilderment at his handiwork. The shaft was powerful enough, but the sinew lacked strength to control it.

"Twist several long sinews together," said Willow.

She was on her feet now, gathering lengths of sinew from her longest drying sticks. Tying the ends together, Willow looped three lengths over a stick and swiftly twisted them into one smooth, compact cord. Then she handed the triple-strength sinew to Hawk.

Eagerly Hawk bowed the shaft again and tied the sinew to either end. He drew it back slowly, a little afraid that it might break again when he let it snap forward. But it merely sang to him, a humming, stronger vibration than before. Hawk rested the butt of a dart against the sinew, drew it back, and shot.

The dart struck the cave's wall so hard that its stone head shattered, and the wooden shaft bounced halfway back to him. Exultantly Hawk swooped to pick it up, and shot again, and again. When the wooden shaft itself was broken, he chose another dart.

Dawn was breaking when he knew that, finally, he had made and mastered a satisfactory bow. He could shoot the length of the cave and hit what he aimed at. Hawk looked grimly at the eight darts remaining in his quiver. The rest were shattered, but he had these left, and if that mysterious power in the animal sinew did not betray him, he might yet win this unequal battle. Hawk went to the mouth of the cave and looked out.

Only four hunters remained to guard the prisoners in the cave. The rest had evidently gone hunting. Soon they straggled back, empty-handed, and stood disconsolately around the fire.

For a moment Hawk stood tensely, then forced himself to relax. Sitting in the mouth of the cave, he fitted a dart into the bow, braced it against his feet, drew the sinew, and took careful aim. As well as he could he calculated the wind, the distance, and what last night had taught him about the bow's strength. When he shot, the dart flew straight and fast, but dug itself into the earth several feet short of the hunters and quivered there.

The hunters stared uncertainly, muttering their astonishment, not sure whether this dart had come from the cave or from some other source. Most of them had paid no attention when Hawk first shot, but now they stood in a close group by the fire, watching his every move.

Now, Hawk decided, was the time to see if the serpent's deadly power would come to his aid. Picking up the dart with the venom-dipped head, he fitted it against the sinew, and drew with both hands. Slowly, letting no muscle quiver, he drew the sinew as far back as he could, and again took careful note of the wind, the distance, and the trajectory which he thought the dart would assume. He moved the bow very slightly to one side and shot.

The whistling dart left the bow. Faster than the swiftest bird it traveled, a flashing streak in the dim morning. It rose in its upward curve, and began its descent, down toward the leader of the enemy hunters. But instead of striking his squarely, the dart's head merely nicked his shoulder.

The hunters milled about, confused by fear and awe of the lone man who could send his little spears such an incredible distance. The leader, however, apparently enraged by the slight wound he had received, was dancing up and down, brandishing his spear. From his actions, Hawk concluded that he was trying to overcome the hunters' fears. Had the serpent's power no effect, then? His hopes began to give way to black despair.

Suddenly the leader of the band took two faltering steps, stiffened, tried to take another step, and fell face down, writhing on the ground.

Bereft of their leader, panic-stricken by the mysterious manner of his collapse, the rest of the hunters took one terrified look and fled into the forest as fast as they could run.

XII

Hawk stood outside the cave, the keystone, and
the bow in his hands. The quiver on his
shoulder held a dozen feathered arrows, which
together weighed no more... was an easy burden, for...
scatter-light, and the bow...
runway-shell.

It had not been an easy weapon to handle,
from several experiments... and
unconnected arrows. It had taken... to feel
the bow by holding it in his hands... right. He could shoot an arrow accurately five
times as far as he had ever been able to throw a
dart. And the arrows were so... that were so
powerful that he had to... to at the
beast's venom. That was always in reserve...
labeled, in his statement, should he ever need it.

RETURN

Hawk stood outside the cave, the dog beside him and the bow in his hands. The quiver on his shoulder held a dozen feathered arrows which, together, weighed no more than a few darts. It was an easy burden; the loaded quiver seemed feather-light and the bow was no heavier than his throwing-stick.

It had not been an easy or sudden transformation. Several experimental bows lay behind him, and uncounted arrows. He had learned to shoot the bow by holding it in his hands, standing upright. He could shoot an arrow, accurately, five times as far as he had ever been able to throw a dart. And the arrows were within themselves so powerful that he had no more need of the serpent's venom. That was always in reserve, a deadly addition to his armament should he ever need it.

The bow spelled security. Even the mighty saber-tooths, which could be attacked with a very rain of arrows whenever they came near the cave, now stayed away from it. Two saber-tooth skins served as beds for Willow and himself, and there were deerskin coverings ready when the weather should turn colder. Now, in reality, Hawk was master of his world.

Willow came from the cave, a new basket in either hand. Hawk and the dog led the way back to the tar pit at their old camp site.

Save for a few tumbled ashes and bits of charred wood, all traces of the fire which they had maintained here, so long ago, were obliterated. The spot had seemed a haven then, but now, accustomed to the shelter of their cave home, they regarded it as a cheerless, exposed place. They had come only to pitch more baskets for Willow's ample supply of storage containers.

Hawk sat down in the sun, the dog at his feet, while Willow began to line her baskets. Hawk's only function was to protect her while she worked.

The first basket was nearly finished when the dog pricked up his ears and growled warningly. Hawk stood up, looking about alertly. Topping a nearby rise he saw a human figure, then another and another. He spoke softly and Willow came to his side.

Hawk was not worried, for his arrows were more powerful than many spears. Besides, the approaching humans had a strangely familiar look. But it was not until they approached nearer that he identified them positively. They were Wolf, Chief Hunter of their old tribe, Kar, the Chief Fire-

Maker, two women, one boy child, and two girl children. They were all haggard, worn, and very thin. Obviously they had eaten little more than enough to keep them alive.

"Come no nearer," Hawk called out warningly. "If you do, I will kill you."

Wolf's voice was weak and husky. "We seek food, and only food."

"From us?" Hawk cried angrily.

"We have no right to expect anything from you," Wolf croaked, "for it was we who banished you. That was an evil day for us, for no one else could make spears that flew as true as yours. When we tried to steal some from another tribe, there was a great battle in which half of us were killed."

Hawk remembered that battle ground, back at the scene of the mammoth stampede.

"Where are the rest?" he asked.

"Dead," Wolf said. "Some killed by wild beasts and some by lack of food. All save us are dead."

"And you seek only food?"

"Only that."

As Hawk hesitated, Willow said softly, "They are our people, and they are in great need."

"Come with us, then," Hawk said at last. "We have food in plenty, and we no longer wander to find game." He touched his bow proudly. "There is no need."

A Note from the Junior Author

Alert readers will notice that most of the animals mentioned in The Hunter Returns are those of Pleistocene North America. The developments in human tools and society almost certainly occurred in Eurasia, before bands of hunters crossed the Bering land bridge. Furthermore, a few of the species of animals never reached North America.

I therefore suggest that readers think of The Hunter Returns as an alternate universe novel, in which crucial portions of human prehistory occurred against a background different from that which we believe happened in our own world.

DAD

Ranks of Bronze
Alien traders were looking to buy primitive soldier-slaves—they needed troops who could win battles without high-tech weaponry. But when they bought Roman legionaries, they bought *trouble* . . .

Vettius and His Friends
A Roman Centurion and his merchant friend fight and connive to stave off the fall of Rome.

Lacey and His Friends
Jed Lacey is a 21st-century cop who plays by the rules. His rules.

Men Hunting Things
Things Hunting Men
Volumes One and Two of the *Starhunters* series. Exactly what the titles indicate, selected and with in-depth introductions by the creator of Hammer's Slammers.

WARNING: THIS SERIES TAKES NO PRISONERS

Introducing

CRISIS OF EMPIRE

David Drake has conceived a future history that is unparalleled in scope and detail. Its venue is the Universe. Its domain is the future of humankind. Its name? *CRISIS OF EMPIRE.*

An Honorable Defense

The first crisis of empire—the death of the Emperor leaving an infant heir. If even one Sector Governor or Fleet Admiral decides to grab for the Purple, a thousand planets will be consigned to nuclear fire.
David Drake & Thomas T. Thomas, 69789-7, $3.95 ____

Cluster Command

The imperial mystique is but a fading memory: nobody believes in empire anymore. There are exceptions, of course, and to those few falls the self-appointed duty of maintaining a military-civil order that is corrupt, despotic—and infinitely preferable to the barbarous chaos that will accompany it's fall. One such is Anson Merikur. This is his story.
David Drake & W. C. Dietz, 69817-6, $3.50 ____

The War Machine

What's worse than a corrupt, decadent, despotic, oppressive regime? An empire ruled over by corrupt, decadent, despotic, oppressive *aliens* ... In a story of personal heroism, and individual boldness, Drake & Allen bring The Crisis of Empire to a rousing climax.
David Drake & Roger MacBride Allen, 69845-1, $3.95 ____
